LAST RITES

FRED NENNER

Last Rites

Aveli Press

Copyright @2019 Frederick Nenner

All rights reserved

Cover Design BooksGoSocial

Dedication

To Judy Nenner
My first reader.
And our daughters, Rachel and Rebecca

Acknowledgments

To my colleagues in Spiritual Care at Lutheran Medical Center who guided me through the difference, importance and power of the sacramental and pastoral ministries.

To Alice Berger for her encouragement and keen literary eye.

To Melanie Shed, a writer and critic, who saw a compelling story, a strong narrative voice and encouraged me throughout.

And to Zoe Deleuil, my editor, many thanks for your patience, skill and knowledge of the craft as we worked from a first draft to Last Rites. A journey that was almost as exciting as that moment when the idea for this book took its first step with a first written word.

Contents

Chapter One

Oscar Ozymandias, always vigilant, first noticed the lights moving slowly across the office wall. Now the room was fully illuminated by what must be the same vehicle returning, but this time parked on the cross street that directly fronted his apartment.

If it were a late Tuesday afternoon when the stores on Main Street stayed open till six, he would pay it no mind. But it was midnight, and the Five and Dime, pharmacy, malt shop and grocery had long since closed.

Even during the day there were few cars on the road, with most folks having given them up. By midnight, the streets were always empty until dawn. Except tonight, and those headlights shining through his front windows.

Oscar went to make sure everything that needed to be out of sight was out of sight. By the time he returned to the office to call Mathers, the cop on duty, the lights were gone.

He sank down into a floral upholstered chair, one of two, and placed his hands on the arms, feeling the worn fabric beneath his fingers. Family members sat in them when they came to make arrangements. Oscar planned on replacing both when times got better.

He reached for a clump of tissues from the ornate box that he kept on the desk and wiped the sweat from his forehead.

"Vigilance, Oscar. Vigilance. Everything has its place and your job is to make sure everything is exactly where it belongs."

There was nothing to do now but wait for the phone call from Doc Radler. The first call had come earlier in the evening from Mae Stevens, the distressed wife of her not-quite-deceased husband. The doctor had just arrived and with the news that the end was near, she telephoned Ozymandias' Chapel, the only mortuary in fifty square miles.

She wanted to wait for her son to return home, which would take at least a month, before having the funeral. Oscar told her anything was possible.

It would be a while before he would need to leave, so he got on with making his supper for the next few days. He had purchased two potatoes, four carrots and a can of beef stock that very day, and taken a package of cubed meat from the freezer, which was probably defrosted by now.

Stew was his favorite meal, especially with fall here and snow coming down. In winter he made a pot of it every five or six days. In the summer he made stir-fry. Mostly the same ingredients but he left out the potatoes, added whatever vegetables were in season, and cut the meat into strips. The freezer was half full of three-pound packages of cubed and one-pound packages of strip. He was partial to his meat and was never sure when the next supply would be available. With the freezer only half filled, he didn't want the three pounds of cubed that was almost defrosted when Mae called to go to waste, so he got to work while waiting for the next call.

~

Morphine for the patient, whiskey for the doctor. That's how they'd get through this ordeal.

Doctor Radler knew this would be the last time he would visit the Stevens' house. Mike had been in a bad way these last three months, and he had told Mae it was only a matter of time.

When he got the call he knew the time had come. Old age and a touch of cancer. Mike was sixty-four and while this wasn't considered old in most places, in Mount Olden, by the time you got to fifty you were old.

It was in his lymph nodes, and a blessing that his age would help with the passing instead of the lingering and wasting that happened when cancer snuck up on young people.

Radler had seen it too many times. Patients with strong hearts that kept beating long after that damn cancer had stripped every bit of flesh from the body. With the few whose passing really dragged on, he wasn't above giving them a little something to help speed things up, telling himself he was doing it for the family and the patient. In fact, he was doing it for himself. He couldn't stand to watch the wasting.

The call from Mae had come earlier in the evening. Mike was twitching and having trouble breathing. He'd been real sick for the past few days and the medicine Doc had left the last time wasn't holding the pain anymore.

He had done a good job on that bourbon, the snow was falling, and the Stevens lived high up the mountain. If Mae had called a half hour later, after one more drink, he never would have made it to his front door. As it was, Doc Radler knew he'd have to take it real slow or else this would be his last professional call and he wasn't ready to say goodbye to it all.

It was no easy matter getting from the garage to the black top. Mostly he liked living so far from the road. Except when the snow came. Thanksgiving was still a week away and this much snow coming this early in the year was a bad sign. The plows were out and he could only hope that by the time he returned from the Stevens' house, Mac would have gotten around to plowing his drive. If there was one thing he didn't want to do, it was walk the quarter mile from the road to his house.

There was time to worry about that. Right now he had to concentrate on the trip out to the Stevens' and keeping the damn car on the road.

Doc, in his state, had the mind to dress with lots of layers. Even with two wood burning stoves, the Stevens' house couldn't hold the heat. Siding coming off in patches, thin insulation, and cardboard against cracked and missing windows left little to keep the warmth in.

"He's been awful, Doc, just awful. It started like this late this afternoon. He's been sleeping on and off now for three days and he hasn't eaten a thing. Ya got to do something, ya just got to do something."

Mae had become old in a very short time. There was fourteen years between her and her husband and although she had been pregnant five times, with three miscarriages and two live births, she was a young fifty until Mike got sick. Their son Ethan was long gone from the house and far away, serving his country. Janie, their daughter, was only on the other side of the mountain, but they saw her so little she might as well have been in another country.

It was up to Mae to do everything for Mike and the worse he got, the more work there was. By the time she called Doc at the end of the summer, she was feeding him, cleaning him and wiping him. She was doing as much for him as she had done with her newborns. Knowing where it was all leading had turned her into an old woman before her time. You could see it in the skin under her eyes and chin, sagging under the weight of worry and grief. Her grandma had told her it was what happened to the women in their family when life became too much for their souls to bear.

"Mae, you stay in the kitchen and put up a kettle. Is Mike in the bedroom?"

"I moved him to Ethan's room. It's warmer in there. Do you need anything, Doc?"

"Just stay put. I'm going to take a look at Mike and then we'll see."

The warmest room in the house, and still cold. People heated these cabins in the woods with coal and wood. Coal cost, wood didn't. It was still too early in the year to use coal and there were two cords neatly stacked outside the front door, and another three in the shed. More than enough to feed the cabin's two wood-burning stoves for most of the winter. Still, come the real cold weather in December, they'd switch to coal. Keeps the place just as warm, but no worry about the fire going out in the middle of the night.

"Mae, bring me the lantern. Can't see a damn thing with the overhead," Doc said, pointing to the naked bulb dangling from the cord in the middle of the room. He looked down at the bed. It was empty, with just a heap of blankets piled in the middle. He started towards the door, assuming he was in the wrong bedroom.

"Mae... Mae."

A faint voice came from the direction of the blankets. Radler turned back and saw a slight movement under the covers.

"Are you under there, Mike? Is that you?"

No response. A bed piled high with mismatched blankets, again motionless. Doc moved closer, looking for any sign of life. He placed his black bag on a chair next to the headboard, and with a surgeon's precision, began peeling away one blanket at a time, folding each back, only to find another.

Another sound, a weak moan from deep inside the covers. He reached for the bottom blanket, gripped it firmly, and pulled it straight down to the foot of the bed.

There, lying on his back in the center of a soiled sheet, was Mike, dressed in long johns that were soaked through. The noise, no longer muffled by the blankets, was the recognizable language of unremitting pain. The putrid smells of leaking orifices quickly filled the room. Doc Radler reached into his bag and took out a tube of camphor. He squeezed a goodly amount on his index finger and spread it along the lower lining of his nostrils, then reached for the flask in his back pocket and took a deep swig that amounted to a quarter of the contents.

Mae, sitting at the kitchen table, staring into a cup of tea held fast in her hands, turned to see Doc standing over her.

"It's not good, Mae."

"Is it his time?"

"He's getting close. The pressure's going down and his heart is going a little crazy. He's in a lot of pain. I gave him a shot for it. Soon it'll kick in and he should be more comfortable. How long has he been that way, smellin' and all?"

"Maybe three, four days. Just yesterday I changed the sheet and look at it now. Couldn't get him warm. All them blankets, and couldn't get him warm. How soon?"

"Where's your boy?"

"Haven't heard from Ethan for weeks now."

"You going to want him here when it happens?"

"He's gonna want ta be here. It's time for me to get him?"

"It was time, Mae. It's close now, close. You still have that bottle in the house?"

"We always got a bottle in the house. You drinkin' too much, Doc."

"No sass, Mae. It's going to be a long night, and it's damn cold in this place; I'm going to need a drink. Now you get me that bottle and a glass. Tend to what you were doing. I'm going to look in on Mike. That shot should have started to work by now."

And it had. Doc Radler had given him a goodly amount of morphine. He took his patient's pressure; it was lower and his breathing more labored. Morphine does that.

Up until the spring, Mike Stevens was a strapping, vigorous man, making his living mining and keeping ice. More than forty years at the High Mountain Ice Company and he hadn't missed a single day. Not missing a day in the ice business meant six days a week in the warehouse tending to the large blocks of ice and loading them on the railroad cars for the trip to nearby cities.

In winter, the real winter when the ice was thick, six days became seven and most of the day, at least for the daylight hours, was spent mining the ice from the lake. This was not work for the physically weak or frail. Up until Mike's visit to Doc Radler, no one would describe him as either.

It had been years since Mike Stevens had visited the doctor and even then, he wasn't there for himself, but for his son. Ethan couldn't have been more than fourteen, maybe fifteen years old and had just started at the icehouse. It was his first winter and his first time with the cutting. No one knew exactly how it happened but sure enough, he'd taken a good slice out of his arm. They knew to wrap it as tight as they could and from the looks of it, they knew he needed to see Doc. Mike borrowed a car for the trip to town. He missed half a day of work, that's how serious he thought that cut was.

As it turned out, while he needed to see the doctor for some stitches, the blade hadn't hit anything major. That was all for the best, since Doc had already started his day's drinking and while his hands were steady enough to sew up a couple of pieces of skin, there would have been some worry if the sewing involved anything more than that.

While there, Mike said nothing about the lump under his arm that was giving him trouble when he put pressure on it. He paid it no mind and was doing just fine for the rest of the winter and through the next when Mae would no longer take no for an answer and told him to go back to the doctor.

She had first noticed that he wasn't feeling his usual self some time before. Aches, pains and general discomfort. Had it been the ice-mining season when the work was the most physical, she probably wouldn't have even noticed. It wasn't unusual for the men to do a lot of complaining during the ice cutting.

This new turn – that's what she called it – started when the harvesting was over, a month after it was no longer safe to be on the lake. The aching was followed by something peculiar, first only at night and then during the day, too. They would be sleeping and out of nowhere, he'd pull the covers off both of them because he was too hot. Mae, a very sound sleeper, wouldn't have noticed this except that when he did it, the cold would wake her up.

Awake, she'd take a look at him and there he'd be, his nightshirt drenched with so much perspiration that the sheet was soaked. A minute later, he'd start shaking with the chills. They talked about these happenings and since neither was the kind of person who ran to the doctor, they were satisfied with the notion that Mike just had got himself one bad infection that would go away with home remedies and rest.

This complacency ended abruptly when Mike came into the bedroom naked, after a bath. Mae saw her husband of twenty-seven years with a distended belly, his legs and upper body obviously thinner than they had ever been. It was time to see the doctor.

Neither Mae nor Mike was prepared for what Doc Radler told them. Cancer. He had lymphoma, and it was probably all over his body. He could certainly feel the cancer in his neck, in his spleen and even in some of the glands in his gut. Maybe if they came a little earlier he could have seen a specialist doctor and something could have been done, but not now.

No big city hospital trip, no X-rays, no tests. Doc Radler assured the Stevens that there was no mistake here, and even though he couldn't give them a date, the cancer would get him.

Everyone knew Doc Radler drank too much. How could he be so sure? But even if there were something that could have been done, Mike would have had no part of it. He had heard that with cancer, the medicine was worse than the disease. He was sixty-three. He considered himself lucky – up until a few months ago he was in good health and maybe it was simply his time.

Even though he didn't go to church as much as he should, he was baptized Catholic and believed if he was going to leave this earth, it was part of God's plan for him. His only regret was that he paid all that damn social security and if he were to die tomorrow, he wouldn't collect a single dime.

Doc Radler had last seen Mike Stevens on that spring day in his office and now here he was, late fall, trying to bring comfort to this dying man.

He had seen this disease many times before, and the way it ate up a person's body always turned his stomach. This was a man who once stood almost six foot, and now Doc could barely find him in his bed. Except for his swollen belly, Mike's skin, a greyish yellow, was paper thin on his bones.

And my God, look at his face. No flesh, eyes sunken, color ashen.

If it weren't for the heartbeat Doc could still hear through his stethoscope and the slow rise and fall of his chest, a casual observer would be convinced he was looking at a man dead for a week.

Doc Radler sat at the side of the bed, looking out the window at the falling snow, while sipping his analgesic. Thank God for the silver flask, his constant companion for all these years since Grace had left. He had been a drinker then but not as much as now and it wasn't the booze that sent her on her way. Being the wife of a small town doctor was more than she had bargained for. She liked the idea of being a doctor's wife. A lot came with being a doctor's wife, she believed: a nice house, new cars, expensive clothes, trips to foreign countries.

Except that the kind of patients who live down dirt roads in houses that won't get warm in winter don't pay their doctor enough money for new clothes or cars, let alone fancy homes and exotic vacations. After too many years to count, Grace Radler wanted none of them, or her husband for that matter. With much planning but no warning, she waited for her husband to make one of his house calls into the distant countryside. When she saw the car leave their quarter mile driveway and make the right turn on the blacktop, she reached for the suitcase that she had hidden in the second bedroom, dumped anything that she thought had value in a carpet bag, and cleaned out all the cash from the top drawer of her husband's bureau. She called for a cab to take her to the bus stop and closed the front door for the last time.

A note on the kitchen table read: *Goodbye. I won't be back.*

Doc Radler returned the next morning to an empty house. He wasn't surprised. Angry? Nope, not angry. He did feel a little sorry for himself, but that faded soon enough after opening a new bottle of Tennessee.

Now, sitting at the side of his dying patient, he gave Mike another injection. The least he could do was be aggressive in treating his dying and guarantee his patient a pain-free passage.

Radler placed the stethoscope in his ears and listened to Mike's chest. There were changes. He placed the back of his hand against his calf; the skin was cold to the touch, above the knee, still cold. It wasn't until he touched the upper thigh that he felt some warmth. Mike was struggling to breathe, reaching deeper to find the energy he needed to pull air into his lungs. It was time to get Mae.

"Come in, we're getting very close."

"How can you tell?"

"Put your hand on his foot."

And Mae did. First with tenderness and then with desperation, pressing the tips of her fingers into flesh and then bone, searching for any sign of life.

"Now move up his leg. You feel how it moves from cold to warm? His heart is having a hard time pumping. He'll get cooler and cooler. Soon his heart will stop."

Mae knew what was coming. Still, hearing the words was overwhelming. Her eyes filled with tears, she placed one hand over Mike's heart and the other on his cheek. Still warm. Both were still warm.

"Let us be. We need a few minutes to be alone, Doc."

"Of course, Mae, of course. I'll be at the kitchen table. I gave him a second shot so he should be very comfortable."

Doc left, closing the door behind him. Mae would be with her Mike, and he with the bottle of whiskey she had put on the table for him.

Mike, we're getting to the end. What am I gonna do without you? You're going to be in a better place, you'll be with our Lord Jesus. If only we had more kids, Mike. You never blamed me for not being able to have more youngins and for this I'm eternally grateful. A lesser man would have given me grief but not you.

I called that army number for Ethan to come home. They got to find him first, and then to get him back is gonna take a few weeks. If it were later on, if we were into cutting season, there'd be no problem. The ground would be frozen and we couldn't dig a grave. We'd put ya inta cold storage. But it isn't the winter and even though the snow's fallen there's plenty of burying time so I called Ozymandias. He said not to worry. He's got his ways. He can keep ya around for the four weeks until Ethan gets home and he can pretty ya up so he can remember ya nice.

Ya been a good husband, Mike. A good husband and a good father. I'm gonna miss ya and I'm never gonna forget ya. Me? You don't worry about me. You just rest, my love, until it's time for you to go.

Chapter Two

There you are my good fellow. Better than I would have hoped. If there ever was a fine specimen to bring out the artist in me, it is you.

Let's check the mailing label. Thank goodness for toes. Michael Stevens. A good name for sure. Your doctor was Radler. You could have done better in choosing a doctor in Mount Olden. Not that there is much choice – Radler the Drunk, Stensen the Feeble, and One Arm Johnson.

If it were me, I would have chosen Johnson. With only one arm he does have trouble with physical exams and from what I've seen on my customers, his stitching is a mess. Still, if I had to choose one of the locals, he'd be the one.

Fortunately I haven't chosen one of the locals. I go to Doctor Kagen on the other side of the mountain. It's a long ride, but look what I get for taking it: a doctor with two arms and an intact brain.

Relax Mike, you weren't cheated of life with Doctor Radler. No matter who your physician was, there's nothing any of them could do when it comes to cancer, especially when it's in those lymph nodes. They're all over your inside from top to bottom, except in your arms and legs and with you, there's not much left of those anyway. Maybe I'll take a look tomorrow and show you. With what you got and what got you, Doctor Radler was just fine.

Maybe even better than fine. He's a man who can't tolerate even the smallest amount of pain. Before he feels the first twitch he has a glass in his hand. I'm sure he gave you whatever you needed to make you comfortable. In fact, he might have even given you a little more than was necessary.

It's late and you have made this a long day for me. Let's put you to bed for the night and we'll begin tomorrow.

Oscar Ozymandias took pride in the very personal service he offered to his customers, both the dearly departed and their living kin. Customer satisfaction is at the heart of any retail operation, and what could be more retail than undertaking? His product was peace of mind for the living, and that's what they got when they did right by their dead.

The call from Doc Radler had come soon after he'd seen the car out on the road. Michael Stevens had just expired. He needed to be brought back to the mortuary. Now it got hard. It had started to snow in the early evening, it was still snowing in the early morning, and the hearse was not the best vehicle to navigate the back roads to bring old Michael back to town. It might be hours before he could get up there and if the snow didn't stop, and the roads weren't cleared, hours to bring the body back.

This last possibility was unlikely since it was only the beginning of November, and major storms that the road crews could not handle were unheard of at this time of year. Still, if the widow thought he was making an extraordinary effort on her behalf, it was good for business.

He explained to the doc that the body needed to be kept cold in order to do everything that the widow was asking for. Was there an unheated structure on the property that was separate from the house? Could they wrap the body in a sheet and move it there? And finally, could they pack the body in snow? All this was very important for a successful reconstruction.

The last detail involved the death certificate. When Ozymandias finally arrived at the Stevens', the doctor was long gone and there was no signed certificate. In its place was a sealed envelope that Doc had instructed her to give to him.

Oscar, it's been a long night and I'm out of here. You know the routine. 'Cause of Death: Cancer.' Note the time, sign my name and keep a copy for me. Thanks, Radler.

The last detail, and no surprise. Ozymandias had a drawer full of certificates he had signed for Radler that had never been picked up.

This had been no ordinary day for Oscar. He hated the snow, even though it was good for business. These country roads were treacherous and there were always a few fatalities. Add to that the work that came from work accidents at ice-harvesting time and these were busy times.

There was the funeral business and the morgue business, and morgue business meant State money. He didn't have to wait for a bill to be paid or chase after a 'grieving' family. There was no hospital in these parts and with his only cold house for a morgue in over a hundred miles, Ozymandias' was where they brought the bodies. And as for the county coroner, that was none other than Doctor Thomas Radler, who did an occasional autopsy and issued death certificates. For big cases – a murder, for instance – they'd no doubt bring in an outside man. But as far as Ozymandias could remember, there never had been a big case in Mount Olden.

The trip out to the Stevens' house seemed endless. It was in one of the remoter corners of the county and the roads were poorly marked once he left the black top. Then there was the snow to contend with, eleven inches on the ground and still coming down. The damn hearse skidded once and after that he went no faster than twenty miles an hour. He had left his place at one and what should have taken no more than an hour became three. He wanted to scoop up his package, toss it in the back and be clear of these damn snow-filled country roads before it became really dangerous outside.

But Mrs Stevens wasn't about to cooperate with his plans. He found her and the mister in the shed, the mister just as he had instructed the doctor to leave him. The corpse, now covered with a sheet, was stretched out on his back on a board that was resting on two wooden horses. The body was completely covered with snow except for the face, which was fully exposed, and the right hand, which the missus held onto tightly. She sat without expression, facing straight ahead.

Oscar Ozymandias knew he was not going to be able to separate this woman from this man's hand. She barely turned her head when he came alongside her and softly whispered her name. She did turn to him when he explained that he had been summoned by Doc Radler to bring her husband back to town. Lord knows how long she had been sitting there with Michael.

For sure it was as frigid in the shack as it was outside, and Mrs. Stevens was turning as cold as her husband. Still she didn't move.

Oscar drew upon every bit of accumulated wisdom he had curried over many years in the business and did what any sensible undertaker might do. He invited Mrs. Stevens to sit in the back of the hearse with her husband for the long trip to town. He opened the folding gurney, draped the body bag over it and rolled it next to the wooden board.

Most undertakers need at least two people to move a body from one surface to the next. Not Ozymandias. He had learned early on to expect little assistance from whoever might be around when he went to fetch a corpse. Except for hospital calls – and most people who died in the county expired at home – family, friends or even neighbors were loath to come into physical contact with the deceased. He also appreciated the economics of the business. If he were to have an assistant for these occasions, and there were fifty to seventy-five a year, not counting coroner cases where someone was always on the scene to help, his overheads would jump and his profits plummet. Old man Olsen had taught him all angles of the funeral business, and how to maximize the dollar was one of them.

~

Before Ozymandias was Ozymandias, it had been Olsen's. Jonas Olsen Junior's father was the first undertaker in the county. Before him the rich called upon Steeds in the next county and the poor just dug a hole in any piece of earth on their property that wasn't too rocky, or found a sprawling meadow well out of town. If they couldn't afford Steeds, they certainly couldn't afford a plot in one of the three cemeteries.

Jonas Senior had learned his trade in a school in Philadelphia and brought the new techniques and equipment of the funeral business to this remote corner of Pennsylvania. He also introduced the low-cost funeral. Couple that with dignity and concern, and after being in business for three years no one was burying their own.

Economy didn't mean skimping on what was important to people. He was always polite and kind and that didn't cost him a penny. He kept a stock of artificial flowers and made sure they were always clean and in good repair. If a family didn't have the money for a real floral arrangement, they could rent one of his reusable ones for a token amount. Of course, if they did have means, the contract stipulated that he handle all floral arrangements and there was a healthy profit margin in that.

Maintaining a hearse was one of the major expenses in the business. At first Jonas Senior rented one when he had a funeral, but that wasn't the best arrangement. If you have to rent something when you really need it, you pay top dollar. At least ten times a year – when there was a fire, or the ice gave in during the harvest, or when one of those stacks of ice tumbled and landed on more than one worker – a funeral involved two corpses or more.

When he needed two hearses, the man he rented from charged so much that he actually lost money on the deal. As soon as he could, and that was pretty soon after he opened the business, Jonas Senior bought two used hearses from a family that ran six chapels in the big city. Most times he had one ready for himself and he rented the other out. He charged fifty dollars cash plus a full gas tank on return no matter how much gas was in the vehicle when he let it out. He didn't supply the driver. On the few occasions when both were rented, he gave the family of the deceased an additional day for waking at no cost. Good economics.

One of his major business principles was to keep the payroll small, and that meant Olsen's Funeral Chapel for many years only had one check to write on payday, made out to Jonas Olsen Senior, and that didn't change until Jonas Junior joined the business. He always paid by check, because that's what business people do. It leads to good honest practice and no problems from the Internal Revenue. He was audited twice by the IRS and proudly told anyone who asked that he didn't owe the government a dime and the government didn't owe him one, either.

The final economy involved coffins. Land was cheap and the county now had a pauper's cemetery where everyone was guaranteed a place in the ground. There were graves that accommodated ten bodies, and a marker. The coffin was the big-ticket item and Jonas Senior soon understood that a family's ability to provide a funeral for a dead relative had little to do with the actual funeral and everything to do with the coffin.

It was better for business to have a funeral, no matter how modest, than no funeral at all. He'd make a little money on the incidentals and the expenses in supplying them were minimal since he had to pay for the chapel, the viewing rooms, the morgue, even the hearse, whether they were being used or not. This was not the case when it came to the coffin, a considerable expense for an indispensable item that would be put in the ground with the deceased. And then Jonas Olsen Senior had an epiphany. Why bury the coffin? The families could rent one and an exchange could be made right in the cemetery.

The mechanics of transferring the body were simple enough and on a few occasions came with a welcome surprise. Most bereaved who opted for the rental, a wonderfully crafted seamless mahogany casket with brass fittings, left the graveside with the coffin firmly resting on wooden planks that straddled the open pit. A few stayed as the coffin was lifted from the planks and placed next to the grave while the cardboard box was assembled.

The transfer was easy enough. The silken sheet that the deceased lay on was in fact a plastic-backed cloth with handles on the four corners that were not visible to the naked eye during the wake.

The surprise? On two occasions the mourners, consumed by grief, devotion to their loved ones, and revulsion at the thought of an eternity stuffed in a corrugated cardboard box, halted the transfer and insisted on lowering the coffin into the ground. Olsen acceded with the understanding that each family would immediately repair to his office where payment in full would be made before a single grain of freshly dug earth was shoveled back into the grave.

Sturdy cardboard, how much could it cost? Charge for a cardboard box, have varying prices for renting reusable coffins, everyone could afford a funeral and Jonas would make a bundle. Within six months no one was having backyard burials and the lines were forming at Olsen's Funeral Home.

Until Jonas Senior woke up one morning, stretched, stood up with every intention of heading for the bathroom to relieve himself, and keeled over. Doctor Johnson, the Olsen's family physician, came right away and pronounced him in the house.

Cause of death: a massive myocardial infarct. He had died of a big heart attack. Known for being a very considerate man, he measured up to his reputation even in his passing. His apartment was on the top floor of the funeral home. All his son had to do was bring him down two flights of stairs and he was ready for funeral preparations. And what a funeral it was. A funeral director is an important member of the community in these parts and Junior spared no expense. He even rented a special hearse to carry all the floral arrangements to the cemetery.

Jonas Junior had been working with his father for many years and knew the business inside and out, and with his son Tom as his helper, he'd keep the business going.

But without his father, Junior lost heart for the business and three years later began looking for someone to take over. It should have been his only son and child, but there were problems.

Chapter Three

There was no explaining what made Tom Olsen so peculiar. He just was, almost from the very beginning. Not that it raised much concern from his parents. He wasn't a good listener but then most kids weren't. They said he was chunky, but his grandma said he reminded her of her youngest brother who was just as uncoordinated as a child and turned out fine.

They noticed but didn't give it much mind till he reached adolescence. He barely got through his first year in high school, missing more days than he was there, and when he did get himself into the classroom he was disruptive. Cheap wine became his only friend and by fifteen he had a drinking problem.

Jonas was prepared to send him away. Not so Mama.

"Tom, he's our son. I can't just kiss him goodbye and throw him out on his own. Let him help in the business. He's a good boy. He just got a few problems, but I can't give up. Not without trying just one more time."

It took Mama a lot of pleading because Papa could easily imagine the harm the boy could do to the business. But she eventually prevailed. He always did show a fascination with the departed, sneaking down to the embalming room and puttering around the bodies. What surprised his parents was that no matter how trivial his assignment, and it included a daily cleaning of the parlor top to bottom, and a thorough scrub of the toilets, he did it without balking.

There were setbacks. Mama could tell when they were coming. There was usually something to set him off. Mostly words with Jonas but there was that time with Sally Jenkins.

Sally was a pretty one. She finished high school with a business degree and got a good job as a bank teller. Tom took a shining to her. Not that he did anything about it, other than mutter under his breath how much he loved her. She never heard these mutterings since he never had the courage to go within a block of her. There were, however, a few occasions when he was close enough to Papa for him to hear of his lust for a girl who barely knew he was alive, and Jonas would torment his son for his inaction.

Mama noticed the missing condom from Tom's underwear drawer but made nothing of it. Since he left school he always kept one in his wallet just in case, and replaced it periodically because it would become brittle after months of just sitting there in wait. It was the change in his appearance that let her know a storm was coming.

Tom never was the neatest but given that the family was in the service business he tried. That meant bathing at least twice a week, clean dungarees and shirt when he was working in the back, wearing his one pair of black pants and the white shirt Mama always had ironed when he was wheeling a casket to a hearse or attending a wake. A daily shave. When he missed a day or two of grooming he was a fright. So much so that the kids would tease him, those who didn't ran in terror to their parents, and customers would take a wide berth to avoid any contact.

A few days after his physical appearance deteriorated, the drinking would begin. Now that he was working, he had moved from cheap wine to cheap whiskey. It didn't take much of that to plummet him into rowdiness and a day or two behind bars. Had this been in a big city, rather than a small town where everyone knew Tom Jr and his ways, it would have been longer.

And then Oscar Ozymandias appeared in Mount Olden. He was polite, well spoken, neat, and pleasant to look at. Sharp features and not a hair out of place. Smart and religious. Mama spotted that right away. He often had a copy of *Life* magazine under one arm and a well-marked Bible under the other.

Jonas took him on to help with the customers, then introduced him to the technical aspects of the funeral business; body preparation and embalming.

But Tom recognized a bully when he met one. He couldn't say exactly what it was about Oscar that raised alarms, but they were going off. Everything about Ozymandias reminded him of every bully who had abused him with words and a punch in the gut. And as he always did when life's challenges became more then he could bear, Tom went on a binge that ended with a full five days in jail.

The best candidate to take on the funeral home was now clear. Ozymandias had a spiritual side to him and had spent many hours volunteering at the funeral home, giving comfort to grieving family and friends. And he wasn't a drunk.

Jonas approached Oscar on Monday, Oscar thought about it on Tuesday, and the deal was signed on Wednesday. An undisclosed sum of money was exchanged and Junior agreed to have his son Tom stay on for six months to teach Oscar every last detail of the business. A good student, it only took Oscar four months.

Six months to the day that the key to the front door was passed to Oscar Ozymandias, Tom Olsen and two other employees who together had accumulated thirty-seven years of service, were let go. The next day the sign that had hung over the doorway was replaced. After thirty-seven years,

Olsen's became Ozymandias' Funeral Home, which didn't go unnoticed by the town. There would no longer be a familiar and comforting Olsen at that moment of loss and grief. Now it was Ozymandias. And what kind of goddamn name was Ozymandias anyway?

Chapter Four

Tom couldn't get used to all the changes that came with his father selling the business to Oscar Ozymandias. It was rightfully his, he didn't see his father's betrayal coming, and took no comfort that enough money had been put away for him to be able to live modestly. This wasn't a father's act of generosity. It was a mother's act of persistence. Mom Olsen's constant nagging that they had to do right by their dim-witted son.

Tom was good with his hands. As Ma would say, "That boy is good at taking care of two. But ask him to put two twos together and he's lost."

For Tom Sr that translated into his son being able to handle a dead body, but ask him to convince someone to buy a casket to put it into, or write up a bill for a funeral, or perform the accounting that comes with running a business, and he was lost.

Tom loved working the bodies, but now the part-time work that Ozymandias threw his way barely satisfied that craving, and was a reminder of what he had lost.

He also missed the apartment above the funeral home, where he had lived since his brutal home birth. As Mama recalled it, "More pain than any woman should endure. Five days counting. The midwife said 'enough is enough. Got to go in and get that sucker.'"

Which was exactly what she did. Reached right in there, the way the local vet did with a pregnant cow, and pulled that baby out. Butt first. Blue as you could imagine and it took more than one healthy slap on that butt to get the boy to take that first breath and start crying.

Growing up, Tom's only friend was his home itself, his magic castle. Right in the center of town on Main Street, it was set back from the street with a large lawn and two sprawling oak trees. Tom likened them to guards, there to protect him from a hostile world. Rumor was that it had been the home of the county's wealthiest ice-harvesting family, who owned three lakes, many ice houses, and distribution from the mountains right into the cities.

While the outside was what folks called stately, the inside was rich in detail. The parlor floor had oak paneled walls, carved beams running the length of the ceilings, gas fixtures in each room for lighting, as well as electric outlets along the base boards for lamps.

There were four bedrooms on the second floor, a large parlor, a second kitchen and a bathroom. Imagine a house with two kitchens and two toilets.

And it had a secret passageway from the first to the second floor that he had discovered and kept secret. It was in the pantry in the downstairs kitchen, which had become the office when the funeral home was established. As a child, Tom liked this room because it was like a maze, with its filing cabinets, metal shelving and scattered boxes on the floor that his dad used to store office supplies and old ledgers.

Tom discovered the secret door quite by accident. He had tripped over a box, fell on his behind, and tumbled backwards against the side wall. He heard a pop, and one of the panels eased open, revealing a three-by-five foot opening and a ladder bolted to the wall, leading up to a closet in the bedroom his mother used for laundry, ironing and mending clothes. Tom called it Magic, his secret that he revealed to no one, even when his mother pressed him about how he could have gotten from the first to the second floor when she hadn't heard him using the main or back staircases.

Just as Tom Jr didn't see that his father wasn't going to leave the business to him, he never realized that he'd have to move from his childhood room in the family apartment when Olsen's changed hands.

The money his father had put aside was enough for a rented room with a kitchenette about a mile off the poorer section of Main Street. There was room for a single metal frame bed, a sitting chair with a lamp, and a small kitchen table. The bathroom was shared with another apartment on the same floor, a studio used by a few women who conducted their business there. A lot of people came and went, which Tom didn't much mind except for the few times when there was a row, usually due to a misunderstanding over money.

Tom once paid a visit to the girls but found it unsatisfying. What they had to offer was no match for a pint of whiskey.

Chapter Five

There was still more for Oscar to learn about the undertaking business. Decreasing overheads increased profits, but how could one man handle all the corpses? Oscar anticipated this problem during his apprenticeship and took appropriate measures. He was an exceedingly strong man and at six feet two could lift and jerk three hundred and forty pounds of dead weight over his head. Of course, a dead person was more difficult to manage than iron disks on a metal dowel. Still, except for very heavy clients, he could easily lift and place them where he wanted.

That worked once the deceased was back at the funeral home. It didn't work when he had to remove them from their home, where seventy percent of people in the county died.

The problem was family. Dignity, the lynchpin of the funeral business, would be compromised if a mother, daughter, wife or brother saw the undertaker handling the newly departed like a sack of potatoes. Dignity and the one-man carry was an impossibility, until Ozymandias found the solution. Within three weeks on the job, he had conceived the adjustable gurney, a contraption that brought the gurney as low as a foot off the floor and as high as four feet from the ground. The first step was putting the body into a supine position, sliding a body bag under it, and finally grasping the handles on the sides of the bag and pulling the corpse onto the gurney. And there you have it, the one-person pick up.

The second matter that emerged wasn't as easy to solve. At a minimum, Ozymandias needed someone to answer the telephone and act as a receptionist. The requirements were very specific. In this business you can't miss a call, and the call usually comes via telephone. Devotion, that's what was needed. Oscar was on a search for a woman, middle aged or older, who lived close by, mostly stayed at home, and had no romantic interests. A church lady would fit the bill.

The answer came in Eva Hoolday. She was a hard worker, lived two doors down and was unmarried. Her only shortcoming; although a Catholic, she rarely went to church. He gave her a telephone with the same number as his so she could take his calls when he was out.

But when the call came in about Mike Stevens, Oscar was in.

~

Mae Stevens wasn't about to let Oscar stuff her Michael into a bag and zipper him up. Oscar was in no mood for an argument, but he was mindful of the danger of traveling on snowy back roads. He could argue with her and waste time, or honor the widow's wishes.

The transfer was easy. Michael weighed next to nothing and all Ozymandias had to do was grasp the sheet Doc had wrapped him in and slide the package onto the gurney.

"It's going to be a tight squeeze in the back of the hearse. Are you sure you don't want to stay here? The Mister will be all right with me."

It was worth a try. It would be better for the both of them, the widow and the undertaker, if she could say goodbye now. The trip back would be even longer than the trip coming, the snow was still falling, and Oscar wasn't looking forward to being in a moving vehicle for an hour or more with a wailing woman.

"I can't stay here tonight. I need to be with kin. I need to go to town. I need to be with my Michael."

Ozymandias knew that the ones who don't cry at the beginning are prone to overwhelming outbursts later on. There was no telling what could happen with him in the cabin and she stuffed in the back of the hearse with her sheet-wrapped husband.

"You come sit up here with me." Soft and non-directive, that's how he asked.

"I need to be near my Mike."

"You'll be near enough. Take a look inside. I'll open the glass partition so it'll be just like we're in a car and he's riding in the back seat. We also need to keep you safe and comfortable. With this snow coming down and the roads the way they are, I can't do either if you're sitting on the floor back there. I hit a hole or go over a rock and you'll be up in the air."

"What about Mike?"

Oscar said she needn't worry; belts would hold him to the gurney and two clasps held the gurney to the floor of the hearse.

When he designed that adjustable gurney he thought of everything: how to keep the body on the thing and how to keep the thing from moving around in the hearse. Once the deceased was on it, the body didn't move until he got back to the funeral home. Even the portable ramp that he used to wheel that gurney into the hearse had been specially built. Oscar had thought of everything and when it came time to start down the dirt road from the Stevens' house, Mae was next to him and her Michael was in the back, just where he belonged.

It's usually hard not to make small talk, especially when two people are alone in a car and it's going to be a long time before they get to where they are going. It's usually easy when there is a grieving person. If they're in the presence of the right person – and Oscar was professionally personable, that was part of being a successful undertaker in a small town – then talk comes easy and it's almost always about what they have just been through, what life was going to be like without their loved ones, or what they wanted from a funeral.

The Widow Stevens sat in absolute silence, just looking at her husband who was now secure in the back. Oscar said nothing, knowing that another part of being the best in what he did was not intruding on people's silence, which he knew was often their attempt to reach out to the Almighty to get the strength to help them through this time of sorrow.

"Ya remember what I told ya on the phone?"

"Pardon?" Oscar was thinking about the meat he'd left defrosting back in his kitchen, and the rich, peppery stew he would make with it.

"I called ya right before Mike's passing, remember?"

"Of course, Mrs Stevens."

"It's Mae."

"Mae, then. You need me to do the special treatment since the funeral won't be for a while. I can give you three, maybe four weeks."

"What will he look like? Our son ain't seen him for a while. Don't want him to see his Papa this way."

"Disease really got the Mister. Cancer, wasn't it? It does that to the body. I'm going to try my best, Mae, and if anybody can bring your Mike back to looking as he did before he got sick, it's me. Mind you, if you were waking him right away it would be easier, but I understand and I'm going to do right by you and your family."

Oscar liked to know things about 'his' families. This was his first encounter with the Stevens clan and now that Mae had begun talking after sitting silent in the hearse for the first twenty minutes, it was easy to get her chatting about her family.

The Stevens had two children. Ethan, who was in the service, and Jane, who lived with her husband and kids on the other side of the mountain. She had moved pretty far away when she could just as well have stayed right here. Family tension was the reason. They were a good Catholic family, except for Mike. He didn't go to church, didn't take communion, and hadn't gone to confession since he and Mae were married. In fact, the day of their marriage was the last time he was in a church.

Mae tried to keep the family on track. Both kids were baptized, and when she could find a ride with a neighbor, they went to Sunday Mass. This wasn't enough for Jane. When she got to the age that kids fight with their parents, she argued with her father about his heathen ways and blamed her mother for her obvious weakness. At fifteen Jane found herself a twenty-year-old who went to church every Sunday and had a good job in the local hardware. A real catch. A year after they were married the bride was pregnant, her husband got a job in the hardware store in the next parish, and the family moved to the other side of the mountain.

Oscar just listened, keeping his eyes fixed on the snow-covered road in front of him.

~

Jane knew her father had been sick and visited him once after an estrangement of many years. She offered him salvation; her priest would be willing to make the trip to hear his confession. The cancer, already eating up his gut, made for a wave of nausea just as Jane had said the Lord Jesus Christ's name aloud. At that very moment Mike Stevens turned his head and vomited putrid-smelling bile. Jane took this as a sign that her father was again rejecting salvation and walked out of her parents' house. That was the last time she saw her father.

Before leaving the house for her last ride back to town with her Mike, Mae called Jane to pick her up for the trip back home. Her daughter was waiting out front when the hearse finally arrived at the funeral home.

The two women rode back home in silence; Jane was keeping her mind on the road and Mae planning a visit to the priest to talk about the funeral. The last time she had been to Mass at Saint Anselm's, Father Reilly had been the pastor. Poor man had passed a few years back and now there was a new priest, Father Paul. He had heard her confession a few times but she had never heard him say Mass. Tomorrow she and Jane would pay a visit to Father Paul to arrange a Christian burial for their husband and father.

~

It was four in the morning and Oscar Ozymandias was still up. Having made sure the body was safely stored in his cold house, he had one more pressing task before he could go to sleep. The cubed meat was just where he had left it more than twelve hours ago, cool to the touch and completely defrosted. He unpacked it from its wrapping, washed and dried it, and seared each piece in a frying pan.

Oscar took pleasure in his planning. Before running off to the Stevens' home, he had cut the potatoes, carrots and celery. All that was left to do was put everything in the kettle, adding stock and seasonings: bay leaf, salt, pepper, and of course Tabasco. He liked his stew hot and spicy. He covered the pot, put it on a very low flame, turned off the light and went to the bedroom where he crawled into bed. His suppers for the next five days would be done by the time he woke up.

Chapter Six

Before St Anselm's was St Anselm's, it was Hackie's Hotel. That was some forty years back, and it was good that the elders who put together the deal to buy the building were no longer around to tell what went on there before it became a house of the Lord.

The thirty families, known as the Founders, put up what little money they had and with help from Monsignor Henry at the Diocesan office, they had a building. Hard work, sore backs and calloused hands made Hackie's into St Anselm's.

It took over a year to fix the place up. The first order of business was to create a space large enough for the pews and sanctuary. The congregation took possession on a Thursday and that Saturday ten men with crowbars, saws, sledge hammers and shovels took apart what had been a living symbol of the fallibility of man; the saloon.

They cleaned out every last bed from every last room on the second floor. Not much furniture in those rooms, but then there was no need for anything more than the bed since no one stayed the night.

There was a kitchen and bathroom up there and that was good since this would have to be the rectory until more money came along to buy a real house for the priest. Forty years later, the rectory was still on the second floor.

There were men who were handy with plastering, painting, and fashioning the windows for stained glass when there was money to buy them. The carpenters started on the pews and the kneelers. They made sure that each accommodated at least ten good Christians and by the time they finished, there were ten pews on either side of a main aisle leading to the nave. The altar was hewn from a section of the bar. There was no trouble making it long enough, it measured roughly twelve feet, but they couldn't get the five feet needed for the width. Still, it was wide enough for the five Greek crosses that were burnt in the corners and the one right dab in the middle.

There was no disagreement about reclaiming the bar, although there was some disagreement about why. Some were partial to this being a symbolic act; a counter of sins now the platform for the Lord's gospel. Others saw it as a way to save a buck.

The timber side altar was for the tabernacle and the locked box containing the Eucharist, the bread that had been consecrated during the Mass. It was unthinkable to have it made from anything from the building's sinful past. Two men went deep in the forest that surrounded the town, felled one of the older trees, and brought back a section of the trunk. The side altar was crafted from this gift of God.

All that was left to do was build a pulpit and a confession box. The carpenters again turned to parts of what had once been Hackie's.

The first Sunday after the last lick of paint and the final nail was put in place, a new house of the Lord was consecrated as a holy space for the Lord's children to meet. A new church was big doings in this part of the country and seeing as there were only five more years before the century ended and the new one began, nothing short of the Bishop would have done honor for the service.

The Bishop got to town on Thursday, traveling by coach through winding mountain roads with his assistants and wardrobe for his vestments. Come the consecration of the church, there were so many who were part of the service, the deacons, sub deacons, thurifers and acolytes, as well as the Bishop's familial, that there was hardly room for the congregation. Every seat in every pew, and every inch along every wall, was filled.

~

The Mass had already begun by the time Mae and Jane arrived. St Anselm's hadn't changed much since its consecration. There was now a steeple but the congregation had run out of money when it came time to buy a bell, so it was still left to the priest to come out onto the street with his hand held bell for the call to worship. Someday the steeple would have a bell of its own. Someday.

Mae attended Mass on Sundays as often as she could. Which wasn't too often, because it was difficult for her to get into town. Janie, on the other hand, was a regular. She went to daily Mass at St Peregrine's, her church. She'd get to the six o'clock Mass and be back home before her husband got up for work and the children got up for the day. She loved her pastor and she loved her church.

Jane always thought it prophetic that she was raised in a church named for a Saint who was a thinker, a man who absolutely proved the existence of God, since the people who called St Anselm's theirs used their hands and not their heads and didn't go very often anyway. When she was growing up there were always seats to be had on the few times she got to church, even though there were enough Catholics in Mount Olden to fill every pew four times over.

It wasn't until Jane married and started attending St Peregrine's that she found the meaning of being Catholic and wouldn't you know it, this was the story of St Peregrine Laziosi. He started out being against the Pope, and look where his holiness took him. He became a believer and a saint.

St Peregrine was the patron to be invoked when you have cancer, and here she was with her mother to speak to Father Paul Dollard about burying her father who had just died of cancer. If only her parents believed, if only her father were part of the faithful, if only they had listened to her, gone to church regularly, and prayed to St Peregrine Laziosi, she had every confidence that she would not be here today.

~

"Mae, my condolences. This is your daughter? Jane, isn't it? It's been years. Let's go to my study. It's upstairs in the rectory."

Years, Jane thought. She barely knew the man. She had grown up with Father Reilly. This Dollard priest had only been at St Anselm's for five years and if he had met her twice in all that time, it was a lot. This sense of knowing her, remembering her, this pastoral intimacy of a preacher knowing his flock, irritated her. She imagined him having a card in the parish files: *Stevens, Michael and May. Children: 2, Jane, last seen 1930.* Knowing a detail about her might impress her mother, but not her.

And as for his looks, she had opinions on that, too. She knew what a priest should look like, and it wasn't what she had her eyes on now. Heavy, sloppy, poorly groomed. And sickly.

Father Paul's study was simple enough, too simple for Jane. No books, a picture on the wall of the Holy Father that could have come out of *Life* magazine, and a yellowing picture in a tacky plastic frame on his desk of a bunch of seminarians. He must have been in there somewhere but she couldn't make him out. Maybe the heavy one in the back row.

She had been in Father Conte's study at St Peregrine's. One whole wall was filled with books, a large carved desk was at its center, and on the far wall, a picture of Father at the Vatican receiving the blessings of the Pope. And he was Italian, just as a priest should be.

"Father, we are here to talk about the funeral."

"Of course, Mae. Come, let's sit around the table. I'm going to have Sada bring some coffee. Would you like some?"

Sada. Everyone in Mount Olden knew Sada. She took care of the rectory and Father Reilly, and now she was here with the new pastor. There was speculation about her age since no one could remember when she was not serving the church. Old but not frail, and she didn't look homely. She always wore a colorful dress, had long dark hair which she kept in a French braid, and wore a wedding ring. Rumor had it that her husband was one of Teddy Roosevelt's Rough Riders and gave his life serving his country. It was known as a fact that he was not nice to his bride, and even hit her once or twice.

When word came that Raulf Weisen wouldn't be coming home, Sada observed the obligatory period of mourning, wearing black for a year. The day the year ended she was back in her colorful dresses, and given the horror that comes with living in an abusive marriage, vowed to stay single and serve her church for as long as God gave her.

Here she was, with a tray holding a pot of coffee, a sugar bowl and creamer for the guests, and a pitcher of water for the priest, doing just that. Before Mae and Jane had a chance to answer Father Paul about the coffee, it was on the table in front of them.

"Anything else, Father?"

"That's all, Sada. If you could close the door."

Sitting around a coffee table was unnatural to Mae. Father filled the first cup and pushed it towards her. In the sugar bowl were little cubes and a small pair of tongs straddling the edge. Uncertain about what to do, Mae sat with her hands in her lap. Sensing her confusion and discomfort, he filled a second cup for himself, plucked two cubes from the sugar bowl with the tongs, added a little milk, stirred, and began drinking. Mae had already done the same by the time Father looked up in Jane's direction.

"Coffee?"

Jane loved her coffee. Still, she shook her head no. This was all too strange for the likes of her. She was used to seeing the priest in the pulpit, in the confessional, and when she was in their study, having them firmly planted behind their desks. This sitting in comfortable chairs around a coffee table was not to her liking.

"It's here if you change your mind. Now, let's talk about Mike. When did it happen?"

"Last night," answered Mae.

"How was his passing?"

"Easy enough, I think."

"And how was his passing for you? For the both of you?"

Mae didn't answer. He was asking the wrong question and that was for the best. Living with the sickness was awful and thinking of a life without her Mike was unthinkable. The dying was nothing compared to that. She needed her strength and if there was one thing she learned in all her years of living, it was to stay strong and focused during times of adversity. If Father had asked the right question there was no saying what she would have come to. For sure she wouldn't have been able to find her strength.

Jane didn't answer either. She was here to talk about her father's burial, not her own sentimentality, which was not to be found when it came to Papa. When she discovered Christ, she also discovered the devil, and the devil was in her father.

Jane couldn't have been more than twelve when she came upon them deep in the woods by the stream. She wasn't sure what they were doing, but whatever it was, she knew her father shouldn't be doing it with this woman. Her bare legs were around his waist as he pushed her back against the thick trunk of a tree. He was moaning, she was emitting bursts of air-filled groans. These were sounds that belonged to Mama and Papa. She knew that because she had heard them more than once as she lay in her bed trying to sleep.

Jane looked and listened with horror. Her only salvation was that her father and the woman were too busy to know she was there.

It was a secret that she could tell no one, not even her brother. She considered telling Father Reilly in confession, but thought better because it wasn't her own sin that she'd be asking forgiveness for. She decided to keep it to herself, hoping that someday she'd forget. She hadn't. Even to this day she still had dreams of the two of them together and when she woke up she'd be nauseous.

Jane's father adamantly refused to seek salvation through confession, no matter how many times she had tried to reach out to his soul. Now it was too late. He was dead and hadn't even been anointed.

~

"We got a problem, Father. My son, he's in the service. He hasn't seen his papa in six months and that was before Mike really got the sickness, before he got the way he looks now. It'll be weeks before they can get him back. Can't put Mike in the ground before the boy gets to say his goodbyes."

Father Paul was seeing emotion for the first time since the widow had sat down and it wasn't coming from a grieving wife, but a protective mother. Knowing it wasn't good or healthy not to grieve, he was thankful for the emotion he was seeing, no matter what was making it come.

He hadn't been a priest long enough to learn about grieving from his pastoral experience. It had been his grandma who had taught him. It happened when his own father and brother were killed.

~

The Dollard family came from two mountains over, right in the middle of coal country. Two mountains to the east might have been as far as Mount Olden was to Paris back then. The only way to get from there to here was to head down the mountains, swing around, and start back up again. When he was growing up he didn't even know there was a place called Mount Olden, although it wasn't more than fifty miles away. Now there was a road, but back then it was like the other side of the world.

Paul's father worked in the mines and that's where it happened.

A cave-in in Shaft #3 during the night shift. No one had to tell anyone when it happened; everyone heard the explosion long before the whistle started blowing.

Mama, Grandma and Paul grabbed what was handy, dressed and got over to the site before the whistle blowing stopped. They had reason to move quickly. Both Papa and Matthew Jr. were working the night shift.

There was smoke coming out of the side of the mountain where once there had been an entrance, and the rescue crews couldn't get anywhere near the mine, let alone down to where the men were.

All that was left to do was look to see who was milling around with a miner's hard hat on. Papa and Matthew Junior were nowhere to be found and within an hour one of the supervisors, whose job it was to keep track of who was and was not in the hole for precisely times like this, confirmed that both men were below.

For weeks after the explosion the fires burned, and it took a few more weeks for the smoke to die down. The mine owners determined that it would be unsafe for anyone to go into #3. They had Catholic, Baptist, Methodist and Lutheran clergymen conduct funeral services, and permanently plugged the entrance.

The day of the service, Paul and his friend Mark stood next to each other, both having lost a father and a brother. After official matters had been completed, Mr. Lundig, one of the mine owners, approached the boys. A physically imposing man, he stood more than six feet, wore a dark three-piece suit, had a bowler hat on his head and a cane with a silver handle on his arm. More remarkable than how he looked was that fact that he didn't have a single drop of coal dust on him, even though there was half an inch of the stuff covering the ground.

"Boys," Mr. Lundig said in a deep, resonant voice befitting a man with a homburg and a cane, "you are now the men of your families. Ya got to be strong. No sniffling or whining. Soon as you're old enough, we'll have you down in the mines. You hear what I'm saying? So long as I own these mines, and I ain't never going to give them up, you boys will have a job with me. Take these," he continued, raising his voice for others to hear, as he handed each an envelope. "Every two weeks there'll be another envelope. Not as thick as this one, but enough. It will be there for you and your mamas until you're old enough to earn your full share down in the mines. Just remember, no crying, no whimpering. You're now the men in your families."

Everyone at the funeral witnessed the public display of Mr. Ludwig's generosity and speculation went on for months about how much was in those envelopes. They were awful thick, everyone saw that. Some thought there was as much as two thousand, others said it couldn't be more than five hundred. Since Matthew and Paul had lost both a father and a brother, no one listened to those who were thinking of it on the low side. The town folks who knew Lundig dismissed the high number. He wouldn't part with so much even though he was a millionaire many times over.

No one, in their wildest imagination, would have imagined the truth – that there were two hundred one dollar bills in each envelope. Matthew and Paul had the wisdom to keep this a secret, fearing that if they told a soul this would be the only envelope their families would receive.

Matthew listened to Mr. Lundig and Paul listened to his grandma. The night of the funeral she came to his bed and saw a child who looked forlorn. No tears and a very long face.

"What is it, child? What's goin' on in that head of yours?"

"Nothing, Grandma."

"Don't be telling me mistruths, child." This would have seemed a rebuke except for the kindliness in her voice and the fact that while she was speaking she was stroking his forehead.

"I can't be talking about it, Grandma. Got to be strong now that I'm the man of the family. That's what Mr. Lundig told me."

"That's one stupid man, child. You should be feelin' dreadful having lost a daddy and a brother and you can feel any old way and still be a man. That is as long as you're feelin' what's measured to what you been through."

That wasn't what was happening to Matthew. His mama didn't allow a squeak of pain or sorrow to come out of his mouth without reminding him of his family responsibility.

After Paul's grandma said what she did, he cried for five straight days. On the sixth day he made some decisions. He'd be grateful for Mr. Lundig's money, but not grateful for the advice. He'd never take a single step inside a coal mine and would instead try to find something to do with his life that would allow him to pass on his grandma's wisdom that you could be a good man and cry.

Matthew, on the other hand, stayed 'strong', went down to the mine and turned his liver into brittle meat from all that liquor he was forever drinking.

~

Mae Stevens had just lost her husband of so many years and Father Paul was asking her how she was doing with that. He knew she might not be able to answer right then and there, but he also knew that by asking the question he was letting her know it was okay to grieve when she was ready and he'd be there to listen to her if she wanted.

"Where is Mike now?"

"Mr Ozymandias came for him last night," answered Jane.

"Excellent. Mr Ozymandias has things he can do so we can put off the funeral for a few weeks. Wouldn't want it to go much beyond that. What have you done to get Ethan home?"

"We were gonna do it today. Call the army. Let them know we need him back right away."

"Let's do that together. Sometimes those military types listen more to a priest. We need to get him back as soon as possible because in a few weeks the ground will be frozen solid and nothing will go into it. Wouldn't want Michael in that mausoleum out at the cemetery waiting for interment until spring."

This Father Paul did know from experience. There had been many funerals in the five years he had been at St Anselm's and the winter ones had always been the hardest on the families. First it was the death, then the funeral Mass and finally the interment. It was hard when months separated the Mass from the interment. It was going through the ordeal twice. Of course, there was nothing to be done when the ground was frozen and that would be coming soon. As for now, if Ethan returned in the next two weeks they'd still be able to get Michael into the ground. More than three weeks and there'd be trouble. The lakes were already starting to freeze over and the icemen were readying their blades and saws for the harvest.

"The funeral, Father. Will there be any problem with that?"

Paul thought this a peculiar question coming from the deceased's daughter and chalked it up to grieving people ask odd questions. "What kind of problems?"

"My father wasn't the best Catholic."

This wasn't coming from the place of grieving. This woman had something on her mind and Paul was a little uneasy about where this might go, especially with the widow sitting in the room. He turned to Mae. "Was your husband baptized?"

"He was, Father."

"He took Communion?"

Jane began to answer, but Mae talked over her. "Father is asking me, Janie. Not as often as he should have."

"Yet he still received the Host?"

"He did, Father."

"And where were you married?"

"In church, Father, in church."

"Catholic?"

"Of course, Father."

"Anointed?"

"No!" blurted out Jane.

What did she want? thought Father Paul. *Clearly this young woman carries a terrible unhappiness when it comes to her father.*

"The children were baptized, Mae?"

"Yes, Father. And Janie was married by Father Conte."

Father Paul leaned back in his chair. He knew what he was going to say and wanted this unhappy daughter to understand that the answer he was giving was thoughtful, earnest and theologically sound. A little showmanship never hurt, he thought, remembering some of his more spirited moments in the pulpit.

After a few minutes of silent meditation, Father Paul sighed, took a deep breath and came forth with his pronouncement.

"It is clear that Michael Stevens was not the best of Catholics. We ask our followers to be part of the community, to respond to the call of the Mass, to take the embodiment of what is good and holy from our Lord and Savior Jesus Christ through the offering of the Eucharist. And of the burdens of our sins, and let it be clear there is no one who is not a sinner, we offer penance and forgiveness through our confession. And where was Michael when it was his turn to speak to Our Savior, asking for His forgiveness? Yes, in the eyes of the Lord, this man, this husband, this father, was wanting.

"Still, he kept many of the Sacraments. He was baptized, he was married in the church and he, with his wife, have two children who number themselves as members of the Faith. Missa, Latin for sent. Through his children, Ite, missa est. Michael Stevens, with all his shortcomings, is a child of a charitable God and the Lord, Our Savior. He will be waiting to have his son return to Him.

"When it is time it will be my obligation and honor to officiate at the Mass. I'm having dinner with Oscar Ozymandias this evening and we can go over some of the details. Now, let's make that call and get your son home as quickly as we can."

Mae, comforted in knowing Mike would be waiting until their son returned, warmly grasped Father Paul's hand as she stood to say goodbye. Jane kept her hands firmly planted in her pockets as they left the study, nodding to Sada who dutifully appeared, tray in hand, to scoop up the cups and saucers.

Chapter Seven

"Let's go, Willy. Time for us to begin. Be a good fellow and fetch Mr. Stevens. He's out back in the cold house."

Willy knew what that meant. Back to work just when he was fixing to have a few minutes of quiet time without Mr. O. barking at him, to sip his coffee and chew on the chocolate-filled donut in the brown paper bag on his lap. He looked up at the familiar room, thinking of the hours ahead of him here.

Two sides of the embalming room were lined with glass-doored cabinets and the room itself was spotless. The walls and floor were tiled in pale green, and there was a drain in the floor to the side of a large, square metal sink in the center of the room.

Three metal tables surrounded three sides of the sink and were anchored to the floor. The tables tilted ever so slightly toward the sink and each had a phalange that extended beyond the rim for neat drainage. A bright light and a scale on a chain hung from the ceiling.

Oscar Ozymandias hadn't slept well last night. Professionalism was the cause of his fitful night and wonderful smells coming from the kitchen were what finally got him out of bed. Seven-thirty was later than he usually slept but very early when you get to bed at five in the morning. Two-and-a-half hours of sleep and so much ahead before he'd rest again. As much as he hated to do so, he had placed the call to Willy Catchum. Oscar was a one-man operation, but he had a list of people for when he needed extra help. As tired as he knew he'd be as the day wore on – and there was a dinner engagement at seven that couldn't be broken – this was a time when an extra set of hands would be helpful. He hoped he'd be able to nap somewhere along the way.

And this was not going to be a simple embalming. The widow wanted her son to see the father he remembered, not one riddled with cancer.

Finally, there was the matter of the soul. The man fashioned himself a Catholic even though he hadn't done what Catholics need to do. His wife told him as much as she prattled on during the long drive back to town with the body.

The widow had yet to speak to the priest, but Ozymandias had every reason to believe Father Paul would find some way to justify a Catholic burial. That might be all right with the priest and the widow, but it didn't measure up to the Ozymandias Standard. The work in the rehabilitation of one Michael Stevens would not be complete until both the flesh and the soul were tended to.

"What a glorious smell, Willy, glorious. That stew has been on a slow simmer all night and soon it will be done. Please, Willy, I'm waiting on Mr Stevens."

Cold storage wasn't as cold as it needed to be at this time of year. The room measured fifteen feet square and seven feet high. The walls were cinder block on the outside and wood on the inside. Together they made a great insulator. Along the perimeters were double-lined large blocks of ice from floor to ceiling. There was an abundance of sawdust, which retarded the melting. In the center of the room, two stacks with three shelves in each. Each shelf accommodated one body. In all the years Oscar had been in the business, he had never needed all six shelves. Once he used five, and several times four, when there was an accident with multiple victims.

With winter coming and the ice harvest beginning, the busy season would soon be upon him. He loved this time, with its endless opportunities to do God's work and make a hefty dollar. But right now, in late fall, the possibility of complications was always present.

One problem was that the warehouses where the ice was stored were by now depleted, with most of the harvest already shipped by rail to the big cities. Keeping cold storage as cold as it needed to be was a problem, and since Michael Stevens had been hanging around for quite some time, Oscar would breathe easier once the embalming was done. He was every bit as good as those Egyptians who preserved bodies for thousands of years, and all he needed to do was keep old Michael for four short weeks.

But who was this at the door? He opened it and found Tom Olsen, staring at him in that blank, resentful way of his.

"You need any help today, Mr O?"

"Not right now, Tom. Willy is here. Later in the season, when it gets busier, I'll let you know."

He turned his back, leaving Tom to let himself out.

~

"Well done, Willy. Now get him on the table and we'll begin. The widow gave me this picture of the Mister before the last bout of illness. This is what I need him to look like. Please get things ready; prepare the instruments and prepare the deceased."

Getting the body ready was easy enough, but Willy dreaded getting the room ready. Mr. O. was very exacting and preparations were never to his satisfaction. Sometimes it was the scalpels, either not having the right ones or not putting them in the right place. Other times the suturing material, the trocars, the hypodermics. The list was endless.

Now Willy was a good learner, he only had to hear something once and he knew how to do it. The problem was the rules were always changing. Sometimes Mr O. wanted the forceps on the left, the next time on the right. As far as Willy was concerned, it would be easier working for a surgeon than for this man. At least he didn't have to mix the embalming fluid. That would be an impossibility, since like the instruments, the proportions of the mixtures always changed.

Ozymandias, always the teacher in his white lab coat, was explaining something about the embalming. Some preparations were for the arteries, others for heart taps, and then there was cavity embalming. A little bit of this, a lot of that – or was it a lot of that and a little of this? And of course there were the body types, the cause of death and when the death occurred. Mr O. was always there to tell his assistant how complex and varied the job was. Willy Catchum knew this all too well, having assisted Oscar dozens of times.

"I need some help getting him up on the embalming table, Mr. O."

Clearly, Willy Catchum had not mastered the one-person transfer. This one would have been easy enough, since the deceased weighed next to nothing. No ambition, was what Oscar Ozymandias concluded. His helper had seen him maneuver cadavers that were five times heavier than Michael Stevens. Willy must have realized there was a technique that could be learned, but he had never asked. No matter how heavy or light the body, Willy needed help.

"Bring the gurney over here. We'll use Station Two."

Willy knew about Station Two; it was used for the more involved cases.

He wasn't pleased they were using that table; it meant this was going to be a complicated case. He waited for Mr O. to ask for the scale. He didn't. There was relief in that. He hated the scale because it meant they would be taking out the organs and weighing them. Usually that only happened in a coroner case, although sometimes Mr O. did it 'just for the practice'.

"Come on, Willy, get him ready. Time's a wasting. And check for the purge. He didn't eat for the last few days but there may be some. I don't want to see purge. Do you understand me?"

Willy was used to this man's irritation. His regular job was at the gas station and the money wasn't so good. If it were he'd say no when Ozymandias called for him to come over. Things as they were, he had his obligations, a wife and kids, and he needed the work. The best way to deal with his boss's nasty ways was to stick with the work and get started.

Willy Catchum pulled up the trash pail, got a pair of scissors and started cutting. The deceased was on his back on the embalming table, his head next to the sink, the eyes staring up at the overhead light. No blinking, of course. Mike Stevens was dead as a doornail.

He had come in his nightshirt and that's what Willy was cutting. Sometimes when they fell through the ice – which happened a lot in late fall and early spring when they were still trying to mine those last few blocks of ice – it was a pain to get the clothes off the cadavers. You've got coats, sweaters, long johns, the works. The nightshirt made for a good beginning.

In no more than two minutes the cadaver was buck-naked. Willy took one good look before he began the washing. It always struck him, this cancer thing. They'd be as skinny as anything except for their damn peckers. Given their emaciated look, it always seemed bigger in death than it could have been in life. If only it were the other way around what good fortune they would have had.

Willy grabbed a sponge and thrust it into the bucket so it could get thoroughly drenched with the disinfecting solution that Mr. O. had prepared. He started on the stomach and went first to the head and then down to the toes. He then grabbed the cadaver by the arm and leg and flipped him over. Mr. O. was right, he was always right. Some purge had accumulated in the mouth and was dribbling out. Willy took a smaller sponge, opened the mouth, and made sure that gravity did its work. A little more dribble was forthcoming. He took some forceps, grabbed another hunk of sponge that was soaked with disinfectant, and cleaned the inside of the mouth, reaching down as far as he could with the instrument. With that done, he got some gauze pads and stuffed them down the throat. He knew this would only be a temporary solution to the purge. Mr. O. would take care of the problem during the embalming when he threw a few stitches into the breathing tube and the gullet. No purge could get past those stitches. Until then, the gauze would have to do.

"The scrotum and rectum, Willy."

How did Ozymandias know? Willy wondered. That damn man was busy at the counter mixing the chemicals and had his back turned to him. Of course he was right. Willy was always cutting corners, particularly when it came to private parts. No matter whether it was a man or a woman, Willy had no affection for touching the rectum or genitals. Oscar was clear that cleansing and disinfecting was the job of the assistant, and the privates, more than any other area, had to be dealt with. "Think of us as doctors of the dead preparing the soul for its final journey, the ultimate journey. We're dealing with a soul's personal resurrection. That's what this is about, Catchum. We have an obligation. Professional, moral, spiritual and religious. Now do what has to be done."

And Willy Catchum did.

~

Michael Stevens, face up, his body tilted to the sink and with cotton stuffed in all his openings, was ready to be embalmed. Willy placed all the instruments and tubing on a rolling table. Oscar Ozymandias brought over the embalming fluid, some in pressurized containers, others in bottles that would be injected with syringes.

"A little music, Willy, I find music so soothing when I am about to begin a procedure. Put a record on the Victrola and turn it up a bit, we need music. A beautiful waltz, wouldn't you say, Willy?"

Willy said nothing. This was not the music he was partial to, and this was not the time he thought he should be listening to it. He knew what was coming and while it no longer turned his stomach, he didn't take to having sweet music in the background when he was mutilating a man's body. Still, Ozymandias was the boss and he did what he was told. If Ozymandias wanted it louder, he'd make it louder.

"We're following in a great tradition here, Catchum. Boyle in 1663, the Hunters, John and William, in the 1780s and Dr. Holmes during the War Between the States. A man before his times, that Holmes. They expelled him from medical school for the work he was doing and that is our good fortune, Willy, our good fortune. He devoted himself to perfecting techniques that we use to this very day. Maybe some day my name will be added to the list. Maybe some day."

Willy Catchum knew what followed next. Every time they used Station Two, Mr O. told the same story about the same people and after he spelled out his hopes and wishes, he reached for the scalpel and made the first aggressive incision to expose the arteries. In a matter of minutes he got to the right femoral and axillaries and both carotids. Then the veins, the large ones near the heart; for these he used a trocar. With all this done, he turned to Willy for the tubing that he inserted with precision. The blood was flowing from the veins into the sink, and the embalming fluid went in through the arteries where once there had been blood.

This was an advancement in technique; the incisions, the lifting of arteries and veins, the insertion of the tubing in vessels and the balanced exchange of fluid for blood. The infusion went smoothly and because dyes had been added, Oscar Ozymandias was able to follow its course through the capillaries that led to the outermost layer of skin. Of course he still needed to use the hypodermic needle for the areas where the embalming fluid had not reached, but certainly there were far less than when using traditional techniques.

"Did you see how quickly I entered the pulmonary vein? Anatomy, Willie, I know my anatomy. Using the narrow trocar with the razor-sharp edge is what did it. There are a few more holes that I'll have to suture, but that will be hidden by the new blue suit we will give this fine gent. One more thing and then we're done with this part. The cavity. Can't chance leaving anything in there. Mr Stevens may be with us for a while and if there is one thing his returning son does not need to see, it's a putrefied father."

Willy hated this part. It was bad enough seeing the sink fill with red. Now there was a good chance the bodily fluids, propelled by cavity gas, would gush from the hollow trocars, spray across the body and run down the sides of the embalming table. This not-so-delicate piece of equipment, a table so sturdy that it could easily accommodate a five-hundred-pound corpse, was built for just this possibility. The perimeter was rimmed with a one-inch lip, and being tilted, everything flowed into the sink. If there was one thing it was designed to handle, it was body fluids. The table was ready, Willy was not.

"The trocar, Willy. Where are you? Wake up and give me the trocar."

"The trocar, Mr O., here it is."

"Not that one you jackass, a number seven. This one is for the brain. Did you hear me say anything about a brain?"

Willy dutifully returned the number three and handed Mr. O. the seven. Oscar held it firmly in his right hand, placed his left on old Michael's chest, felt for the sternum, placed his thumb and middle finger on each clavicle precisely where it joined the sternum, extended his pinky directly down, found his anatomical landmark, and placed the sharpened end of the instrument in the precise place he had been looking for.

He worked it back and forth until he pierced the skin and when he saw some ooze, he thrust it in and up. First gas, then bile, and finally tinges of blood gushed through the hollow opening. He waited a moment, pulled the trocar back, letting it come to rest just as the tip was about to emerge from the skin, and then thrust it back again, only this time at a different angle. Ozymandias repeated this over and over again, adjusting the trajectory so that by the time he finished, every internal space and organ had been pierced.

Michael Stevens' naked body was now splattered and stained and there was liquid coursing its way down the embalming table towards the sink.

"Clean up, Catchum. I can't work like this. Keep up with me, man. Pay attention."

Oscar was starting. Every word was as sharp and coarse as the thrust of the trocar, and if a man could bleed from repeated thrusts and parries at his spirit, Willy Catchum would be as bloodied as old Mike Stevens there on the table.

Why did a man like Willy put up with it? If you asked the question, you really didn't understand what was happening in this county. There was so little work and the pay was so darn poor. Sure, the ice industry was booming, because no matter how hard times were people in the cities needed their ice. But beyond that line of work, which was only there during the cold weather, there wasn't much more that a man could do to feed his family.

It was time for a break, a cup of tea, thought Oscar. The work was intense enough without having to put up with the likes of Willie Catchum. Keys in hand, he climbed the long flight of stairs to his private quarters. He struggled with the lock, which needed a touch of oil. Tomorrow. For now it was to the kitchen and the kettle.

Oscar could smell it. Couldn't see it; everything looked as it should. But something wasn't right. It was in the air, a defiling, an intrusion. He inspected each room, but found nothing out of the ordinary, so he retraced his steps, closed and locked the door, and walked down to the parlor floor.

"What the hell!"

~

Tom had used the magic passage to get upstairs to his childhood home while Ozymandias was busy with a client in the embalming room. He had found the keys, and been unable to resist the opportunity to be in the house again.

And now, he couldn't figure out what he was seeing.

In the living room sat a locked double door wardrobe next to a perfectly good clothes closet. And a locked structure made with highly polished wood and metallic hardware four feet deep and five feet wide was set against the far wall. A piece of material caught in the door looked like it came from a priest's vestment. One of those bowls on the coffee table was similar to the ones he remembered seeing in church. And in the kitchen, shelves filled with sealed jars with strips and chunks of meat. Canning was usual in these parts. Mama used to put up all types of summer vegetables, fruits and berries for winter eating, but nothing like what he was seeing.

Tom didn't know what to make of it, but it all did seem peculiar. Again, lots of twos but no fours, as his mother would say.

The noise of feet clomping on stairs and the jingle of keys raised the alarm. Tom left his snooping and headed for the secret passage. Panicked, he almost missed one of the steps as he climbed down to the parlor floor. He got down with just enough time to be clear of the secret passage, but not in time to avoid an enraged Oscar Ozymandias as he came charging into the room.

Tom was no match for Oscar Ozymandias's accusation that he had "smelt him" in the apartment, or for the threat that if he ever caught him again, even though they both knew he hadn't caught him at all, Tom Olsen would never put a foot in the embalming room again.

No one saw Tom for days after the incident. He went on a bender. It was a wonder that he didn't do anything during those dark days to get himself locked up.

Chapter Eight

It was a wonder that a man like Ozymandias made a living. Folks in the county were still dying but when you're really poor, you find other ways to bury family. That public health law helped some. Maybe ten years back there was a bad outbreak of disease. It was traced to the water and it got there from decaying bodies. People weren't burying their kin properly. They'd just dig a hole willy-nilly, plunk the body in it, and that was that. Most graves were too shallow and if the animals didn't dig up the corpse, the decay and rot would leach right into the drinking water. The law didn't say who should do the burying, because in this county that would be called communism. It did say how it should be done and if you didn't, the fines were big. Lots of people still did their own burying, but with the new law there were some who didn't want to take the risk.

If you were Catholic, there was another compelling reason to turn to Ozymandias. Rumor had it he knew how to prepare bodies in the fine tradition of the Church and when he did the preparing, the soul went right to heaven. He liked to call it a resurrection, and that had great appeal. He fashioned himself a funeral director, not merely an undertaker, and made it a point to meet with next of kin to hear the story of the dearly departed.

There were two reasons for this attentiveness; bereavement and healing began with the telling of the story, and salvageability could be determined. This was more complicated to assess and only applied to Catholics, since the Methodists were beyond redemption. The local Methodist pastor would marry anyone and bury anyone before the altar of God. Didn't matter if they were baptized, ignored every tenet of their church, or lived a life deep in sin. You come, you ask, and Pastor Stenson delivers. Some religion.

The Catholics, and Ozymandias numbered himself among them, were different, but not as different as he would have liked. Since Paul Dollard took over the parish things had been slipping. Still nowhere near the damn Methodists, who were going in the wrong direction. Father Paul did ask if a person was baptized and looked to see if they had been married in church. That was it. What about the other sacraments? Confession, communion, the rest. What about them? Oscar Ozymandias listened to the Catholic families to see if their dearly beloved needed anything from him to assure the ascension. It also helped that he was a close associate of the priest and was known to give the family a break if Father Paul asked him. These were bad times when it came to funerals, and anything that Oscar could do with the price was greatly appreciated.

And there was coroner work. Someone was always dying from an accident that had to be investigated by the local authorities. The local authorities were one sheriff Heinrich Smith. When circumstances were unclear, and unclear meant one of the docs in town couldn't attest to the cause of death, Heinie needed to investigate, and that could mean an autopsy.

Doc Radler was the official coroner, as no one else wanted that job – it didn't pay much and most coroner cases happened in the middle of the night, and who wants to be pulled out of bed at two in the morning?

Radler didn't mind. Most times he was too drunk to leave his house when the call came and he just let Ozymandias go fetch the body. As for the post mortem, he didn't have too much stomach for that either and anyway, ninety-nine percent of the time the cause of death was evident. Either the deceased had frozen to death from falling through the ice, had hit his head falling down drunk, or ran his vehicle into a tree. There was no foul play in this Christian county, at least none that anyone could remember.

Oscar Ozymandias knew enough to do an autopsy and report things like Cause of Death: exposure, trauma secondary to alcohol intoxication, and so on. At the beginning Radler would go over to the funeral home, put his eyes on the deceased, and sign the autopsy report and death certificate. In recent years, he figured why bother? Oscar would call, tell him what he did and what he thought, and Radler authorized his signature being affixed to the appropriate documents. This worked out especially well during these hard times.

Suicide was never reported as the cause of death even though Doc Radler knew that it was the likely cause of some of the unexpected ones. Some were his patients and they'd speak of their despair, the strain of being unable to put food on the table. He knew for a fact, well almost a fact, that some of these unexpected deaths were caused by the deceased's own hand. What good would it do for that to be known? It would tear the families up and if they were Catholic, their souls would forever be in a restless state.

Between falling through the ice, drinking too much, and doing yourself in, there was a lot of coroner's work and the county paid for these burials. With everyone else it was a wonder that there was enough money for a decent funeral. Still, getting to heaven was taken seriously in Mount Olden, so people were willing to give their last dollar to assure a peaceful journey.

Between that and the coroner business, Oscar Ozymandias was one of the county's wealthiest citizens. Willy Catchum was one of its poorest. He didn't work for the ice company and had to rely on odd jobs that came his way. Between the few dollars he earned and the garden his wife tended behind their trailer, there was just enough money to put a good meal on the table for himself, the missus, and the four kids. His most reliable odd job was in the funeral parlor. Mr O. called him four or five times a month and paid him five dollars an hour in cash after each day's work. What better reason to put up with this man's nasty mouth?

~

"Keep up Willy. You like this work?"

"Sure do, Mr. O."

"Then you need to attend better to what's happening here. Time is important. Let the cadaver linger and we got putrification. That happens and it's not so easy to take it away. Slow down with the embalming and the arteries collapse and nothing will go in. A pint in, a pint out. Do you understand, Willy?"

"Yes sir, I understand."

"Now clean up and hand me the forceps, needle and sutures."

How could two things be done at the same time, Willy wondered. Logic would have him clean up before Mr O. moved to the next step. Experience taught him to keep his mouth shut. In one hand he had a big sponge soaked in disinfectant, and in the other the forceps.

"Not the dissecting, the arterial," barked Ozymandias. The embalming fluid was beginning to ooze through the punctures. The packing soaked through and he needed to close them quickly. Willy corrected his mistake and quickly finished sponging down the body, hoping to avoid another Ozymandias outburst.

By the time Mr O. was ready to begin, Willy had finished. He reached for a large watering can, also filled with disinfectant, and began pouring the liquid along the ridges of the embalming table to rinse away the residual blood, body fluids and embalming materials that had accumulated along the edges. He would hose down the floor when Mr O. was completely done.

Oscar knew this to be one of the most demanding ingredients in embalming. Suturing, along with restoration, required the highest levels of skill. He didn't have to concern himself with what was happening under the skin and after what he had done with the trocars, he knew a lot was happening. He began with the incisions that had been made in the groin and armpits, beginning the stitching before he fully withdrew the tubing. The holes left from the cavity embalming required surgical buttons. That's what Oscar called them. A more fitting name would have been surgical nipples but that affected his sensibilities.

The buttons were one of the many innovations he brought to the embalming table that he hoped would one day result in his name being listed among the luminaries. He had invented them after noticing that it was not always easy to fully close the trocar holes in the abdomen. Even though the cadaver was placed in a tight-fitting garment, a dead man's union suit, to contain the embalming solution, there was always significant staining with cavity embalming. When burial came within a few days of death, he never used this technique. When it didn't, the damn holes were so big and the sutures didn't provide a good enough seal.

Oscar Ozymandias saw opportunity where others saw problems. He needed to find a way to help the sutures contain the fluid. The solution evaded him until one day when providence struck. It was a Sunday, and the epiphany happened during the seven o'clock Mass. Oscar, a good Catholic, rarely missed a Sunday at church with Father Reilly.

He chose the early Mass because he had little patience for noisy children who were in great abundance at the ten and eleven o'clock services. He didn't fault parents for bringing their children; this was how good Catholics were made. He just didn't want anything to do with them. He even went as far as discouraging families from bringing the little ones to wakes in his funeral home.

It came to pass that on a particular Sunday, while Father Reilly was delivering his homily, a piercing, irritating noise emerged somewhere behind him. By the time he turned around to identify the source of this irritation, it had stopped. A few minutes passed and there it was again. A baby, a wailing baby. This time he had no difficulty spotting the three pews behind and to the left. A mother and infant, she holding him with one arm while reaching into a bag with the other. Out came a bottle and in went the nipple, right into the child's mouth, and catastrophe was averted. Father Reilly could finish the seven o'clock Mass before the eight o'clock began.

It was on his way home that the bells and whistles began in Oscar's head. Bottle, rubber nipple and controlled leakage through a tiny slit at the head of the nipple. If that slit was closed and the rim of the nipple was inserted in the wound made by the trocar and held in place with both glue and sutures, it could work. Oscar attempted the insertion on the next call. The procedure wasn't necessary but he couldn't wait till the appropriate candidate for cavity embalming came along. Whatever he did would be out of sight, so what difference did it make?

After the eighth try, Oscar Ozymandias was finally able to achieve a good seal. He jotted down each step in the procedure, quickly dressed the cadaver, and by the time the family arrived for the wake their dearly departed looked just as he had in life. What difference did it make that this man, this husband and father, now had five nipples, two that were given to him by our maker, and three more compliments of Oscar Ozymandias? Ralph Jackson's wife Cynthia, his sons Joseph and John, and his daughter Mary, never knew.

~

Oscar took a step back to look at his work. Before closing the last incisions of the carotids, he used the dissecting forceps to snare the esophagus and the trachea and dissected and sutured each, thus almost eliminating the possibility of further purging.

"We're now ready for the hypodermics."

"What about the eyelids and mouth, Mr O? Shouldn't we tend to that before we begin with the needles?"

"Do as you're told. Begin the massaging."

Willy had been Mr O's helper for eight years and knew enough not to be surprised by his strange ways and sudden changes in the order of doing things. Mr Stevens' eyes and mouth would stay open until Mr O. was ready to sew them shut. With the windpipe and feeding tube cut and tied, and a wad of cotton stuffed down the throat, leakage from the mouth shouldn't be a problem, even when the cadaver was flipped on its stomach so they could deal with the buttocks.

"Willy, I want to rotate the cadaver, putting the head here and the feet there."

Now this was really odd, and it didn't sit comfortably with Willy. He had seen enough bodies that death no longer upset him. It wasn't even a curiosity, so long as everything stayed in its place. On the embalming table, the place for the head was next to the sink. That's the way it always was, that was natural. Now Mr O. was asking him to switch everything around. Not sewing up the mouth was one thing, putting Mr. Stevens in this most unnatural position was quite another.

"Are you sure, Mr O?"

"Do it!"

"It don't seem right."

"You are impossible. Move away."

With that, Oscar pushed his assistant away, reached over the table, lifted Mike Stevens with the classic one-man carry, and in no more than a second the head and feet were reversed and the buttocks were facing up.

"Now massage."

Willy did what he was told, trying to avert his eyes so he didn't have to take in the whole of Michael Stevens. Looking only at the left buttock, he kneaded it as one would dough to be made into bread. The embalming fluid, which had a flesh-like tint to it because of an additive Mr O. had mixed in, began to emerge in the flesh under his hands. There were places it didn't reach and that was now easily seen. He used a hypodermic needle to fill in the gaps, especially the face, notably the cheeks.

"Good," said Oscar. "Now the wax."

It wasn't exactly wax, although there was some wax in the preparation. He filled a second syringe with a needle with a wider bore, injecting the substance subcutaneously, filling the syringe over and over again. This, he later explained to Willy, along with regular chemicals he had used, would delay the decomposition of the body for a few more weeks until the deceased's son arrived.

"We're done, Willy. Set up my cosmetics, do a cleaning, and then you can leave. Let's see. Two hours. This should be more than enough."

Ozymandias handed his assistant an envelope. Willy folded it, put it in his pocket, and proceeded to attach the hose to the spigot. He cleaned all the instruments, put out the makeup on the counter, and washed down the room. Thank goodness for that drain in the floor.

~

Oscar's workday was only half done. It would be hours before he'd be finished with Michael Stevens and even longer before dinner with Father Paul. He needed to fortify himself for the rest of the day.

His apartment, all five rooms, was to his liking, and why wouldn't it be? He had chosen everything, from the furniture in the living room, to the cups and saucers in the kitchen cupboard. The kitchen, his favorite room, had enough space for a small oak table, a freezer, and cabinetry for every device that would ever be needed for the preparation of fine food. Oscar Ozymandias, by any measure, fancied himself a gourmand.

Fortunately, lunch was already prepared. Oscar placed a modest portion of stew in a saucepan, heated it under a small flame and evenly distributed what remained in the pot into four glass jars, which he placed in the freezer for other dinners. He took a small package out of the freezer and left it on the counter to defrost.

Presentation is essential for a man of elegant sensibilities. Oscar Ozymandias was such a man. While he abhorred the reconstruction and application of cosmetics that would come when he returned to work, he did appreciate the absolute necessity of dining in refined surroundings.

The first order of business was choosing a tablecloth. It was a dreary, cold fall day. For balance he chose linen embroidered with springtime flowers. He plucked a rose from a vase in the living room. The flowers, although artificial, were of the highest quality. He placed the vase exactly in the center of the table next to a silver candlestick that cradled one long white tapered candle. Two dozen bottles of wine were in a rack. He picked one that he thought would be a worthy complement to the stew and opened it so that it could breathe. A crystal wine goblet, a cloth napkin, a silver setting, and the table was ready. He placed the copper saucepan on a trivet, selected a Puccini opera from his collection of seventy-eights, and he was ready. All that remained was to say grace and begin. A wonderful stew for a chilly fall day.

Oscar took a full half hour for the midday meal. He ate slowly, deliberately, cutting each cube of meat into even smaller pieces, placing morsels into his mouth. He stopped only to take sips of wine, letting the liquid move from one side of his mouth to the other before swallowing. Every taste complemented the other, every texture enhanced the experience. When all the stew on his plate was gone, he broke off an ample piece of crusty bread from the loaf that sat in a wicker basket and soaked up the remaining gravy.

All done, Oscar placed the napkin back on the table, blew out the candle and readied himself for his afternoon work. Cleaning up would come later. He reached for the small package he had taken from the freezer and took it with him. It had started to defrost.

~

Michael Stevens was just as Oscar had left him. Now well preserved, there was no longer worry about his turning foul and beginning to rot and smell; at least not for the next few weeks. Oscar took the picture Mae had given him, taped it to the shade of the overhead light, and returned to work.

Some undertakers considered restoration the art of the profession. Not Oscar Ozymandias. It was a step up from the work Margaret Hastings did for the wealthy ladies of Mount Olden. Every Saturday they were to be found in Margaret's Beauty Salon getting their treatments. They too were looking for restoration. It was just that theirs was not from death to life but rather from now to then.

Mind you, just because Oscar didn't like this part of the business didn't make him any less of an expert. Many of his clients were forever grateful and he was sure Mae Stevens would soon be one of them. He looked at the photograph, looked at Mike and looked at the tools of the trade that Willy had laid out. It was doable.

"Okay, Michael Stevens, let's begin. We've got two tasks before us, one more difficult than the other. The easy one is restoring the flesh and the hard one has to do with the soul. For the first, I make no guarantees. Your wife wants me to make you the father that your son last saw. If it were a stroke, a heart attack, even a fall through the ice, I'd say what she wants is very doable. You, my friend, died of cancer. That's a disease that eats you up. Mind you, I'll come close. That boy will know it's his daddy in the coffin. You just won't be exactly the way you were. I'll fill out your frame with some padding under the suit we'll put you in and he won't see a thing. You've got a nice head of hair and that beard will help. Looks like you haven't had a haircut or trim for some time.

"You look a little scruffy in the picture. Lots of hair means less exposed flesh. Still, that cancer had no kindness in it. Your hands, your face, and that damn beard. That's what I'll be working on and while I can't make any promises, you'll certainly look presentable for your last showing."

Oscar reached for the scissors, trimmed the hair and beard, and painted a little color into the cheeks. Not much he could do with the wasted hands, but folding them below the waist and placing a linen cloth with an embroidered cross over them would work just fine.

"Now for the hard job. Your soul. This is the beginning of the journey and you're not exactly prepared. I know, you are going to tell me the priest at St Anselm's has no qualms about your ascension.

"But Father Paul is just one step beyond those damn Methodists and nowhere near what a Catholic should be. He's not here carrying our Lord's message to make us feel good. A priest is here to lead his flock into everlasting salvation and that path is eminently clear. The sacraments, Michael Stevens, the sacraments. It's not enough to be baptized and married in a church. Was there a confirmation? Mae didn't know. When was the last time you went to Confession? Mae didn't know. And Communion? Mae didn't know. What she did know was you didn't receive the Extreme Unction. Or the Last Rites, as you would call it. You didn't just up and die, my good man. You were sick and you knew what was coming. With all that warning, how could you not have received the final sacrament? Still, I am told you were a good man. You stayed with your wife and your kids, and your daughter is a follower of the teachings. You did the right thing by them. Not enough, but something."

Something wasn't right. Oscar took a step back and repositioned the light. It was the cheeks. The color was good, but still? With so few teeth in his mouth and with the ravages of the cancer, Michael had that cadaverous look. He needed a bit of heft in the face. Oscar reached for two hunks of cotton, rolled them and with a pair of tweezers inserted them behind each cheek. Too puffy. He tried again, this time using some gauze. Better, much better.

"If you were a Methodist we would not be having this conversation. To join our Father, to join Jesus Christ our Lord and Savior, you needed to do more. It's too late for some of the doing. There's no longer time for confessing and you're too long gone for the Extreme Unction. All that is left is the Communion, the Eucharist, the making of Lord's flesh and blood part of who we are so we can walk in his righteous steps. It is a path that leads to Heaven itself. Understand what is being said to you, Michael Stevens, a good man with no belief. There is still hope for the resurrection of your soul to live in lasting peace with our Savior Jesus Christ."

Oscar pulled down a wooden box he kept on one of the high shelves. In it were the trinkets and religious ornamentation that often added that special touch. He pushed aside the costume jewelry; necklaces, earrings, a few bracelets, and rosaries. There it was, Christ on the Cross. He crossed himself as he placed it on the chest of the deceased, knowing it would mean so much to the widow.

With the intense concentration of a master of the craft, Oscar did a final inspection. Michael Stevens was ready. And so was Oscar Ozymandias, as calm descended upon both of them.

"Your Mae tells me you are a Christian, a man wanting to leave this world as he entered it, a Catholic. When you were baptized a priest anointed you with oil in the name of Father and of The Son and The Holy Ghost. With these words you accepted Jesus as our Savior and Catholicism as our community.

"Now you are poised to begin the last journey, the return to our Lord, and to begin this journey we again offer, and you will accept the Eucharist, the Offering, and The Host. You will accept the flesh and blood that I will consecrate in His name and that you now take into yourself."

Ozymandias went to the far cabinet, reached to the top shelf, and brought down a silver plate and chalice. He carefully unwrapped the package he had taken from the freezer, exposing a perfectly square piece of meat that measured no more than half an inch on each side. A beaker of blood that had come from Michael Stevens sat on a shelf under Table 1. Oscar poured the contents of the beaker into the chalice.

Ozymandias, by now almost in a trance, held the chalice and tray above his head saying, "Lord, you are holy indeed, the fountain of all holiness. Let your spirit come upon these gifts to make them holy so that they may become the body and blood of our Lord Jesus Christ."

He put the chalice and tray on a table next to Michael's head, and with forceps, reached deep into his mouth and pulled out the cotton swab that Willy had inserted a few hours ago. It was damp and smelled strongly of formaldehyde. He replaced the swab with the meat, took a clean swab of gauze, immersed it into the chalice, and then placed it, too, down Michael's throat, pushing it as tightly and deeply as he could until he felt the resistance of the sutures in the esophagus. He did all this while chanting the liturgy in Latin.

It was now time to do what Willy thought should have done before; suturing the mouth and eyelids shut. This took Ozymandias no more than five minutes to complete.

It was done. A soul would go to heaven. Ozymandias slipped a tight undergarment on the cadaver to assure no leakage of embalming fluid and dressed the body in a dark suit.

He pulled in a coffin on a gurney, placed the deceased in it, and wheeled it back to the cold house. Now embalmed, Mr. Stevens didn't need to be there as much as he did before. Oscar brought him there as a practical matter. He needed a place to store the body until the funeral.

It had been a long two days. Oscar had two hours before his dinner engagement. Enough time for a shower and another glass of wine.

Chapter Nine

Oscar left for his dinner engagement at exactly 6:45. It had been a long and taxing day, and dinner could come none too soon.

Tilly's Coffee Shop was also on Main Street, and although only a short walk, Oscar took the car. He didn't like walking. The only time he used his feet was when he was on a coroner's call and had to remove the corpse. Accidental deaths always seemed to happen outdoors and deep in the woods and he could only get the car but so close and then he'd have to walk.

Couldn't they just once in a while fall from a ladder in their kitchen or slip in the tub? A broken neck is a broken neck and even for the master of the one-man carry, it was quite an effort when the death occurred a hundred yards down a hill and in the woods.

This was an evening when Oscar needed his 'just in case' ten minutes. He put the key in the ignition and nothing happened. The sun had set some time ago, the temperature had dipped well below freezing, and the Ford was being temperamental. It was the first time he started the car today, and it would only get worse as it moved into winter and the thermostat outside his kitchen stayed below freezing for the next four months. Bad for the Ford, good for the icemen.

He had considered buying one of those premium cars, so there'd be no trouble with its starting, but it would be bad for business. The people of Mount Olden would have problems with a man making a living off their sorrow and flouting the profits. He had the money – even in bad times the undertaking business was good – and people expected their funeral directors to be comfortable. They just didn't want it shoved in their faces, which is exactly what driving a new Cadillac would do.

Oscar's almost new 'peoples' car was temperamental and finicky – another thing he had little patience for, especially after having paid good money. That was one of the reasons he liked the undertaking business: there were no machines. He even resisted using one of the new electric pressure pumps for the embalming infusion, which had to be done with precision if the embalming was to be successful. Oscar's embalming was always successful and he attributed this to his skill and physical strength, using his powerful arms and shoulder to pump just the right amount of air into his embalming tanks.

After turning the ignition to the Ford three times with nothing happening, he lit his lantern, popped the hood and began his inspection. Wearing only a sweater and a windbreaker, the cold was beginning to seep in. He had worn enough for the short ride to Tilly's, but not enough for what he was doing now.

He hadn't come prepared and that bothered him. He liked to be prepared. After one quick and complete look under that hood, he found the culprit. The choke was stuck in the wrong position. After some minor manipulation he was back in the car and on his way to the diner.

He would soon see the glow emanating from four of the five neon letters affixed to the metal frame on the roof. The middle letter had been out for more years than he could remember. D I E R.

At seven o'clock Oscar and his Ford pulled up in front of Tilly's. His table, right in front of the picture window, was waiting for him.

Coulton's would have been his choice of restaurants if he didn't have to worry about what the neighbors would think. Always the businessman, Oscar knew that neighbors today become customers tomorrow and the citizens of Mount Olden liked doing business with simple folk. Even though Ozymandias' Funeral Home was the only one on this side of the mountains, there was too much competition for Oscar to take chances. Anyone in the county with a shovel could fashion himself or herself an undertaker when it came to burying their kin. People in this part of the State never spent money on things they could do themselves, and there was no one who couldn't dig a hole. Embalming was a different matter, of course, especially if there was a wake, and having a wake was the preferred way of doing a burial.

Everyone knew the story of the O'Briens. Everett died of natural causes at the ripe age of forty-six. It was either his heart or a stroke; no one was sure which. All they knew was he was having his morning coffee on the porch one minute, and gone the next. They waked him for four days, right there in the living room, in a casket his youngest son fashioned out of some trees that came right from his back yard. By the time Sean, Everett's oldest, made his way back home from a visit in the next town over, expecting to see his father as he left him, it was day three of the wake. Sean didn't have to see that something terrible had happened, he smelt it a quarter of a mile before he got to the porch steps.

Even though the family had stuffed cotton in all the places where cotton had to be stuffed, poor Everett had started to rot.

Everyone in the county told the story, and at the last telling, the quarter of a mile had grown into a mile and a quarter. Embalming was the answer so long as the embalmer wasn't uppity and fancy. Oscar made a point to be neither and in that regard, choosing a restaurant was as important as choosing a car. There was nothing simple about Coulton's with its linen and silver on the tables and pricey menu. In contrast, everything was simple at Tilly's, from the oilcloth tablecloths to the ample and cheap offerings – hamburgers, pasta and the special of the day. It was Tuesday, and Tuesday was always meatloaf day. Every corner of the diner smelled of meatloaf, even the john, where he washed his hands before taking his seat at his favorite booth in front of Tilly's picture window.

Passersby who glanced in would see Oscar with a plate of meatloaf and Dollard in his Roman collar. All very good for business.

Oscar was very hungry as he waited at his table, with its seasonal oilcloth depicting a winter country scene with farmhouse and barn, surrounded by a smattering of thick evergreens. Partial to linen tablecloths, Oscar found the winter rendition particularly objectionable because of its Christmas ornamentation scattered throughout. The fall oilcloth with muted colors and the tapping of maple trees was a better match for his aesthetic sensibility.

Wine was part of Tilly's offering. Burgundy and Chianti when it came to reds, and a sweet carbonated Asti Spumante.

No sooner had Oscar taken his seat than Jake was at his side.

"Something to drink, Mr Ozymandias?"

"Red wine."

"A glass of Chianti or burgundy?"

"Burgundy, Jake."

Why burgundy? The answer was simple enough. Oscar detested sweet wines and last week he had the Chianti.

In a moment, there was Jake with a glass of red. Oscar would have preferred a high stem wide-mouthed wine glass, as it let the wine continue breathing and enhanced the taste. He only used high stem when drinking wine at home. But this was Tilly's and he had come to expect the six-ounce glass filled to the brim. That was the smallest size glass Jake had. At breakfast he used it for the orange juice.

When it came to what others could see, Oscar Ozymandias always opted for the simple. His tastes were not simple, but there were other considerations when making choices.

Somewhere around seven-thirty, a breathless Paul Dollard wandered in, a half hour late. This defect of character always irritated Ozymandias and he made no exception with his Tuesday night dinner companion. Taking Holy Orders was no excuse for not being punctual. So much of the priest's work had to do with being on time. Oscar was convinced that if the rectory weren't directly above the sanctuary, the seven o'clock Mass would begin at ten to eight.

He looked beyond their table to the counter that ran along the far wall. Jake was behind it taking orders, and Tilly, portly Tilly with her apron wrapped tightly under her ample breasts, came out of the kitchen to see who had just come in. She wasn't looking for a hello. This was a business of regulars and supper was a busy time. For Jake it was Father Paul coming through the front door, for Tilly, spaghetti, not too soft, with red sauce. After nodding to her new customer, she returned to the kitchen and put up a kettle of fresh water.

When Dollard came to Mount Olden as a recently ordained young priest, Oscar resolved to make the seven o'clock Mass. That resolve ended on day two, when for the second time, this stranger to the town wandered into church ten minutes late. On day three Oscar returned to his own sanctuary, a splendid private room tucked away in a corner of Ozymandias' Funeral Home that only he knew about. It was there he continued to reaffirm his devotion in his own way to our Lord Jesus Christ.

"Sorry Oscar, a parish call," the priest said, seeing Oscar glance pointedly at his watch. For Oscar Ozymandias, apologies were not enough to excuse rudeness. Dollard's list of excuses was endless. There was always something to do around the church, with the parishioners, in his personal life. Given this significant flaw in his character, Oscar thought the Diocese had made a good choice giving this man the out-of-the-way parish of St Anselm's. It was a one-man assignment. In all the years that Oscar could remember, and that was well before Dollard arrived, there never was a second priest.

What put this place on the bottom of everyone's list? Lots of reasons, and any one of them would have been enough. Most, however, had to do with money. Whorehouses were not built to be churches, the cost of constant repairs and maintenance was enormous, and no one in the congregation had more than a dollar to his name. A priest of stature would never put up with that.

Dollard had only been away twice in the five years he was in Mt Olden, once for a medical problem that he wouldn't talk about, and the second time when one of his brothers died. He didn't talk about that either and there was probably something to say since James was only in his early thirties and people didn't get old in these parts until they were at least in their mid-forties. He said nothing about the hospitalization and nothing about his brother, and secrecy like that was unusual in Mt Olden.

For whatever reason, Father Paul was gone both times for weeks and the Diocese couldn't come up with a priest to take over. The congregation was told to go to St Augusta, clear on the other side of the mountain, when only a handful of people had a car in Mt Olden.

"You've already started, Oscar. Your first or second?"

Oscar smiled politely but offered no answer. He didn't take to this intimate locker room chatter between two male buddies. He and this priest were no buddies. Small town business associates, that's what Oscar considered their relationship. He reached for the bread basket, squeezed a few of the rolls until he found one to his liking, and turned to Dollard.

"A drink?" he asked.

"I'll wait until Jake comes over."

An answer from the priest and another source of irritation to Oscar. Jake waited on tables, that was his job. Why not ask him to do what he was there to do? An act of kindness? Out of respect? Maybe misguided egalitarianism. The man was there to wait on tables, to wait until they had a need and then respond. Dollard wanted a drink, Oscar knew that. He even knew he'd be asking for a beer and a pitcher of water. Every Tuesday he had two beers, one before ordering and one with his food. Enough of these games, Dollard, enough. He raised a hand to summon Jake.

"Yes, Mr. Ozymandias?"

"Bring Father Paul his beer and his water."

Two businessmen on their Tuesday nighter. When Oscar took over the funeral home from Olsen, his first call was to the rectory and Father Reilly. He told him he was more than an undertaker; he fashioned himself a funeral director, and his calling was not only to prepare the deceased for the final journey in accordance with the teachings of the Church, but also to help the grieving family.

This, a radical concept, was nothing new to Father. Wasn't he charged with both a sacramental and pastoral ministry? Publicly he was prepared to embrace Oscar's far-reaching vision since even the shepherd needs help with his flock, particularly at the time of passage. Privately, he was very pleased. He was more comfortable with the prescribed structure of ritual and less comfortable with the unexpected that comes from giving counsel and comfort in times of great emotion. A wizard in the confessional, he knew exactly what to say no matter the sin, and was always prepared with the appropriate penance. Come a family tragedy, anything beyond *it was God's will* and *we will pray for you child* and he was lost.

No sooner had Oscar proposed this holy alliance than it was put to the test. The Fitzmours, Hattie and Gerald, worked a small farm a few miles from town. Married eight years and after four miscarriages, Hattie finally became pregnant with her Annie. Father Reilly told the Fitzmours this was a testament to their faith; Jesus had heard their prayers. This was also an answer to his prayers. He had been there for each of the misses and for each baby lost he had administered the sacraments of the Baptism and the Last Rites.

Each time the parents, Gerald with his stare and Hattie with her tears, asked why this was happening to them. They were good people, honoring the Lord, taking confession and doing penance even though they never sinned. Why, they asked. Why? Reilly gave the only answer he had, and while it might have given some comfort the first time, by the fourth miscarriage he could feel their bitterness at what was happening, at their church, their God and yes, even with their priest.

Everyone celebrated Annie's arrival, especially Doctor Gardner, who, now in his sixties, had been both Hattie and Gerald's doctor since each was no more than two or three weeks old.

Doc's happiness turned sour when Annie came for her first exam. He couldn't put his finger on it, but something didn't look right. Probably Hattie would have noticed too if she hadn't been so taken with just having a live baby in her arms.

Three weeks after that first visit to the doctor, Doc Gardner was on the phone to Father Reilly. The unthinkable had happened. He was at the Fitzmours, little Annie had just succumbed and he needed him to be there with the parents. The parents wanted a real funeral so he better stop by Ozymandias' and bring Oscar along. Lord knew where they'd get the money for a funeral.

Ozymandias went in the priest's car and by the time they were driving down the dirt road to the Fitzmour's one-room shack, he knew all the particulars. It was clear from what Reilly didn't say, that the shepherd wasn't up to what needed to be done.

They came into everything that could be sad and depressing. Whatever had happened was clear to be seen; in a one-room house there are no corners to hide in. Hattie was in the bed and next to her, her dear beloved Annie. Dead for more than an hour, her skin was grey and rigor mortis was setting in. At the table, Doc and Gerald, each slumped and each with his head in his hands.

Father Reilly said a few prayers and then awkwardly moved from the bed to the table, not knowing what to do with himself.

"Mrs. Fitzmour, Mr. Fitzmour, I am Oscar Ozymandias. Father Reilly asked me to come to help you make the arrangements. You need to know that I know how disastrous losing your Annie is to both of you. No one can ever know how you feel. The most we can do and the least you can ask of us is that we be here with you in whatever way brings you comfort."

There was silence, even quieter than it had been before anyone had spoken. Oscar pulled up a chair and sat with hands folded in his lap, looking first in Gerald's direction and then towards Hattie. He took a deep breath, let it out softly, and started talking again.

"Your Annie will soon be returning to our Lord, sooner than anyone would have wanted. Even our Lord Jesus will shed a tear when he greets her. All He will have to offer is eternal peace and comfort in place of the love she would have gotten at the bosom of her mother. Maybe knowing where she'll be will give both of you some comfort as the grief of the loss moves to your eternity of sorrow."

Oscar's soft voice again moved into silence as he leaned back in his chair. This time the silence was broken by Hattie, who, summoning all the energy she had, lifted her head towards Oscar and began to weep softly.

"Hattie, pray to Jesus for strength," Father Reilly offered. She turned away, looking at her Annie and away from the crucifix above the bureau. She might be able to hear what Father Reilly was here to say in a day or two, but not that night.

"Hattie is a strong woman," answered Oscar to no one in particular. "She is grieving and if ever there was a time to do just that, it is now."

"Whatever it takes to get my baby ready to be with our Lord, then that's what I want."

"Of course, Mrs Fitzmour," said Oscar.

No one called Hattie by her last name. This was Ozymandias showing respect and she appreciated it.

"There's some money in this farm and if we need more, Gerald, tell him we'll pay it out. Tell him that's the way we will do it. Tell him we're good for the money. You tell him, Gerald."

"Every last penny Mr. Ozymandias," answered Gerald. "We're good for it, I swear we are."

Oscar Ozymandias, on his own in his new business, turned to the Fitzmours and said something remarkable, something that no one had ever heard come from his mouth before and only a few times since that day. "No money is going to pass from your hands to mine to take care of little Annie."

Doc Gardner, nervous by such talk and thinking that he had to protect these two children at such a vulnerable time, cautioned Ozymandias not to be playing with them.

Oscar, hearing every word he had said, kept his eyes on the Fitzmours who both were looking at him. He unfolded his hands from his lap, placed them on his knees, leaned forward and spoke to the grieving parents as if they were the only ones in the room.

"Hattie, Gerald, there's no playing here. These are not idle words. You children are beginning," Oscar said, knowing he might be taking some liberties since he was not much older than they were. "There's a long life ahead of you and in that life there will be children, whether they come from you, or if it's just too hard to make them, from adoption. You're going to be wonderful parents and whatever way that those children arrive, you will be the Mama and the Papa. You need this land. This is what's going to feed you all. No money. You continue to serve your church and when the next one comes along, you let me know so I can be there at the christening."

A professional relationship was sealed that night between St Anselm's and the Ozymandias' Funeral Home, and between Oscar and the folks of Mount Olden. There were no false expectations here. Everyone knew the desperation of poor Hattie and her husband and that's what compelled Oscar's generosity. In all the years that followed, there were only three more gratis funerals, and all came after Mount Olden got its new priest. None were children and all shared common features. All were portly men with no kin who had led exemplary lives in service to St Anselm's as members of the congregation. They had all died suddenly: Henry Weid and Lemwell Jenkins on the lake during the harvest, and George Fowler right during the eight o'clock Mass. The congregation was on the kneelers praying to the Lord and when it was time for everyone to get up, George didn't. His heart just decided to stop beating.

Like the other two, George was a young man and he, too, had left explicit instructions in the case of his demise. 'Closed coffin, no wake, put me right in the ground and say farewell.'

~

After the burial of little Annie, Father Reilly and Oscar began the long tradition of Tuesday evenings at Tilly's and the town folk turned to Oscar when they weren't going to bury their kin in their own back yards.

When Father Reilly retired, he spent a whole month with the new pastor, Father Paul Dollard, showing him around the rectory and church, and doing a lot of introductions. Come Tuesday nights, for the four weeks that St Anselm's had two priests, there were three men sitting at Tilly's window table.

It didn't take long for Oscar to see the difference between the two priests. Dollard was long on the pastoring and very short on the sacramental ministry. He attended to it but not with his heart or soul. It seemed more like a chore to get through and his Latin was wanting. Oscar, who became more devout with each passing year, knew his Latin and was probably the only person in Mount Olden who knew that Dollard cut corners.

Still, keeping up the Tuesday tradition was good for business. It gave Oscar and Father Paul a chance to chat and Oscar some knowledge of what business was in store for him. Such was the opportunity this very night as Oscar and Dollard readied themselves for the meal that Tilly had cooked and Jake was bringing over.

"Another wine and beer?"

"Please," answered Paul for both of them.

"Someone sick?" asked Ozymandias, thinking about the call that had kept Dollard from being on time. More often than not these calls were because someone was not well and in these parts it didn't take too much of a sickness to put you in the grave. The sick calls always sparked Oscar's interest, which wasn't driven by concern for the sick, but rather the need to plan.

Was death imminent, would there be a funeral, and would the diseased be buried in the coffin? This last piece of information, if it were known, was critical. The county people were poor folk and when Oscar took over the business, he decided to dispose of the catalogs that Olsen used since no one ever bought a coffin from them. Families would look at the beautiful colored glossy pages, see the price, close the book and walk out, opting for a backyard burial. If they couldn't have it all, if they couldn't afford the coffin that would give the living the peace of mind that they had done right by their dearly departed, they'd just as soon dig the hole themselves.

When Ozymandias bought the funeral home, he made some changes. You could now rent a coffin for the wake and buy the less expensive cardboard one for the internment. Instead of catalogues, he had three offerings if a family wanted their own coffin. The basic, the least expensive of the three, was part of his arrangement with the county. Accidents or suspicious deaths, and there were a few, were brought to Oscar's for the autopsy. Since these cadavers couldn't be embalmed until after the autopsy, they had to be kept cold until the coroner was done and had signed the death certificate. For seven to eight months of the year, this was no problem; it was plenty cold in the cold house. During the hot summer months he had to constantly replenish the ice and that cost plenty, so the county paid to keep the building always ready.

There was money to be made and enough cases to make it. He got five dollars a day as a storage fee and two dollars for the use of the embalming room where the actual autopsy took place. In recent years, since Doc Radler became the coroner, there had been fewer autopsies. Radler, never one to leave an open bottle of liquor unattended, was more often drunk than sober. When he'd had a few too many and there was no suspicion of foul play, he was inclined to just stay at home and take the word of his resident expert.

Oscar fetched the body, called the doctor and told him what he got; looks like a heart attack, could have been a stroke, a tree fell on his head, the ice gave way and he drowned.

Whatever it was, when Doc Radler didn't feel like leaving his house, he'd hear Oscar's story and tell him what to put on the certificate. Sometimes he'd tell Oscar to hold the paperwork and he'd be around to sign it, other times he'd authorize Oscar to sign his name for him.

The real money came from the burial. The county didn't like bodies being buried willy-nilly. This, they said, was a matter of public health. When someone died who had no kin and it was a coroner case, or if the kin had no money, the Commissioner of Health contracted with Ozymandias' Funeral Home to do the burial, coffin and all. Oscar charged twenty-five dollars for the plain pine 'coroner's' box, opening the vault, that's funeral director talk for digging the grave, and the trip to the cemetery. He stocked the coffins, always having ten on hand. This, and cardboard, were enough for most burials.

There were times when people wanted something better than the basic pine box. There were two offerings, a mid line and a deluxe. The midline, a polished mahogany with some trimming, sold for one hundred dollars on top of the other costs. He stocked two. The deluxe, and it was deluxe, was a different matter. In all the years, he had only five orders for it. It too was highly polished mahogany but also had a carved cross on the lid, brass handles for the pallbearers, and a silk lining for the comfort of the deceased. Three hundred dollars worth of luxury and it had to be ordered from a catalog. When the weather was good, so long as his supplier had one in stock, it was in Mount Olden in less than eight hours. When the weather was poor, eight hours might become a day or more.

Families, at times of great loss, should never be offered something that cannot be delivered. Oscar learned this the hard way. He had shown a family of some means a picture of the deluxe only to find out after they had made the choice that the supplier didn't have one in stock. Enraged, the family hauled grandma out of the cold house, put her in the pick up and went clear to the other side of the mountain to his competitors. This wouldn't have been so terrible if the family hadn't told everyone how Oscar Ozymandias had let them down in their moment of need. For six months following that terrible time, there was a run on backyard burials. Oscar learned an important lesson. Keep the picture of the deluxe out of sight unless it's available and make the call as soon as you think you might need it. How could you know that someone near death's door might be in need of a deluxe coffin? Talk to the priest.

~

Oscar, nursing his second glass of burgundy, asked Dollard if his parish call had been to a sick congregant. Indeed it had. Old man Hinton was soon to go. Frail, bedridden, and having trouble breathing, he had been there to give him his last rites. He knew Hinton as a fellow businessman who owned the local hardware store. No backyard for these people and certainly the top of the line. He would place the order tomorrow morning and have the casket waiting for Hinton's arrival. Money would not be a problem. His supplier would wait for his one hundred and fifty dollars until the family settled the account.

"Tell me, Dollard, was this man a good Catholic?"

Father Paul was neither surprised by the question – Oscar always asked him about how devout his congregants were – nor offended by Oscar calling him by his last name. In his mind they were colleagues, two men who were in different ends of the same business; tending to the body and soul of their fellow man. He took no disrespect in Oscar's informality. That, however, was Oscar's very intent. He had enough good sense to refer to the cleric as Father when in the presence of others, but when the two were by themselves, he made it a point never to address him as Father.

Oscar took his religion very seriously and being a Catholic, that meant the sacraments. Setting the standard and administering those very sacraments was the sacred duty of the ordained. This Paul Dollard was no Father Reilly, who was the very epitome of the parish priest. While he didn't reach the highest standard when it came to pastoring his flock, no more could be asked of any man who took the vows when it came to leading his congregation to the gates of heaven. That damn Dollard couldn't even get the words right when it came to conducting the mass, a reason why Oscar was an infrequent visitor to services.

He made it a point to be in church on all holidays, but when it came to Sundays, he often offered the Mass himself at the altar he had constructed in the recesses of his home. Of course he couldn't give himself communion or hear his own confession. That was where his Thursday trips to the Pines came in. The Pines, the county seat, was almost big enough to be called a small city. As far as any one in Mount Olden knew, he was going to his supplier to fill in his stock of embalming fluids, needles, sutures, and all the tools of the trade. What they didn't know was he got to the Pines early enough for the seven o'clock Mass at St Olav's, a large church for a large parish with a large congregation. Oscar was just one of the many in attendance and his receiving communion and giving confession went largely unnoticed. Between his private sanctuary and his weekly trips, he felt more than comfortable with his Catholicism. All he needed from Paul Dollard was a steady stream of dead parishioners to keep his business thriving.

As for his curiosity about who the deceased were; he wanted to know if they had lived decent lives and honored their sacramental obligations. If they had, Dollard was good enough to start them on their trip to heaven.

If, however, there had been lapses, Oscar felt the calling to assure they left this world with what this priest could not give them. That's what Oscar had done for Mike Stevens and what he did not have to do for Jarvice, a childless widow who was a churchgoer all her life, regularly received communion until three weeks before she took ill, and went to confession even though there was nothing to confess.

Oscar Ozymandias, redeemer of lapsed souls destined to rattling in the desolation of purgatory.

Guiding them by word and deed in those moments when their heart has stopped. Bringing them to the gates of a now forgiving Peter and the promise of an eternity among the angels.

Father Paul's spaghetti was unremarkable, Oscar's meatloaf was barely edible, and they were both ready for coffee and a piece of Tilly's apple pie.

Paul looked to Jake as he did each week to indicate that they were ready for dessert, but then hesitated, turned toward Oscar and leaned forward. The space between them became less than comfortable. Something to be said, but not overheard.

"I went to the Petersen's a few days ago. You did Joseph's funeral last month."

"Yes, I remember," Oscar answered, puzzled by Dollard offering this information. He was always visiting someone and only spoke about a week being busy or slow, never mentioning who he was busy with unless asked.

"What do you remember?" Paul asked with eyes now fixed on Oscar's.

Oscar, a little uneasy at first, began to relax as he considered the question and who was asking it. There was nothing coy about Dollard. Curious, but not coy.

"Nothing special," answered Oscar. "Let's see. Joseph was laid out for two days, a coroner's coffin and then the burial."

"Anything special about preparing him?"

"It took a bit of doing to get some color in him and getting him set just right in the coffin."

"Any particular reason?"

"After the fluid goes in, the body starts to set. Joseph was a big man and I did everything by myself. Lifting and moving was not easy and there wasn't as much room as I could have used to position him once I had him inside. Why so curious, Dollard?"

"I went out to Sally to see how she was doing. She's a regular at church and I knew this wasn't going to be easy for her. I didn't know him very well, in fact I saw him only once and that was in town last year.

"Sally, always hospitable, sat me down with a cup of tea and one of her biscuits. She let me know it's been hard for her and then she began to tell me about the old times, she and Joseph tending the farm and raising the children. She had a family picture on the mantle and set it on the table while she talked. There he was, in front of the house with the kids, under a big old tree full of leaves and the beginnings of apples."

Oscar began fiddling with his coffee cup. He took one last sip and signaled to Jake for a refill. Father Paul, involved with his story, noticed nothing.

"Something was not right. Was it something in the picture that didn't belong or was there something not in it that did? I looked, stared, and turned it in every direction until I got it. Joseph, it was Joseph. I was looking at a man with only one ear. Joseph Peterson was missing his left ear. Ordinarily that would have meant nothing to me; this time I noticed.

"The strange thing is, I went to the wake. His head was nestled on the pillow in the way you place most bodies. If anything, we only get a good look at the right profile. But I anointed him Oscar; I went over to the coffin and reached inside to make the sign of the cross. I saw all of him, the side of his face that was towards the back of the coffin. And I noticed nothing. I'd remember if that man had only one ear."

Father Paul's voice trailed off in an uncomfortable laugh, as if he were questioning his own recollections.

Cool and composed, Oscar pondered what Dollard was saying. Only the back of his neck, well below his high collar that was securely buttoned in front, revealed the slightest of discomfort. It was beginning to soak through with perspiration. Oscar usually didn't perspire, even in the middle of summer.

"Are you sure, Dollard?"

"At first I tried to convince myself that I was mistaken. Still, I keep having that picture of Joseph in the coffin and he's looking just like you and me. I went so far as to go back to the Peterson house thinking that I got the picture wrong. No mistaking what I was in that picture. The man only had one ear. What do you remember Oscar? Think."

"I'm thinking Dollard, I'm thinking. It was a busy time back then. Right after the summer, is that right?"

"Early September."

"Lot of fool hunters were in the woods back then and there were several nasty accidents. That and the drowning with the boat turning over at Stockwell Lake and the regular deaths of people who couldn't make it through another summer and it was a very busy time. You did a number of funerals then, as I recall."

Father Paul did remember. It seemed like he was offering a funeral Mass every other day.

"I had more funerals than you had Masses. I have some memory of one of them missing an ear but I can't be sure of that and I certainly can't remember who it was. In fact, I think there were two. And then there was that drifter who was missing a hand. That one I remember for sure. It looked nasty. A new wound, no more than a year old and it looked like he got it caught in some type of trap. That one I remembered."

Of course, Oscar remembered each and every time the opportunity for restoration came his way. Ears, nose, even one or two partial penises. A Robin Hood of sorts, taking from the well endowed and giving to the less-endowed. All in service to his sacred mission to make whole what is broken. Or at least as whole as could be for the final sacred journey.

"Peterson and one ear, I really can't say, Dollard. You sure?"

"I wouldn't be asking if I were sure. Like I said, his head was far down in the pillow. Could have been some of that fabric that looked like an ear. Could have been that. Could have been."

~

Two glasses of wine, two beers, and two pitchers of water and another Tuesday night had come to an end.

"Come to church this Sunday, Oscar, it'll be good for your soul. Next week at seven?"

"Seven," answered Oscar, as he left his share of the bill on the table and headed for the door. By now his entire shirt was awash in sweat.

Thank goodness it wasn't the widow Peterson who noticed. He needed to be more careful.

Chapter Ten

"Ite, missa est." The Mass was over.

The words came none too soon. No need to look in the Missal, he knew his *Ils* by heart. After so many years of both hearing and giving this Sunday ritual, he should have known each and every word, every chant of the Proprium Missarum de Tempore. Five years at St Anselm's, the years at the seminary, and how many Sundays at St Thomas Aquinas, the church where he was baptized. By now it should have been part of his gray matter. It wasn't.

The Mass was in Latin and that was both good and bad. Father Paul had difficulty in front of large groups, fearing a mistake, and that made him anxious. Conducting the Mass in Latin was very forgiving. At his worst, all the congregation noticed was that he lost his place and that was easily remedied since his missal, after all these years of struggling, was well marked and tagged. As for mispronunciations? Even missing a word or phrase, so long as it was in Latin, went unnoticed. Unless a member of the clergy was in attendance.

Ozymandias was in attendance.

"Ite, missa est. Go, the Eucharist has been sent forth."
Another Mass had come to an end.

~

"You did very well today Father. The homily had us thinking."
"Do you think so, Sada?"

"Most definitely. To bring the gospel into our very lives is a gift. It means something to us. Now, let's think about lunch for you before you make your calls. What will it be?"

"Whatever. Sada, do you remember the Petersons?"

"Joseph and Sally. Of course I remember them. Sally comes to church every so often and Joseph, he wasn't a regular by any stretch. He died a month or so back, that's right, isn't it?"

Of course she was right. There was nothing that happened in St Anselm's parish that Sada Weisen didn't know about. Births, deaths, who was coming to church and who was staying home to sleep late, she knew it all. The last time Joseph Petersen had been to church, before being brought in to be buried, was when his youngest was confirmed, and that was many years ago.

"What do you remember about Joseph?" Father Paul asked.

"Not much to remember. He was a good man, devoted to his family, and worked hard, not a church goer."

"Physically, what do you remember?"

"Nothing remarkable. Nice-looking fellow when he was younger. In good health until he got sick except for that frostbite that got him one winter."

"Frostbite?"

"He was working the ice and it was bitter cold. Couldn't explain why it happened but it sure enough did. Lost an ear to that frostbite."

"When did that happen?"

"A long time ago. So long ago that even Father Reilly was a young man. What has you thinking about all this?"

"A conversation with Oscar Ozymandias a few days ago. It was nothing. Forget about it, it was nothing."

Sada knew it was something. Father wasn't one for idle conversation, at least not with her. Now with Father Pat, it was different. They had a lot of history between them, he and Sada, even before there was even a Raulf Weisen in the picture. Nothing shameful, nothing that either would have to speak about in confession. That was not altogether true for Sada. She had her crushes when she was a young woman and Pat Reilly was one of them. She never said anything and she was almost certain that he didn't know what she was thinking or imagining. She stopped that thinking the day that Pat went into seminary.

Sada had quite an imagination back then and still did, even to this day. She no longer thought about men the way she thought about boys when she was a girl, but she was still intrigued by people, who they were and why they did what they did.

Father Paul did not escape Sada's speculations. She knew few facts and most had come from Father Reilly. Sada made tea for Father Reilly every night at eight and then they would talk. Nothing intimate, nothing that the priest and the widow who takes care of the rectory shouldn't talk about. The conversation had to do with things, doings, what was happening in town. Father Reilly would say this was one way he found out where he was needed. If someone was sick, if there were struggles in a marriage, if a mother and father were having a hard time with their kids, if there was a family unable to put food on the table, Sada would tell him.

It worked well because the good Catholics of the town weren't about to come to him. Too religious, that's what they said. He'd listen to their first ten words and then tell them what to do and that usually had to do with what was in one of his religion books. Father Reilly was at his best when he was in the church doing church things and tending to the needs of the hungry. At least then he brought some canned goods to go along with the Hail Marys and admonitions that they had best get to church on Sunday if they wanted to get out of their pickle.

Sada Weisen was Father Patrick Reilly's eyes and ears when it came to his flock and in exchange, he'd tell her what little tidbits he'd find out along the way. The coming of the new priest was one of the larger morsels he shared with her during eight o'clock tea.

Father Paul Dollard came from the western part of the state, coal country. He took his time before deciding to be a priest. Father Pat didn't know how many were in his family but he was fairly certain that all the male Dollards made their living underground because that's what life was like in those coal company towns. Mother, father, his kin? All that was known was that he was the first in the family to answer the Call, although these people were church goers, even the men. Father Paul was the youngest of a string of them and the oldest was killed over in France during the war. Sada did some quick math, figured this new priest was somewhere in his thirties, and that she at fifty-eight was old enough to be his mother.

Sada wondered if this new priest would be the one to say her Requiem Mass. She didn't want just anyone; he'd have to know her. It was a great comfort that Father Pat was there to bury her dear Raulf, and she thought he would be there for her. There was good reason to think that because he wasn't going anywhere as long as he had his health and like her, he was in his middle fifties. A long life in these parts was late forties, early fifties. If you got past that you had every reason to believe you'd die very old, at least your seventies, maybe even into the eighties. So long as you didn't fall through that damn ice or get hit in the head with something, you'd be around.

Father Reilly looked like he was going to make it and then he got that emphysema. Couldn't even walk to the altar without losing his breath. Doc Radler said it probably was all those cigarettes.

Now that Sada was as old as she was and still kicking, she'd be kicking for another fifteen, maybe even twenty years. It was the new priest she was worrying about. He was no kid, not if he was in his early thirties, and if he spent a lot of time with that coal, the Lord would be taking him sooner rather than later. She needed to be attached to her priest to not be in fear of her final passage. These good feelings don't come overnight and while she moaned that it wouldn't be Patrick Reilly standing by her coffin, she did take some comfort in knowing that there would be time to get to know this Father Dollard before her own passing. When she found out he came from coal country, her comfort went out the window.

It was now five years since Father Paul came to St Anselm's and Sada had been there since day one with every intention to keep him at a great distance from getting to the place in her heart. She didn't think this was going to be too hard. She was a very proper widow, that's how she was with most people in town, be they men, women or children. Some people went so far as to describe her as cold and standoffish. She knew they thought that, Sada knew everything, and she didn't mind one bit. It kept the distance between them that she liked. Nor was she worried about herself and this new priest. Come eight o'clock teatime, they only discussed business; what he would be doing the next day and what he needed her to do for him. He never entertained the idle and mindless gossip that brings people together and that suited Sada just fine since they both seemed to be working on keeping their distance.

But soon it didn't work, at least not from Sada's side. First, she was taken in by how hard it was for this new priest when it came to saying Mass, especially when the church was full, and still he was there trying. She knew if there were a way for him to have someone else at the altar, he'd do it in a minute. He was pretty good with the preaching. When he was in the pulpit giving the homily, he had a knack for making the gospel come into everyday lives and it felt like he was talking to just you. But the rest of the Mass, the Kyrie, the Epistle, the Sacramentarium, the whole of it, he never got it right. He looked down at the missal, he was forever flipping the pages looking for the right part and always having trouble finding it.

And his Latin, oh help us, Lord, with his Latin. She was convinced that only she and the one or two clergy who had occasionally attended Mass over the years knew how he massacred the Latin. Yet he tried every Sunday in spite of his suffering. She admired him for that.

And then there was the caring. When he spoke each day about his plans for the next, it had to do with people, with his congregants. Sada could tell from his list that he was a listener. Father Reilly was a ten-word man. Not this priest. When Father Paul came for visit, or when you came to see him in his study, he listened to all you had to say and sometimes his giving was just in the listening. Sada liked him for that too and as much as she didn't want it to happen, he was finding a place in her heart.

Paul Dollard kept a journal. It wasn't an everyday thing. He used it to keep track of things, events; thoughts that struck him during the day that were worth remembering. There were many days without an entry. The last was the sick call to Michael Stevens.

November 18 - Visit to the Stevens. Mike looks like he's holding his own. Sitting up comfortably in bed. Still he is gaunt, cheeks sunken, neck no wider than my arm. Everything is just sinking in. He worries that his soul will be caught in purgatory because he never got to church. Offered him the Last Rites. Got very upset with me; 'I ain't goin anywhere yet Father. There's plenty a time.' Not so much time from the looks of him. He's just not ready to hear about it. Mae holding up okay.   *Plan: return in five days. Maybe he'll be ready then for the Rites.*

Dollard leaned back in his chair, looking at this last entry. Had he done the right thing? Three days after the visit, Mike Stevens was dead. Faster than anyone would have thought but not entirely unexpected. Should he have given him the Last Rites in spite of his protestations? Thinking that he was not about to die may have given him more comfort than having a prayer said to get him ready for his death. What was more important? Dollard knew what he thought, he just didn't know if he was right. He prayed that if a sin had been committed, the Lord would welcome his child Michael Stevens anyway, settling the account whenever he himself arrived. Paul Dollard had every confidence that was the way it would be with the Lord Jesus that he prayed to many times a day.

Father Paul dipped his pen into the ink well and began his entry for November 24.

Dinner with Oz. Nothing remarkable about the evening at Tilly's, same food, same wine. Asked about the picture, the ear. Lots of deaths, lots of funerals that month. He's right. Seemed like another funeral every day. He can't remember and now I'm not sure what I saw when I anointed Joseph. Too late now, he's long buried.

It had been a long day and it still wasn't over. Every night during the cold months, before he went to sleep, he tended the furnace and filled the wood box for the potbelly in his study. It's a good time for a man's mind to wander and Paul was thinking about the journal. Something about what he had just written and something he had written before.

That old lady, Stella Reese. Eccentric, that's how he remembered her. A woman in her eighties who came one day and told him a wonderful story about her grandfather fighting with the Union under General Grant and her father and Teddy Roosevelt. And then, when it came to telling you what she did yesterday or what she had for breakfast that she couldn't remember.

After listening to her for more than a half hour, she started talking about her brother's death. It had happened years before Paul came to St Anselm's when Olsen owned the funeral home. Something to do with the Rough Riders and her father's exploits in Mexico, that's why she found her way into his journal. He couldn't remember what she had told him about her brother Henry, except that it was bizarre and could easily have come from an old demented woman.

Paul had a journal for each year. With no clear memory of when she had come, he took down his first St Anselm's volume and started turning the pages. He found what he was looking for midway in the second volume.

September 18- Old Lady Reese came to my study unannounced. How she made it up the stairs I'll never know. Her legs are bowed and she is permanently bent at the waist. Has a walking stick, which probably keeps her from falling over. Must be in late eighties, early nineties. Wearing clothing that is old, but clean. Socks don't match. Straw hat with a feather and too much rouge on her cheeks.

Father was one of President Roosevelt's Rough Riders. Rode with the President....

Dollard started skimming the pages, finding what he was looking for on page eight.

After more than a half hour of this very interesting story Stella finally got to what brought her today. A wild and unbelievable story about her brother's burial. Henry came to an unexpected and violent death. Was out hunting and got shot. An accident. A six-footer and carried a lot of weight. Olsen buried him and Father Reilly conducted the service. Because he was shot in the face, there was a closed coffin. She was alone with him at Olsen's where he was waked. When no one was looking she peeked inside to make sure it was him. She said only a sister could tell that was her brother.

Now it became very strange. Have to judge it from where it comes. She opened the bottom half of the coffin and there was something missing - his belly. In death he was flat as a board. She touched him and there was nothing there. Stella said she couldn't ask anyone because she wasn't supposed to be snooping. She figured to leave well enough alone. Let him go into the ground and be done with it.

Got more confused after telling hard-to-believe story. Thought I was Pat Reilly and got upset when I wasn't.

'Stella, how long has it been since your brother passed?'

'A long time Father Reilly, a long time.'

'Father Paul.'

'What, Father Paul?'

'I'm Father Paul.'

'Where is Father Reilly?'

'You're crying. Please don't cry, everything is all right.'

'What have you done with Father Reilly? What have you done with the Father? Did you hurt him? You hurt him. I know you did. Who are you? What are you doing here?'

'Father Paul. I am Father Paul. I took over for Father Reilly.'

'Imposter, imposter. Get away from me! Get away!'

Paul Dollard, his mind having wandered to memories of this forgotten encounter with a broken old lady, returned to the journal entry.

Couldn't speak to her, or ask questions. At end she became more than confused. She thought I had done something to Father Reilly. She started to cry, and then got angry, then stormed out. Need to find out who she is. Ask Sada. Stella needs our prayers and then some. Put her on the 'to do' list.

Paul closed the book, returned it to the shelf, and mused about his one and only encounter with Stella. He had asked Sada about her, saying nothing of the story about the brother. Stella was well known in Mount Olden. She had never been well balanced and with the passing of each member of her family, became more 'off'.

The last to go was her brother Henry and after that she stopped coming regularly to town. Lived on the few things she grew in her garden and the one pig she'd kill and butcher each year. Never the friendly type, she'd scream at people who came to see how she was doing and once even took a shot at one of them. After that everyone left her alone. She did make the trip in twice a year to shop for staples, once in the spring and once in the fall. That's how the people who cared about her in town knew she was still alive. Not many people cared.

Nothing more was said until Sada came to him the next fall. Paul returned to the bookcase and looked for the journal that had that entry.

November 22 – Sada came to me yesterday, Stella Reese is late. Didn't know what she was talking about or who this person was. She reminded me about the old lady that stopped by last year. Relatives fought in Civil War and with Roosevelt. Remembered her now. Should have been in town in October. She's late. Rode over to her farm. No Stella Reese. Gone. Looks like she's been out of there for a while. Walked around property. Nothing. May have wandered off. The last of the Rough Riders. May the Lord bless and keep her immortal soul.

~

"Oh, it's you, Sada. You startled me."

"I saw the light and just wanted to see if you needed anything, if you were all right."

Sada Weisler; always standing guard over her charge. How long had she been doing it? Father Reilly was a young priest when she came to the rectory. He grew old, she grew old. He's gone and she's still here, as strong as when she first came as a new widow. It had happened right here in Mount Olden. His heart gave out; went to bed and didn't wake up. The doctor said it was unusual for so young a man but these things do happen. He was laid out right there in Olsen's. Given the tragic nature of his early departure and her devotion to the church, old man Olsen spared nothing and charged little. There was even a floral arrangement in red carnations across the coffin that said 'Beloved Husband'.

A year after her husband's death, while still wearing her black mourner's dress, Sada came to Father Reilly offering herself in service to God. He spoke to her about a convent and taking vows, she spoke about keeping both feet planted in this world. They reached a compromise; she would take care of the rectory and its priest and for as long as anyone could remember, she had been doing just that.

On two separate occasions, while tending to Father Reilly's needs, she had come upon him while he was in obvious distress. She immediately called the doctor and was told that if she hadn't acted as quickly as she did, Father Pat would have gone on a premature journey to heaven. Diligence in the service to God, that's what she said her vocation was all about.

Sada also kept a close eye on Father Paul. Sometimes he'd look so sickly and take to his bed. She knew he had grown up in coal country and was sure the sickness had something to do with that. She resolved early on, just like with Father Reilly, she'd need to be ever vigilant with this new priest.

"You need to go to bed, Father."

"Soon."

"Reading one of your journals?" Sada asked, curious about what in the book would compel a man who was so regular in his habits to stay up past his bedtime.

"Yes," Father Paul answered, with a slight trace of annoyance, wanting to be left alone.

Sada, not one to pick up on the subtleties of communication, kept on going. "Not the latest," seeing that he had one of the older books in his hands. "Reviewing a little history?" she asked with a chuckle. "B.A. or A.A?' she asked.

Father Paul, confused by her question, stared back blankly.

"Before or after St Anselm's."

"Ah," Paul smiled. "This," he answered pointing to the book, "is since I came. A.A Volume Two," he answered playfully.

"Not quite ancient history," she answered, keeping up her end. "What has you looking back then so late at night."

"Stella Reese."

"Oh, Stella. A peculiar lady, Father. The kids tormented her when they found her on the streets. I felt so bad for her, but what could I do? She had such wonderful stories about her grandfather and father. What was true and what wasn't? Didn't make much difference. If you took the time to listen, it was always entertaining."

"Did she ever tell strange stories?" Father Paul asked.

" Strange, weird, a little crazy. Did she ever tell stories like that, Sada?"

"All her stories were a little off, Father. Are you thinking of something in particular?"

"She had a brother."

"Yes, I remember him. Chubby. Dropped dead as I recall."

"Accidental shooting, Sada. Hunting season."

"How would you know that?"

"Very heavy?" asked Dollard, evading Sada's question, at least for the moment.

"What are you thinking, Father?" Sada asked, sensing something was not being said.

"A year after I came to St Anselm's, Stella came to me. She began babbling about her brother. He must have died a goodly number of years before. She kept talking about him being smaller in the coffin than he was in real life. Smaller around the middle, she said."

"It sounds like one of Stella's nutty stories, Father," she said, as her voice trailed off so she could barely be heard. Sada became distracted, distant, she was gone. Now it was Paul Dollard who was concerned.

"Sada, are you okay?"

She kept looking into some unseen point in the distance.

"Sada!" Paul said with a low but forceful voice.

"Yes, Father, you were saying something?"

"Are you all right? Where did you go?"

"Nowhere, Father. Nothing."

Impatient with what he thought was evasiveness, he almost commanded her to speak through her silence. What had he said that left her without words?

"Stella's brother being small, I never heard that one before."

"That one?"

"Yes, Father. That's one story about the dead that I never did hear."

"There were other stories, Sada?"

"Many, Father, many."

"How long ago, what are we talking about?"

"Many years ago."

"Before I came to Mount Olden?"

"Before you came to Mount Olden."

"Strange that Father Reilly mentioned nothing of this," mused Father Paul.

"Maybe because there was nothing to say. We paid no mind to the stories. Preposterous, Father Reilly would say, preposterous. Who could believe dead people with parts missing or parts added? There was even one tale about a needle stuck in this man's chest with a little flag attached to it, which was supposed to move if his heart started beating. There was always someone who knew someone who had seen something. And the people who had seen what there was to see were always a little off, like Stella Reese. Except Joe Collins. He wasn't like the others."

"Why Joe Collins?" asked Father Paul.

"Like I was saying, all the others were crazy. They told horrifying stories that would get you up in the middle of the night. Strange people telling unbelievable stories."

"And Joe Collins?" Dollard asked.

"He was different. Had himself a regular job, he was a barber, and a regular family; a wife and three kids. Actually two, that has to do with this story. The Collins lost their middle child, the fourteen-year-old, a boy. He was a rowdy, that boy. Got caught more than once drinking and carousing with the girls. Rumor had it he singled out the Robbin's youngest, twelve year old Cynthia, and did her."

The 'did her' almost did Sada in. She blushed, turning bright red in front of Father Paul.

"Sada, you're telling me a story. Now take a deep breath and continue."

Catching her breath and cooling herself down, Sada drew in a big one through her mouth and let out a long slow one through her nose before she continued.

"Rumor had it that he did what I told you. No one saw it, mind you, but the evidence was compelling. Some months later, word of an accident came. Joe Collins' middle child had come to a sudden end. Broke his neck while diving into the lake down by the ore pit. Everyone heard of the terrible accident, but given the child's reputation, only the immediate family felt the loss. For those in town with young daughters, there was unspoken relief.

"They laid Joe Jr. out in Olsen's and waked him only that one night before they buried him. It was more than enough time. All that was coming came within the first ten minutes. With a half hour to go, the Mrs took the two children home, leaving poor Joe to stay just in case someone came in the few minutes that remained. The next day was the funeral and Father Reilly did the officiating.

"Long after Joe Jr. was deep in the ground and the family was safe and sound back in their cabin, Joe Collins came knocking on the rectory door. Father Pat invited a distraught father to join him in the study for a cup of tea. When I brought it in Joe was at the beginning of the wake story. Because they were putting Jr. in the ground so soon after he expired, they figured they could save a few bucks by skipping the embalming. Tim Olsen, that's Olsen's youngest and only son, a strange pug himself, tried to discourage foregoing this important step. What happens if putrification started before Jr. was down and under? It was going to be a closed coffin so they'd take their chances. These were hard times, Joe Collins had his responsibilities to the living, and an extra fifty dollars in his pocket would come in very handy.

"When the Mrs. and children left Olsen's, and he was by himself with his son, profound grief compelled Joe Collins to say one very private goodbye to his wayward son Joe Jr. Prepared for the worst, the smell of rotting flesh, he pinched his nose and lifted the top lid. Nothing, no odor. His son almost looked handsome in his Sunday suit. Even had a little color in his cheeks that he was sure came from one of those bottles Olsen kept on a shelf in the back room. Without thinking he lifted the bottom lid and as he did, he turned as grey as his son's hands that were folded across his chest. In his middle, his crotch, that's his words Father, I remember them just like he said them, and his crotch was a bloody red right through his pants. He couldn't help what he did next. Joe Collins reached down to where his son's privates were and felt around. He felt nothing but mush. That's what he said, mush. He couldn't bring himself to open the boy's trouser, that would have been more than he could take. As it was, he feared passing out right next to the casket. Joe reached into his pocket, pulled out a hanky and wiped and wiped his hands. When he got almost all of it off, he reached back, looked at his son for one last time, and gently closed both the top and the bottom.

"Joe Collins said nothing the day of the funeral. The first and last time he spoke about what he had seen and what he had not felt was right there in Father Reilly's study. He made Father and I swear not to say a word about what he had told us. He was sure it was the hand of the devil, taking the offending part, making him go to the other world without the very instrument that had robbed that poor Robbins child of her chaste entrance into womanhood.

"We were sure that it was the hand of grief that made him hallucinate things. That's what they call it, Father, when you see things that aren't there. That would have been the end of the story except for what I saw. It was time to leave and Father Pat, who was preparing his homily for Sunday's mass, returned to his work, leaving it for me to show Joe Collins out. As he was leaving, his back to me, I noticed a rag hanging from his back pocket. It was red, Father, red. That hanky was stained with the blood of Joe Jr. I told Father Pat what I had seen as soon as Joe left. Father Pat said if I keep this idle talk up, he'd think I was as crazy as Mr. Collins.

"I knew what I saw but I said nothing about it again, at least not till tonight."

~

Before Father Paul had a chance to say a word, the siren went off, a loud and piercing sound that could be heard in a ten-mile radius, and they both began to count the blast of the horn that followed. Two long, one short. Two long, one short. Three short, a pause and then a final short blast. The siren again and then the same sequencing. This was repeated four times in the next five minutes.

Sada would remember this moment and how she felt it was the soul of Joe Collins Jr. speaking to them of his pain and sorrow at the precise moment she had told his story to the Father.

Paul Dollard, listening carefully to the blasts, heard it as a summons for all to report to North Lake with their rescue equipment. It was a level three, possible loss of life, with three or more victims. Father Paul, still in his collar, only needed to slip into his heavy pea coat and pull his knit cap down over his ears. He reached for his equipment, his bible and stole and oil, in case he needed to give Last Rites, and slipped them into his coat pocket.

"You be careful, Father. Walk around and not across or else the next sound of the horn will be for you."

"I'll be careful, Sada. You go home, it's very late."

Father Paul didn't need Sada's admonition, even though if challenged, she would readily say she'd seen him crossing that damn lake many times to get to Main Street without knowing if it was frozen solid. The blasts of the horn told him that whatever happened, happened at the lake and given the time of year, probably the ice had given way and people had fallen in.

It took only a few moments for Father Paul to get to North Lake; it was behind the rectory and down the hill. He could tell from the lanterns that the activity was on the other side. Remembering Sada's warning, he began the long walk along a path that circled the lake. It would be another fifteen minutes before he got to where he had to be, and with no moon or lantern, it might take even longer.

Chapter Eleven

By the time Father Paul got to North Lake the rescue was well under way.

To an outsider it looked like chaos. But if you knew what you were seeing, it was a well-oiled crew doing what they had done more often than could be imagined. Come the busy season, there might be four or five calls a month. Most were false alarms.

From the looks of it, Dollard could tell this was not.

"Frank, is that you?" he asked, making out what he thought was a familiar face.

"Ya Father, it's me."

"What happened?"

"Can't stop now, Father. They need me and this," he said, as he headed for a cluster of men standing around a lantern on the frozen lake. A coil of rope was strung over his shoulder.

Father Paul's eyes slowly adjusted to the dark expanse of the lake. The activity was at the east end, not quite opposite the church. There were thirty or forty men, and more coming.

A clearing at the shoreline, marked by a lantern hanging from a pole, was where the bodies would be put. Two were already laid out.

Twenty to thirty poles permanently planted in the ground marked the shoreline. They were for tethering the safety lines that the men wore when they walked out on the lake. Didn't matter if it was winter or summer, if there was a rescue and you were going on or into the lake, you better be tethered. Mount Olden learned that the hard way; lost Jack Finch when he cramped trying to rescue a ten-year-old boy whose boat turned over.

They were both lost, the child and Jack. And if that wasn't enough of a reason, there was the Horror of Twenty-six when eight men on a cold moonless night, just like this one, fell through the ice during a rescue. They all drowned.

Father Paul counted eight separate lanterns on the lake, each with four or five men around it. "Why do these disasters always happen when there's no moon," he mumbled to himself. "And now it's starting to snow."

"What was that, Father?"

A portly man, hair matted and unkempt, was standing so close to Father Paul that he could feel the man's breath on his neck. Just seemed to appear through a sudden gust of the snow.

"You were saying something about the snow, Father? It's coming down real heavy."

"Do I know you?" the priest answered uneasily.

"I have been to Mass at St Anselm's," the man answered, his face now illuminated by a lantern.

Not a pleasant face, thought Dollard. His skin was pockmarked, his teeth protruding, and a scar ran across his cheek. There was no comfort coming from this man's eyes. Even in the dim light, the priest could see he rarely blinked his eyes. Had he been alone with this stranger instead of in the midst of all the rescuers, his unease might have quickly turned to fear.

"Sorry, I don't remember you," he said haltingly.

"I'm not one of your regulars. Terrible night, wouldn't you say, Father? I knew it was going to be a bad one when

Oscar Ozymandias called and told me to be here with the flatbed. That usually means big trouble. When he has more than he can handle he calls Willy. When there's more than he and Willy can handle, he calls me. The name is Olsen, Father, Tom Olsen."

~

There was more to do than think about this coincidence; Tom Olsen's name coming up twice in one evening.

Two bodies had already been fished out of the lake and Father Paul had his sacramental obligations. He reached for a lantern, placed his stole around his neck and went to where the bodies were laid out. The going wasn't easy. Falling snow had already covered many of the rocks and ruts that littered the path. His legs came out from under him once and it was only with the grace of God that he was able to regain his balance before the lantern came crashing to the ground.

The bodies had been left uncovered, one face down. Father Paul, placing the lantern by his side, reached down and turned this large man over. His skin was cold to the touch. Poco Stevens. He came to church, not often but he came. He wasn't from these parts but had been in Mount Olden long enough for people to know him, doing odd jobs when there was work, and when there wasn't hanging out waiting for something to come his way. A nice man even when he drank too much; he often drank too much.

Paul turned to the second man and began brushing the snow off of him. Rob Church. A husband, a father, now dead. The smell of whiskey lingered on his near-frozen face. After what happened here, nothing would be the same for his family. This was the man who worked at the pharmacy. He made the sodas and when a medicine needed to be delivered, he was the one who took it. He didn't make enough to keep his family going but then no one made enough to do that. Still, the few bucks bought what couldn't be grown in the backyard or sewn by his wife. Now with him gone, there would be nothing for his wife and kids. Was he Catholic? No telling since the family never came to church.

Father Paul thought for only a moment before making a decision. He would anoint both men, even though he was only certain about one. Rob Church, if not Catholic, was probably a Methodist, and Father Paul felt some certainty that if being a Methodist didn't keep you from going to heaven, receiving the Last Rites wouldn't either.

~

The wind was picking up and the storm worsening. The snow, now coming in on an angle, stung when it hit his bare skin. Unable to see more than a few feet ahead, Father Paul pulled his knit hat down on his forehead and his muffler up on his face.

The lanterns on the lake, swaying every which way, made for an odd sight as the light unevenly illuminated the crews. The priest, becoming lost in the spectacle in front of him, imagined a cluster of dancers as the men in the crew moved in and out of shadows. He felt faint, knew he needed sugar, and fumbled for one of the peppermint candies he always carried in his pocket.

A noise came from the middle of the lake. It was hard to make out what had happened but it was clear that whatever it was, it wasn't good. Light was coming right off the lake's surface and the muffled sounds of raised voices began reaching the shoreline.

"The lamp, the lamp. Bring it out there!"

A man was coming in from the lake. It was Len Hinton, Old Man Hinton's son, the hardware store man.

"What's happening out there, Len?"

"It's you, Father. The hat and all, I didn't recognize you."

"What's going on?"

"It's worse than awful. Damn lamp blew over, got knocked over, don't really know. Anyway, it busted open and a number of us got splattered with burning oil. Got to find a doctor. You seen any of them?"

"No. You need me to look?"

"Need you to bring that lantern out there."

With that said, Len Hinton was gone. Father Paul, holding the lantern in front of him, saw where he had to get to, saw where he was, and became nervous. He was certainly used to walking on the lake, but never this early in the year, never during a storm, and never when two men had already been pulled out dead. He took a first tentative step, put all his weight on that foot and pushed down. It felt firm. The next step wasn't as comforting. He heard ice shifting beneath his foot.

"Stop. Stop!"

A familiar voice. Father Paul couldn't figure out which direction it was coming from or who it belonged to.

"The rope, you need the rope."

What was he saying, what rope? Len Hinton told him to take the lamp to the men, not the rope. This was all very confusing. In spite of the thick covering of snow on the lake, it felt like he was going to lose his balance. Was the ice giving way under his feet or were his feet giving way on the ice? He should be able to tell. He couldn't.

"The rope needs to be tethered. Tethered!"

The voice was coming closer and more insistent. What was this man talking about and why was it important? Paul

Dollard, his hands still tightly clasped on the lamp, felt his legs give way.

"I've got you, Dollard. Just take it easy and you won't fall."

A firm hand was holding him by the arm, the familiar voice now no more than a foot or two from his ear. This should have been comforting, being held, being supported. Instead it made for more confusion. Father Paul pulled away and for a moment it seemed like both men were falling.

"Dollard, for God's sake. Some control. Stop pulling or we'll both be on the ice."

Dollard? It was Ozymandias. Only Oscar called him by his last name. They were close to the shoreline, no more than a foot on the ice, and at that moment Paul Dollard realized he would survive, at least for now.

"Oscar, it's you. I became terribly confused but I think I'm all right now. The lantern. There's been an accident out there. Something or someone was burning. I have to bring the lantern to the men. I have to go."

"You have to be tethered."

"What are you talking about?"

"Just turn around," commanded Oscar.

Father Paul did as he was told. He felt a sudden tug at his belt, and looking down, saw Oscar attaching an end of the rope to him. He unfurled the large coil, found the other end, and tied it to the nearest pole.

"Now you're ready. Just try to keep it untangled and watch out for the other ropes. Not so easy to do when you're out there, but go out there without it and there's a good chance you'll find yourself where you don't want to be."

Under the ice.

~

A man, running and out of breath, emerged from the falling snow. This was the second time that someone had simply appeared without Father Paul seeing him coming. This time it startled him.

"Who is that? Who are you!" he asked, not seeing a face under all the clothes and yet recognizing the voice. This familiar man reached for his cap, pulled it up and leaned forward.

"It's you, Vincent, it's you. Where did you come from?"

"Take your lamp out to the men over there," Vincent Stasser, the local postmaster said, pointing in the direction where, just a few minutes ago, Father Paul had heard the noise.

"What happened?" Paul asked.

"Nasty business. A pole blew over, got knocked over, don't know," an out-of-breath Vincent answered with difficulty.

"What's that? It seems like it's moving on the ice."

Vincent turned from Father Paul and leaned forward, raising his hands to shield his eyes from the snow as he looked in the direction of the commotion.

"Damn, they haven't gotten it out yet. Nasty business, nasty."

"What's not out yet?" pressed the priest.

"The lamp fell from the pole and broke up, splattering some of the men with oil. They need the lantern. No time for talk. Take it to them."

Father Paul had come to care for men's souls and now he was being asked to be a messenger, delivering a lantern instead of the Lord's message. If that's what was needed, that's what he would do. This was yet another test of faith. He knew it because he could feel it. His fingers started to go numb, his stomach pained, the sweat was all over his body under his many layers of clothes, and his legs felt like they no longer had the strength to hold him up, let alone take him to where he had to be. No stranger to all this, he nonetheless hated it when it happened.

Always fear, always in his body before it got to his mind; that's how he knew this was another trial. And in every trial he carried the uncertainty of whether he would make it, and the hope that this time would be the last so he could put to rest the time he didn't.

Paul, at the age of eight, was a strong youngster. At the rate he was going he'd be down the mines by the time he was fourteen, two or three years ahead of most. The sooner the better, his folks needed every penny he could bring in to help the family make ends meet. No matter how many of the kids were down in the mine with their fathers, the ends never met.

With six more years before manhood, Paul's plan was to take advantage of every moment he had. That meant school during the week, church on Sunday, and hanging out in the summer. When the days started getting long, it was always warm enough for Paul and his cousin Judd to go down to the ore pit for a swim. That's where it happened.

It was mid May and it was warming up. After Saturday chores, the cousins headed for the pit. It was too early, ten in the morning, and too cool for anyone other than these two eight-year-olds to be at the swimming hole.

Paul didn't see it happen, he just heard it.

He was swinging on a rope tied to a tree when Judd started screaming, gasping and coughing. The child, over his head in water, was bobbing up and down. Paul, timing his release, let go of the rope and plunged into the water no more than a few feet from where he thought his cousin should be. He came to the surface and began looking. No one. He saw no one. Now it was Paul's screaming that filled the air; "Judd, Judd, where are you!!" He yelled out the name two, three times.

No answer and no one around to hear.

Finally, after what felt like more time than could be imagined, the quiet surface of the water broke and a gasping Judd rose out of the placid lake, almost his entire chest exposed to the air. The child tried to pull in air before he plummeted back down, coughing and heaving swallowed water. Paul, no more than five feet away, began swimming to Judd, getting there just in time for the next descent. He reached out and grabbed hold of his cousin's arm and as he did, Judd grabbed onto his. Paul, no match for a panicked and struggling swimmer, began to go under as the drowning Judd tried to use him as leverage to get to the surface. They both, one entangled in the other, only went deeper.

By now, Judd's strength was going and Paul was weakening as he exhaled the last bit of air in his lungs. Without thinking, Paul put his free hand on his cousin's head and pushed down as hard as he could. Judd, with his last bit of life, released Paul's arm and tried to free himself of a watery grave. Starved of oxygen and very confused, Judd went down for the last time. Paul, out of breath and throwing up, kept himself afloat on the surface.

The families were devastated. They were used to losing kin, but not to water and not when they were so young. Five days after the drowning, Judd's parents buried a son and Paul tried to bury a terrible memory. It didn't work. Feelings of guilt and shame were never far away.

~

Father Paul's first steps on the lake were careful and studied. He registered every sound that came beneath his feet. The further he was from the shore, the fewer the sounds, and he took this as a firm sign that the lake was frozen and safe. He kept this silly notion in his head for only a few minutes and then remembered why he was here; an accident had happened and men had drowned. When the lakes in these parts are really frozen, when it's dead winter, a man could bring a truck onto this surface and there'd be no danger or sounds of shifting ice down below. It wasn't the middle of winter, and if this weren't humbling enough to Father Paul's overestimated sense of well being, he began to make out the form of a man coming towards him pulling what he was sure was a toboggan. He knew about toboggans, hadn't he grown up in ice mining country? They were used to move heavy objects from one part of the lake to the other, mostly the blocks of ice that had been cut from the frozen lakes. There was no mining of ice tonight.

"Watch it, man. Watch where you're going before we get our lines tangled."

The voice was easier to make out than the man it belonged to. Gene Turner, a member of the parish, was wearing one of those special caps that completely covered his face except for the eyes and mouth.

"That you, Turner?"

"It's you, Father. Be careful with that tether. You'll get hurt if it gets tangled."

"Who's in the toboggan, Gene?"

"Don't know, Father. They hauled him out and had him on it before I got there. It's bad. Looks like the whole damn lake gave way by those rocks. No knowing how many more there'll be by the time this messy thing is over. Wouldn't be surprised if some more pop up with the spring thaw."

"He's dead, is he?"

"That's what I'm saying."

"Let me give him his rites."

"Don't even know if he's Catholic. You bringing that lantern out there? They need that more than this one needs your words," said Turner, making the decision for the priest. "He'll wait for you, Father. He's not going anywhere."

Given the choice, Father Paul would rather have tended to the sacrament than go towards the men on the ice who were now fifty or sixty feet in front of him.

A loud noise, thunder. No, not thunder. It wasn't coming from above him and it wasn't that loud. Loud enough to startle him, though. Father Paul reached behind to make sure the rope was tightly secured. His lifeline, nothing could happen as long as he was connected to the shore, even if the connection was no more than a quarter inch rope.

What was he feeling? It was coming through his feet. This was not the crunching of the ice that he felt taking his first steps on the lake. He had been on this lake many times, sometimes even walked across it when he went from the rectory to town and had felt the shifting of ice before. This was different.

For a moment Father Paul lost sight of the men he was heading towards. Was he gettting confused? With no light in the sky and the snow continuing to fall, he could only see but a few feet in front of him. He stopped.

There they were, the lanterns, the shapes. He inched his way closer, small tentative steps, one after the other.

Something was wrong. What he was seeing now was not what he had seen a moment before. Now he could see what was different but didn't understand what that meant. That would come all too soon as he got closer.

Calamity. This was no well-oiled crew. It was chaos.

"How many?" yelled a large man whose face was hidden under his hat and a full unkempt beard, leaving nothing but his eyes exposed.

"Dunno," someone shouted back.

"What the hell do you mean 'don't know?' Who was doing the count?"

Someone was supposed to be doing the count of who was out on the ice doing the mining, and, God forbid, how many when a rescue team was called out. That's the way it was done. They'd had enough experience with these rescues to know that when you got to the site, one man had to keep count. It was dangerous enough to send a man into the water under any circumstances and especially when it was like this with the snow and all.

You didn't want to send someone in if there was no need and you didn't know if there was a need unless you did the counting. The man with the beard didn't want to hear that the counter didn't know how many men were at the hole and how many of the crew were in the water.

"We started with a crew of eight," said the counter. "Two men on lanterns, two minding the security poles, me and Gary, and four dunkers."

"So that's eight."

"More than eight. Pulled out four and people were coming and going. Lost track as soon as we pulled the first one out."

"How many you seen go in?"

"At least three. Two of them are over there. There are two dunkers in right now looking for the third."

"Let's pray to God there's no more than three," said the bearded man. "How many on poles? What's the count now?

"I'm working on it, it ain't so easy."

"Make it easy, man!" he barked. "The ice gives way again, we're going to be losing more men. There's one coming towards us. Behind you, damn it. Turn around. A lantern. Good, we need the lantern. Who the hell are you? Speak up, I can't hear you?"

"Father Paul," Dollard said, in a voice that was louder and firmer than the first time he had responded that night.

"You, Father. We don't need a priest now. Another pole man, that's what we need. Bring the torch over there. No, Father, there," he said, pointing to two men who were no more than five feet from the edge of a gaping hole in the ice that must have measured fifteen feet.

The two rocks that had marked the edge of the original breakthrough were now completely surrounded by a goodly amount of water. The men, wielding sledgehammers, were driving two new stakes into the ice. When the spikes were firmly anchored, they screwed an extension on to each that was capped with an eyelet.

"You got two in. Bring over their lines. We're ready to tie them on," said the man with the beard. He was telling everyone what to do and everyone was listening. It was Phil Shaw, the head of Mount Olden's three-man police force. He was also the head of the Public Safety Committee, which gave him authority over the volunteer fire department during emergencies, and this was an emergency. Chief Shaw was now giving the orders.

"Hurry up with those lines and get those men tethered to the poles. Get the other two poles into the ice. Do it over there, on the other side. The next crew will be going down in a few minutes. How long have those men been in?"

"Five minutes," answered the counter, who was also responsible for keeping time until the pole man was ready to take over.

"Then hurry up with the other poles. We got to bring them in real soon. Now tie them on."

The ropes of each of the two dunkers were being held fast by three men, not the safest arrangement since they could easily lose their footing. If that happened when a dunker had a body in tow, the weight of the bodies in the water could easily pull one or more of them in. This had happened before and was why poles were used to anchor the lines. A pole held by ice was more secure than any number of men holding a rope while standing on the ice. That is unless the margins of the opening in the lake gave way, toppling the poles. That never happened because the men drove the spikes a distance from the edge of the ice, and the ice was usually strong enough to hold a lot of weight.

What never happened had just happened. The ice gave way exactly where the poles had been planted, and now there were more men in the water. With no accurate count and more going on than anyone could take in, they'd have to wait until they got back to the town building to put the whole story together.

The rescue crews were no longer looking for the men they had come for. If there were any more of them in the water they'd be dead by now. The effort now concentrated on members of the crew who had fallen in. Three confirmed; two were already pulled out and a team of dunkers was looking for the third. They could see no bobbing on the surface. The job now was to get as many dunkers safely in the water to check under the ice at the margins to make sure there was no one alive under there.

Father Paul knew he had more than one job to do; manage the poles to ensure they didn't move, make sure the lines of the two men he was handling didn't become entangled, and pray that the holders didn't get pulled in. So far he knew of at least three dead. He needed to concentrate on what he had to do and that made him forget how afraid all this made him.

Father Paul took a deep breath, and concentrated on nothing other than his poles, his lines and the two men in the water.

It was going to be a very long, cold night on Eastern Lake. It must already be midnight with no end in sight.

Chapter Twelve

"What the hell happened out there?" said Chief Shaw, barely containing his rage. "We go through this year after year. We know the drill. What happened?"

The men in the meeting hall said nothing. They knew what happened. Disaster. How many had they pulled out? How many were still under the ice and wouldn't wash up until the spring thaw? Every time someone turned around, there was another body being hauled out on a sled.

"Who was doing the counting? Speak up, goddammit. Who was supposed to be keeping track?"

No answer.

"Are you telling me no one was doing the counting?"

"Too much snow, Chief."

"*Who said that*?" Shaw, about to explode, looked around the room in the direction of the lone voice that was sharing the air with him.

"It's me, Chief, Meyerson. Meyerson."

"You were the counter? Where the hell were you? What were you doing, man?"

"Easy, Chief, you're scaring the boy," Father Paul interrupted, walking to the front of the room. "We've all been through more than any of us can handle. Now tell me, son, what happened with the counting out there?"

"I couldn't keep track, Father. I was trying. I was doing okay until the snow started and then I couldn't see more than a foot past my nose."

Meyerson was having trouble getting the words out, with his sniffling and all. He was more upset than scared. At sixteen he had never been near anything as horrible as what just happened. He knew about the big one, the Horror of Twenty-Six, the one his daddy talked about, the time before they used the poles and ropes.

A lot of people went in and under the ice. There was more said about that than the big war. Mount Olden only lost six of their sons in the war. How many had they lost when all those men fell through the ice? God, thought Ray Meyerson, this could be worse than that and he was supposed to be doing the counting.

"I tried to keep the count, Father. I just couldn't see and then, Father, and then it seemed like they were coming out of everywhere. They were supposed to come past me, Father, so I could keep count of how many were out there. They were supposed to and they didn't. I tried, Father Paul, I tried."

Paul, now standing next to the youngster, put an arm around him. The boy could hold on no longer as his whimper turned to tears and then sobs. The others, including Chief Shaw, stayed silent, averting their eyes, to spare this broken soldier the embarrassment of his comrades seeing his distress.

"It's okay, son," said Chief Shaw, breaking the tension that had filled the room. "We all did what we had to do. It was dark, it was storming and I know the men were coming from every which direction. How many? What do we know?"

"We don't know," answered Len. "There were two bodies up on the shore. Isn't that right, Father? Stevens and Rob Church."

"There was the one I brought in on the toboggan. Remember, Father? The Last Rites or the lantern." It was Gene Turner, standing at the back of the hall with a mug of coffee in one hand and a donut in the other. Speaking to no one in particular, he quietly took charge as he always did when matters of grave importance in Mount Olden were getting out of hand. He had gotten his training for these big moments in France where he had been in the trenches. He had seen everything there was to see and knew the best chance that anyone had to get out of a tight spot was to not lose their head.

"Now look, Chief," began Turner, reaching for yet another donut from Tilly's. Jake always brought over urns of coffee and dozens of donuts when the town turned out for one of these disasters. "We got to figure out what happened and how many we lost. Everyone that's a goner is over at Ozymandias' by now. He had some helpers tonight, he had to. Who was out there?"

Silence.

"Okay," continued Turner. "Where's Willy or Olsen?"

No answer.

"Oscar, are you here?"

Still, no one spoke.

"So that's it for how many we lost, or at least how many we got out. No need speculating until one of them gets here."

Of course he was right. They'd have to wait for Willy, Olsen or Oscar Ozymandias, or for someone looking for a missing husband, brother or son, or the thaw, before they'd know no one was still under the ice.

"So now, Chief, help us find out what happened out there and if we did something wrong."

~

"Willy, you see Tom Olsen out there?" asked Oscar, who was already at work by the time Willy pulled up with his truck. He should have been complaining at the amount of work in front of him, but always the businessman, Oscar understood this was a moment of great opportunity. He, too, had heard the telling and retelling of the Horror and by any account that night would soon be taking second fiddle to the 'Great Lake Break Through'.

"I saw his truck Mr. O, but I never put an eye on him."

"How many do you have?" Oscar asked matter of factly, trying not to give any hint of his true feelings about such bounty.

"I brought in four. Two trips. Four altogether."

"Do you know any of them?" This was an important question that Oscar would be asking again. With so many bodies, he needed to know the county's from the privates, and of the privates, how many of the families would be doing the burying themselves. Then there were the death certificates. Better to wait until Olsen came with his truckload before calling Doc Radler.

"A couple," answered Willy. "These two are the Johnsons. This one is a cousin to that. The one over there with the red hair, I seen him around but don't know his name. Maybe he has kin. I don't know. The muscle man, the heavy-set one, nobody knows. Came into town three days ago from out of state. Stopped by the hardware looking for work. Must have hooked up with the others and tied one on. What you want me to do with them?"

Ozymandias knew exactly what had to be done; the Johnsons and the redhead to cold storage, the stranger on the gurney stays on the gurney, and then Willy could leave. So far the number was six, Willy's four and the two he had brought in. Both were from these parts and unless Tom Olsen brought in something extraordinary, the heavy-set stranger would do just fine.

"I put them outside, boss. Anything else before I go?"

"If I need you, I'll call you."

Willy got in his truck and headed for the meeting hall. Oscar Ozymandias pulled up a chair and stared at his trophy, hoping that Olsen would soon arrive with the final load. He needed to get things going.

~

"Ah, there he is," bellowed Chief Shaw. "You coming from Ozymandias'?"

"That's where I come from." Willy Catchum looked cold and uncomfortable. It seemed like he'd been moving for hours, pulling bodies, carrying bodies, hauling bodies; a lot of dead weight when there's no life in the flesh. The snow hadn't made it any easier, that was for sure. When he was carrying that big one, one of the Johnsons, he even fell, nearly hitting his head on a rock. That alone could have made him one of the ones to be counted. It was good to be indoors and not have to carry anything but himself.

"Get yourself a cup of coffee and come up here. Hold it down there, fellows," ordered Shaw. "This man may have an answer to one of the questions. How many?" he asked, turning to Willy, who now had both coffee and a donut.

"Six when I left," he answered, trying to speak and swallow at once.

"What do you mean 'when I left'?" asked Len. "What about Pico Stevens, Rob and the one I brought in on the toboggan?"

"Is that you, Len? Can't see ya from here."

"It's me, Willy. What about those three?"

"They were there. I brought one of them in and Mr Ozymandias brought the other two."

"And there were still three more?"

"That's what I counted, Len."

"And what's this 'when I left'?"

"Olsen hadn't got in yet with his truck."

"Oh my God!" said Father Paul. He was saying it for all of them in the meeting hall. There were already as many dead as in twenty-six and there was still Tom Olsen out there with his truck.

"Quiet down," ordered the chief. "Before we leave tonight we got to start making sense of what happened out there. We had the poles, we had the tethers. What the hell happened?"

More than twenty-five men began telling what they did and what they saw. Twenty-five men and twenty-five stories; hard to believe they were at the same place at the same time. While some were impatient with this, Father Paul understood it all too well.

Between the dark, the snow and the adrenalin pumping, as much as everyone had been part of the same catastrophe, the catastrophe was different for each, depending on where they were standing and what they were doing. Still, it was important to get a single picture of the unfolding night. This way they could start to answer the question of what went wrong so that it could be fixed. Isn't that what happened in twenty-six when they decided to use poles and ropes? And hadn't that worked; not a single rescuer lost? That is, at least until tonight.

~

"Very good, very good." It was Oscar Ozymandias, intense in thought and busy at work, talking to no one but himself. He knew he'd be alone for the next few hours now that Olsen had come and gone with his delivery and all the others were locked up in the meeting hall with Chief Shaw.

Somewhere in the night, after they'd done their talking, the Chief would break out a case of booze that the local VFW chapter kept locked up for their first of the month Friday night meeting, to help with the process of healing and soothing.

Oscar knew, from looking at what had been brought in, that each of the men had been through more than they had bargained for and it would take every last drop from every last bottle to get them through the night. By the time Shaw was ready to open the door and let the men out, the moon would be setting and the sun would be rising. Oscar Ozymandias would have all the time he'd need.

~

"Quiet. Goddamn, we need a little order if we're going to make some sense of all this." Chief Shaw had a way of making himself heard, no matter how many people in a room and no matter how loud they were talking. "So let's see what we got so far. The alarm sounds ten or ten-thirty."

"More like ten-thirty," came a voice somewhere in the back. There was reason for not being sure in this matter. Before the horns started blowing, there were always bells, loud bells. They were located in strategic places throughout Mount Olden so people could call for help in an emergency. The lake was such a place. In fact, there were five bells around the lake. That's how big North Lake was. The routine was, if you heard a bell you rang a bell and when the alarm finally got to the firehouse, the horn would be blown. There was none, as long as they were willing to listen, who couldn't hear the horn blowing. A series of blasts every minute for four minutes, silence, and then repeat the sequence three more times. By that time, it was usually known what had happened and where it had happened.

Fact: at exactly 10:43 Jeff Smithfield, on evening watch at the firehouse, hit the horn; two short, three long, two short, a pause, and then repeated it two more times to make sure everyone had a chance to hear, whether they were sitting at their kitchen tables or asleep in their beds. Whatever was happening was at station four at the lake.

"Too much time between the first bell, no matter what time it was sounded, and the horn. Write that down, Smitty," he said to Jeff Smithfield, who was not only a volunteer fireman, but also Shaw's deputy. "We got to fix that one; too much time. Don't want to forget it so write it down. You said you got on the lake first, Hinton. No trouble finding the break?"

"Kids who sounded the first alarm pointed me to it," answered Len Hinton. Fortunately there were poles and a rope box right there. There were a few of us. Mike stayed by the poles and me and Jonny got tethered. We were out there in no time, but no time was already too late. The two that we pulled out were floating on the water. Stinking drunk, from the smell of them, and very dead. We sent a dunker in and he came up with a third body that was trapped under the ice."

"You thought there was more?" the Chief asked.

"A pretty good chance of that," answered Dick Gray, who owned the package store. "Six of them came in early evening and bought four bottles of whiskey. When I got onto the lake, I let them know there might be more and we'd have to keep looking."

No one was about to argue that point. Each man could tell a story about someone pulled from under the ice who looked dead, should have been dead, but came back to life. In fact, Seamus, who was right there in the hall, had been such a man. He was working the ice when it gave way under him. Went straight down and couldn't be seen. It took forever to get a dunker tethered and by the time he went into the water, everyone was sure Seamus was gone. The dunker went down three times looking and it wasn't till the fourth dive that he spotted Seamus' limp body floating under the surface. Pulled him in, did mouth to mouth, covered him with blankets and five years later he was here telling everyone that you simply can't give up the search.

~

"Here's your money, Olsen. Thanks for helping out tonight."

Oscar knew that Tom Olsen's departure would be the last of the night's intrusions. He needed time to get done what needed to be done and now there wasn't enough. Soon people would be coming over to see if their family and friends who never made it home were in his mortuary. Oscar figured he had an hour, maybe two at most.

"You sure you don't need any help moving the corpses?" asked Tom.

Oscar knew this wasn't a gesture of consideration. Olsen had a fascination with the dead and the longer he could stay around a lifeless body, the better he felt. Lots of people in Mount Olden thought the younger Olsen was strange in the head but couldn't put their finger on it. Oscar Ozymandias knew exactly what he was dealing with. It was Tom who showed him the business when he was buying it from his father and he got to know the young man very well. He was a strange bird and Oscar knew that some day that might come in very handy. As for now, the sooner he could get him to leave, the better.

"I can manage everything now. Go home, Olsen. Leave. Out. It's been one very long night and it's a long way from being over for me. Go."

"Okay, if you can manage it. I suppose I'll go over to the Meeting Hall." He heard Mr. O's impatience; it was in his voice as much as in his words. Some day he'd call him on it but not this night. Every time he took Ozymandias on it was months before he'd get a call to help out and he didn't want that to happen right now. Tom Olsen, using every bit of control he had, simply said good night. Oscar in return said nothing as he walked this last intruder to the door and double locked it now that he was alone. Pouring himself a glass of sherry, he took a moment to organize his thoughts and work out a plan for the next hour.

The first order of business was the doctor. He hadn't seen him at the lake.

"Radler, it's me, Ozymandias," said Oscar in a firm and commanding voice, as he woke a groggy Radler from what was obviously a deep sleep.

"Who's this?" grunted the doctor.

Very good, thought Ozymandias. He was almost sure he was hearing a slurred Doctor Radler.

"It's me, Radler, Oscar Ozymandias. We need to talk."

"What are you bothering me at this hour? What hour is it anyway?"

"Do you know what's going on? Didn't you hear the horns blowing?"

"What are you talking about?"

"The lake, man. There was an accident."

"Yes, so?" answered the doctor, now looking through his bedroom window. "Where did all that snow come from? What are you bothering me about?"

"A lot of people got pulled out tonight, Radler. You're the coroner, you have to be called."

"Screw you Ozamodis, mandias I mean. You don't tell me what I'm supposed to do. Supposed to do."

"Don't be falling back to sleep on me, Doc." Oscar could hear in the man's voice that falling asleep was a clear possibility. When this man was on one of his binges, he'd disappear for days and that would not do tonight.

Be aggressive, Oscar said to himself. Focused and aggressive.

"Look, Doc, stay awake and listen. This won't take but a minute and I don't think there's much need for you to come out if we take care of our business."

Oscar heard a clear sigh from the other end of the phone. He needed more than a sigh. "If this is not a good time, then you'll surely have to come over in a few hours to take care of the business yourself."

Doc Radler looked at the half-filled bottle of bourbon on his nightstand and the empty one right next to it. With the liquor he had drunk, the half bottle that was still waiting to be drunk, and the snow on the ground, he knew he wasn't about to leave this room for at least a day or two. Concentrate, you idiot, concentrate, he said to himself. You've done this before, just ask the question. The question, what's the question?'

"What's that? Who's talking? What? What?" a confused Doc Radler asked into the mouthpiece of the telephone. A voice answered, bringing him back to the here and now.

"It's me, Radler. Oscar Ozymandias. Oscar, the undertaker. There's been a big accident at the lake. Nine men are dead and you've got to either tell me what to do or get your sorry self over here!"

Oscar's words sobered Radler up, if for only a minute. He knew what Oscar was asking; there had been other calls like this.

"Tell me again, Oscar. How many?"

"Nine."

"Nine? On my god! Do we know them all?"

"Most."

"Who?" asked the doctor.

"You're in no shape to remember. The names will be on the death certificates."

Radler knew he was right. He'd have a hard enough time remembering the call, let alone the names of the dead. "All drowned?" he asked.

"All nine."

"Okay. Make out the certificates and sign them."

"Like we always do?" asked Oscar.

"Like we always do."

It was done. Oscar prepared nine certificates and signed Radler's name nine times. Three were townies, four were from the rescue crew and two were names of men who were not from around these parts. If anyone asked, Doc Radler would say he came right over to Ozymandias when he got the call, examined all the expired, and certified the cause of death.

Nine bodies, nine certificates. If anyone asked Oscar, he'd say the same. All that was left to do was bring the nine bodies into the cold house; there'd be time to deal with them tomorrow.

As for body number ten, a well-developed and muscular man whose face Oscar did not recognize, his place was in the special chamber behind the embalming room.

This corpse belonged to Oscar and there wasn't time to wait for tomorrow.

~

"What happened at the hole? How did we lose our men?" asked Chief Shaw. This was the heart of the tragedy. A bunch of men get drunk and wander on to the lake. They're where they oughtn't be and there's an accident. Their families grieve, if they have families, friends and acquaintances say a few kind things about their stay on this earth, and the rest of the town folk speak under their breath about how they had it coming since they were out drinking and carousing. The rescuers were a different matter. Good people doing good things for others shouldn't come to so bad an end.

Anyone near where it happened had an answer about what had happened and while there were differences, a few basic facts were common to all. The rescue team did what was supposed to be done. The first men who got to the hole were tethered to poles at the shoreline. A dunker got in quickly and pulled two bodies out. To go down deeper into the water, for the dunkers to be able to swim around under the ice, poles needed to be set near the hole. Three poles were planted and immediately used. Then it happened. It started with a low growling noise, then silence, and then a large chunk of ice gave way. Men were just sliding and flopping into the water. More of the ice caved in and with it more men and the three poles.

"Do we know how many fell in?" asked the Chief.

"Don't know for sure cause we don't know how many was right there," answered Rolphie Turner, Gene's younger brother. "I saw at least five. Between going in because there was nothing under your feet, slipping off the ice, or being pulled in from all those poles and tangled ropes, I saw at least five."

"Ask the priest, he was there."

It was Tom Olsen and no one had noticed him come in. He knew everyone would want to hear from him since he'd been working for Oscar Ozymandias that night, and yet he just got lost in the back of the hall and said nothing.

"When you get here, Olsen?" Deputy Smithfield asked, with an edge to his voice.

"Long enough to know what you're talking about so ask Father Paul, he was there. Saw him going out to where all this was happening."

Father Paul turned in the direction of a familiar voice. Standing no more than a few feet behind him was Tom Olsen. Again this man had come almost next to him without being noticed. He could see his face more clearly now, the matted hair, the scar, a strained and contorted grimace that seemed a permanent part of who he was.

"The priest," Olsen said for the third time. "Ask the priest."

Paul Dollard turned away from Olsen, whose unblinking stare was locked on him. He hadn't meant to turn away, it happened all by itself.

"What about it, Father? You were out there?"

Who was asking? Where? Find the voice and lock onto it. The sweat was starting and his heart was beating faster. Soon he would know what was making this happen. The feelings first, then the thoughts; that's how it was with him. That's what happened when he said Mass and had to stumble through the Latin.

Anxiety.

It began with a light sweat. A few minutes later he'd pick out a face in the congregation, and with that he'd feel his heart speeding up. It happened when he first got to St Anselm's when Sada Weisner, dear Sada who now looked after him and the rectory, came to mass, and thank goodness it didn't happen with her any more since she was in church seven days a week. It was always there with Oscar Ozymandias. No problems during their weekly dinners at Tilly's, but every time that man came to church Dollard knew he'd get one of those attacks. Fortunately he didn't come often. Paul found that puzzling, since Oscar was more devout in his Catholicism than even he was. Ordinarily he would discuss not coming to church with one of the congregants but when it came to Oscar, he was frankly pleased that he wasn't there, satisfying himself with the possibility that Oscar Ozymandias was going to the next parish to assure a place for his soul in heaven.

Sometimes Father Paul's anxiety attacks were triggered by a woman, sometimes a man; old, young, it was always changing and because it was always a little different, he couldn't figure out what it was about these people that was making him so uncomfortable. He did, however, know something about the fear. It had to do with being exposed, found out, being publicly embarrassed or humiliated.

"Father, are you all right?" asked Chief Shaw.

"The priest, ask the priest. He was out there. He knows how many they pulled out."

This time Father Paul didn't have to see who was speaking to know who was speaking; it was Olsen again. And he didn't have to turn around to know that Olsen was still staring in his direction. He could feel those unblinking eyes on the back of his neck.

"Yes, Chief. I'm all right. Was I out there? I was out there."

"Good," answered Chief Shaw. "You were out there with the crew. Very good. Not too many people who are not part of the team are willing to get that close to the action. A brave man," said the Chief, turning to the men in the hall. "What did you see, Father?"

"Did it take you long to get out to the hole, Father?"

It was Olsen again. Dollard, now beginning to feel his heart beat, couldn't understand why this man was asking this question. Dollard knew it took him a while to get out there and that the only reason he got to where it was all happening was because of Gene Turner. He told him it was more important to take the lantern to the rescue crew than give the last rites to a dead man being hauled to shore in a toboggan. And no one but he knew that when he finally got to where the men had drowned, he quickly handed the lantern to the first outreached arm and then took ten good steps away from the hole despite the need for another able-bodied man.

Paul Dollard knew all these things about himself and what he did, not this Tom Olsen. And yet this man was asking questions like he knew something; like he had been standing right at Father Paul Dollard's side from the moment this all began to the moment that it ended.

~

"Okay Number Ten, let's see if I made the right choice."

Oscar Ozymandias was in the middle of a one-way conversation with a man who had now been dead for at least five hours. He had already made decisions that let him get this far.

Opportunities like this did not come often; three of the ten corpses were not known to many in Mount Olden and since he knew all the families in these parts, Methodists as well as Catholics, he knew the three had no kin close by. The official count was nine and the body count ten. Doc Radler would be certifying the official dead and with all the confusion that comes with these tragic events, especially when they happen at night in a snow storm, Oscar would be the only one who'd ever know about the extra body. Now for number ten, his potential was enormous. It was Oscar's good fortune that Vern Wasby, this wonderful physical specimen of a man, carried his life story in his wallet.

Wasby, Vernon C and Kathryn J. October 1, 1933 – Vern and Kathryn Wasby of South Kaden died in a one-car accident on

Route 35 in Perkins County. The police said the driver appeared to have lost control of the car during last night's storm. Vernon, a veteran of the Great War, fought for his country in France. The Wasbys were members of St. Thomas R.C. Church where Kathryn served on the Parish council. Sole survivor is their son Vern Jr. age 22 at home.

A good Catholic, thought Oscar.

Oscar Ozymandias was a fundamentalist by nature but an intellect by temperament. If something didn't sit right with him, he questioned it, no matter if it were dogma, or if it had been part of tradition for centuries. He never considered moving away from his church. He was born a Catholic and would die a Catholic, but that didn't mean that he was prepared to follow what didn't make sense. The confession was a perfect example. He firmly believed deed and action over time, not a few recited Acts of Contrition, was the road to forgiveness and absolution, no matter the sin. A progressive and conservative all at once.

Ozymandias had a fundamental difference with the Eucharist; a cracker becomes the embodiment of Christ because the priest says a prayer. He did believe that Christ lives in all of us, and by incorporating Our Savior into our very being we foster the possibility that we might walk in His footsteps. His issue was with that damn cracker. A cracker is a cracker no matter what prayer is said. This symbolism in fundamental matters of faith was wanting. That's not to say Oscar didn't recognize or believe in the power of prayer, but if it was to turn the ordinary into the extraordinary and the extraordinary into the fundamental element of the Sacrament, you don't start with a *cracker.*

Vernon Wasby Jr. had every appearance of being a good Catholic, from the article in his wallet to the crucifix around his neck and right down to his uncircumcised member, which was clearly visible now that he was buck-naked on the embalming table.

The last item of business was to make a judgment on Vernon's state of health before his untimely demise.

"Let's take a closer look, Wasby Jr.," said Oscar, as he meticulously moved his hands across every surface of visible body. "No scars, very good."

When his hands hovered over the liver, he gently pushed down with his fingertips. He had seen Doc Radler doing this more than once, feeling for something hard when it was supposed to be soft.

"Just the way it's supposed to feel. A healthy liver, Mr. Wasby."

Oscar again picked up the wallet and began searching through all its compartments. "A card from a doctor in Kadem and a date on the back from a year ago," as he turned it over several times in his hand. "Should I be worried, Vernon? Or should I presume that you were simply under a doctor's care, and given the good shape you seem to be in, are in perfectly good health?"

Oscar was almost ready for the final step, the autopsy, where he could tell if Vern's other organs were up to snuff. If there was any disease, that would be the end of it.

The first step was draining the body of all fluids and since there would be no replacement, it would take considerably less time than an embalming. Oscar reached for the trocars, tubing and scalpels, then glanced at the clock on the far wall. He was still doing all right with time. This, for Oscar, was a matter of pride. With all that had to be done before the first intruder came knocking at his door as part of the investigation of the night's tragedy, a man of lesser skill would have considerable difficulty. Having opened up all the lines and inserted all the trocars with great precision, the purging would soon be complete. Now it was time to start examining the insides.

"Okay, sonny, let's open you up. You've got an expert here in Oscar Ozymandias," he said with a chuckle, "and this shouldn't hurt a bit." And an expert he was. With a steady hand and sharp scalpel, he penetrated each and every layer of skin and muscle with a single incision, from the base of the sternum to the pubic bone, exposing poor Vern's guts.

"Well done, my good fellow," he said aloud. "Now let's open the sack and take out the organs and entrails. Ah, a wonderful healthy liver, just as I thought. Fantastic!" Oscar loved it when the pathology confirmed the clinical examination.

"With the wrong crowd tonight, Vernon? Too much to drink, Vernon?" He could smell the alcohol in the now exposed organs. "But a fine, healthy liver. No cirrhosis in this bright item. Anything else? No. Everything looks just fine. Pancreas, stomach, intestines, etc. etc. etc; fine, fine, fine. Now for a look up top." Oscar pierced the diaphragm, reached for the heart and pulled down. Faster than spreading the ribs and for his purposes, just as effective. He grabbed a piece from each lung; the tissue pink and subtle.

"One good healthy Catholic," declared Oscar, almost giddy from this good fortune. A few more things to do and he'd move Vern Wasby to the back, the room that he, and only he knew about, where the final and most important work would be done.

Oscar went to the base cabinet on the far wall, reaching at the same time for the key in his pocket, and unlocked the padlock that guarded the contents from unwelcome eyes. He removed a circular saw that could just as well have been in a garage, but instead was secreted away in his embalming theater. After meticulously cleaning the spotless blade with several applications of alcohol, he brought the saw to the table, where Vern Wasby, face up, was spread eagled, with his intestinal cavity now empty and exposed to the air.

"No need for you to see what happens next, my good man," Oscar said to Wasby, as he placed a towel across the expressionless face.

The sound of blade on bone filled the room. Slivers of bone jumped into the air, white dust hovered above his 'patient's' crown. After one last swipe around the circumference, Oscar reached down and lifted a now severed portion of bone from the skull. Staring down and in, he was in awe; that unremarkable remarkable place where body and soul met, where God had given to humans what he had given to none other of his creatures: the knowledge of His very existence, and the capacity to love the Lord with all our hearts and all our mind. Oscar felt no embarrassment as a tear moved slowly down his cheek.

Satisfied that there was no obvious disease, Oscar slid Vernon back on the gurney and rolled him to the back room and the beginning of the sacred work.

There, he picked up his scalpel, sharpened it to assure that each precise cut would leave no ragged edge, and began harvesting large sections of still-pink flesh, wrapping each in brown paper that he then carefully bound with white cord.

~

A persistent Tom Olsen was going to make sure Father Paul gave a full account of what he had seen and what he had done on North Lake. Had Olsen seen him with the body in the toboggan, wanting to give a man his last rites rather than put himself in harm's way? Had he seen the anxiety that swept over him? Was that what Olsen was after? Expose and humiliate the priest in front of his flock? *Just tell them what you saw,* Dollard commanded himself. *Stick to what you saw and it will keep you away from the panic you felt.*

"Chaos, absolute chaos," began Father Paul Dollard, as he started his account. "It seemed like any number of men were thrashing in the water, tangled in a mass of tethering lines. When one man moved to the left, a rope became taut, pulling another man down. When that man finally came up for air, his motion and his tether brought someone else under the water. Was there anyone in charge? At first no, but within a few minutes someone began giving orders and restoring some sense of order."

Someone in the back of the hall asked who that person was. Father Paul had no answer. It was too dark and it was snowing. All he knew was that someone did take charge and everyone was dutifully following orders. New lines were tossed into the water and secured by three or four men on the ice. Father Paul was one of these men. He was at the end of the rope, furthest from the water. He told them everything but this.

"Who took charge?" asked the chief. "Come on, man, no one's going to shoot anyone here. We just got to get to the bottom of this while it's still fresh in our minds and before we start making things up. Got to find out what we did right, and from what we know happened, what we did wrong. Who took charge? Who did Father see?"

"Me," came a voice from the middle of the men; high-pitched and so soft that it was barely audible.

"Who's me? Who said that?" the chief asked, raising his voice with some impatience.

"Me, Chief," came the voice again, only this time a little stronger.

"What did you say? Speak up!"

"This is as loud as I get before I start screaming. It's me, Chief, Rolphie Turner."

"You, Rolphie," Shaw answered with disbelief. Come up here, son. How old are you?"

"Fourteen, sir."

"Make room for the youngster, let him through."

Rolphie Turner, all fourteen years of him, was already a gangly five foot nine. Not much meat on the bones but under a pea coat at night in a snowstorm on a frozen lake he'd look like most grownups.

"Get over here and speak up, boy. What the hell happened out there?" asked the chief, who was now more than impatient. The men were getting tired and surly, Shaw wasn't sure how long he could keep them there. "Hold it down back there so we can hear what the boy's got to say."

"Well, sir," Rolphie Turner began in the loudest and deepest voice he could muster, "it was terrible. Like Father said, there was more people in the water than should have been and there was all that thrashing and bobbing with heads coming up and heads going down. The break in the ice was enormous. It's those rocks, Chief Shaw, that's what made the ice so weak out there. Anyway, all the tethering poles were gone; fell right into the water with the men. The men on the ice were trying their best, really they were. I just saw another accident about to happen. That's what I saw, Chief."

Silence, the boy went silent.

"That's it, son?"

"That's what happened, Chief."

"Tell us about what you thought might happen, Rolphie," asked Father Paul, knowing there was more to the story than the boy was telling.

"You were there, Father. The men were running this way and that. They meant well, we all did. We had to get those fellows out of that cold water. It's just that the way they was running it was a surprise more didn't fall in, let alone get anyone out."

"Yes, now tell us what you did."

"I grabbed one of the lanterns from someone."

"That was me," interrupted Father Paul.

"Then you saw what I did, Father. You tell them." The boy was feeling uncomfortable in the crowd of silent men, moving closer around him so they could hear every word. Still the story had to be told. No telling what would be important when it came time to changing the rescue plan.

"It's not what I saw, Rolphie," answered Father Paul. "It's what you did that we need to know. You're doing fine, son. I know this isn't easy for you but you got to tell us. Now you go on."

Rolphie took a deep breath, let it out slowly, and looking only at Father Paul, continued. He knew what had to be done; he wasn't sure exactly how to do it. The first order of business was establishing a new perimeter around the opening in the ice where the rescuers could safely work. The second was to have the men hold the tethering ropes securely now that there were no poles. Finally, a counter was needed so they would know who was on the lake and who was going into the water to fish out the men. That's what had to be done. His voice wasn't strong enough to carry and one of the men went so far as to push him down on the ice when he told him what he ought to do.

"Who was that?" demanded the chief. "Who pushed the boy?"

"Any one of us, Chief," answered Father Paul, for all the men that were in the hall. "Grownups are not used to taking orders from a fourteen-year-old. Now you go on, Rolphie. How did you get us to listen?"

"I pulled my hat down as far as it could go, took the lantern you gave me, and marched into the middle of the men. No good talking, this was no time for discussions. I already knew that."

"So what did you do?" The question came from the back. It was Tom Olsen, who probably wasn't near enough to Rolphie when he did his thing.

"Well, I just took the lantern, sir, and threw it hard to the ground. The oil splattered and caught fire, making for quite a scene. This made the men near me take notice and when they did I handed the rope to four of them and told them make a ring around the hole maybe ten feet from the edge, using the rope like a safety fence. They were to make sure only dunkers and a few of the stronger men who could haul the bodies out were inside the circle."

"I saw that lantern explode from the shore but couldn't figure out what I was seeing," said Olsen. "Very clever, kid. Very clever."

And it was clever, his knowing what to do and doing it. If there was a hero, it was Rolphie Turner. By the next afternoon, this boy would be part of Mount Olden's folklore. All that was left was the count. They'd worry tomorrow about who was pulled out alive. For now, the chief needed to know how many were confirmed dead and who hadn't been accounted for.

"How many you take to Ozymandias, Olsen?" asked the chief.

"Three."

"So how many does that make it?"

"Mr. O. said he had nine. My three, Mr. O. said he and Willy Catchum each brought in three. Nine."

"You seen 'em all?" asked Dick Grey, the package store owner where the men had bought their liquor.

"Saw five of them. That's including my three. Big place over there at Ozymandias. He might even have a couple more bodies out in the cold house that have nothing to do with what happened tonight. A good time to be in the undertaking business," Olsen said, with jealousy lingering on every word. "Man's making a lot of money on a lot of people's misery." That's what he said, figuring it was best not to say what else was going through his mind. Damn his father for selling the business to that bastard Ozymandias. Those corpses sitting in that funeral home could have been his if it weren't for his damn father and that lousy good-for-nothing Ozymandias.

What Tom Olsen did say was more than enough for them men closest to him to move back a few steps and stare at him in disbelief. In the face of this tragedy, all he could think of was his bitterness over a lost business opportunity.

~

Oscar Ozymandias had done more than a night's work. Vern Wasby was no longer. The harvest was in, now in neat packages weighing no more than five pounds each and safely stacked on the shelves of one his three refrigerators. He had bathed the rest of poor Vern in a disinfectant that contained embalming fluids to help slow down the rotting and placed the remains in the bottom of a county coffin under one of the strangers who had perished that night. He chose the skinny one and thought to himself how perfect all this was working out, as he nailed the coffin shut.

There was more to do but that could wait now that the meat was safe, sound, and would not spoil. Oscar retreated to his kitchen, heated a little more stew, finished the last bit in the bottle of port, and went to bed. There was always tomorrow.

Chapter Thirteen

Tomorrow came very late in Mount Olden. The town didn't want to wake up after what it had just gone through.

Only Sada Weisner, in her black dress and cloth overcoat pulled up high around her neck, sat in a cold and empty St Anselm's, waiting for the seven o'clock Mass that she knew would be unattended, even by the priest, Father Paul. She was in the rectory when he left after the first sound of the horn, and saw him from her window when he returned at five-thirty in the morning. Now alone in St Anselm's, Sada sat contentedly, eyes closed, hearing the priest in her mind conducting the Mass. She knew every prayer, every word in both English and Latin, and took great comfort that another day had come and she was sitting in her pew in the third row. There would be plenty of time later in the day for confession and receiving communion.

By eleven o'clock the morning edition of the *Standard* was flooding town. A big city paper, it was trucked in daily and in town by the time most folks had their morning coffee. The paper didn't get to Mount Olden till ten. Usually not a word was to be found about anything to do with the town or the people who called it home; that was left to the *Record*, a weekly that had just come out the day before.

Today Mount Olden was on the front page of the *Standard*. The story was so big that the presses had been held till six a.m. It was obvious that a reporter had been on the scene and called in the story. Reporters from big city papers rarely came to Mount Olden and in the weeks that followed there was as much speculation about the identity of M. S. Hoffmann, the reporter's byline, as there was about the event itself. At least five men who were near or on the lake that night spoke with great authority of being interviewed by this man. No two accounts described the same person.

~

"Ah, there you are, Father," said Sada, acknowledging the obvious. The Mass was done and he had returned to the apartment. The *Standard*_had said there were nine dead; Dollard's face gave meaning to that number. Now in his pajamas and bathrobe, the priest sat on the hard wooden chair at the kitchen table, drained of all color, eyes sunk and face expressionless.

"It was that bad, Father?"

Dollard drew his arms close to his body, slumped further into the chair, and began to rock slowly, trying to make sense of what he had been through. Nine men, nine lives and the families of three of the men who were no stranger to him. He had gotten back to the rectory at five-thirty, leaving the men in the meeting hall still putting the pieces together. He had heard enough by then; the details could wait until later. This was a story that would be talked about for years.

At least nine men had been fished out dead and any more down there would have to wait for spring to pop up. Nine men – what else was there to know?

"You're looking a little peaked, Father. Let's get you some tea," Sada said gently. "Some tea, Father, take some tea," she repeated, now standing over her charge as she added more than the usual tablespoon of honey into the steaming brew.

"What, woman, what?" he snapped, seeking the source of irritation with fixed and vacant eyes.

"It's me, Father Paul," Sada said more firmly, worried now that he was having one of his spells.

No response. Just staring at and through the window towards the lake. Looking for what? Confused now as he had been then? Trying to understand what he couldn't make sense of but a few hours ago?

"Father Paul!" A firm hand now pressing down on his shoulder. "Father, you must have the tea."

"Sada? Yes, Sada. Tea. I need to take some tea. I haven't had anything since last night. I have to do things," he said, as he mindlessly put another tablespoon of honey into the already sweetened tea. "They need their priest. I need the strength to do what needs to be done. My calling. My calling."

~

Disasters were the reason for Paul Dollard becoming a priest. Catastrophes happened throughout his childhood, although he didn't think of it that way then. Not until the mines took his dad and brother, that is.

It seemed that whistle was always blowing, no matter what the season. Cave-ins and explosions in mines don't pay attention to the time of year. Growing up, Paul didn't pay the whistle no mind, unless it sounded with three short blasts, and then he only worried if it was at night. The three blasts meant it was his daddy's mine and night was when his daddy and brother were down there.

It never happened till it happened and then he and his mother went running. There's no second chance down under. If disaster strikes and you're in the hole, there's a good chance you're not coming up.

Paul's mother knew what she would find when the whistle blew. Her husband and son were good providers and that meant if they were working, they were there with the coal. You got paid by what you brought up and if you weren't in the ground, there wasn't going to be food on the table. When the whistle blew three times that night, Paul's mother knew she was a widow before she stepped out of the door.

The Dollards were good Catholics and when this godawful thing happened, they turned to their church and their priest for comfort. Father Coviello did right by all the Catholics whose tomb was deep in Mr. Ludwig's mineshaft. He said the right prayers, even gave them their last rites without knowing exactly who was down there.

'To all our Catholic brothers who lost their lives in Ludwig's mine,' was how he started.

The next Sunday Paul and his mother were in church for the nine o'clock Mass. Mother wept. Mathew Jr. was always there on her left. This Sunday there was only an empty space. After the final *ite, missa est*, they sat quietly until everyone had gone.

"You're still here, Mrs Dollard, and you, Paul," the priest said as he came back into the church.

"Paul has a question, Father," said the widow Dollard. She knew that was why they had waited and knew her son was too shy to speak up himself. She also knew the question and was wondering about it herself.

"Yes, son?" asked Father Coviello, in a voice that made sure mother and son knew he was the priest and the church was his building. This message did not escape Paul, who was now thinking twice about his question.

"Go on, Paul. Ask Father your question."

The words were not enough for Paul to know if it was safe to ask what was on his mind. He turned and looked into his mother's eyes to see what they would tell her. Mother could lie with her words but never with her eyes.

"Speak up, son," said Father Coviello, sensing Paul's hesitation.

"How come you didn't say my father and brother's names when you had the service at the mine? They were down there and they are gone. Why didn't you say their names?'

"I said no one's name son."

"Then why is that, Father?"

"The sacraments aren't for everyone."

"They are for Catholics."

"Not all Catholics, son. A man can't decide when he's going to follow the Church. Being born a Catholic, being baptized a Catholic, that's only the beginning. Do you understand what I'm saying, son?"

Paul wasn't sure this was a real question. It sounded like Father Coviello expected to be understood and if he wasn't, there was something wrong with the listener.

"Are you following me, son?" asked the priest again, this time with clear annoyance in his voice.

"My father and brother were Catholics and you didn't say their names," Paul responded, more a challenge than a statement of fact. Father Coviello set his eyes on Mary Dollard and she began shifting nervously in the pew.

"Your father was one of the reasons I didn't say the names at the memorial. You can't stay away from St Thomas Aquinas, you can't ignore the sacrament of the confession for years at a time and expect to receive the last rites when your time comes. Your father, son, was one of the reasons I said no one's name. What would you have me do? Speak the names of some and not others. How would that be for you? How would that have been?"

Paul Dollard did everything he could not to start crying. There was no way he wanted to give this man that satisfaction. That Sunday was the last day Paul Dollard set foot in St Thomas Aquinas. He made it a point to go at least four times a year to Our Lady of Perpetual Help to receive communion and give confession. The twenty miles was a small price to pay to stay devoted to his church.

~

Paul Dollard had answered the call to the priesthood to be different from Father Coviello when the time came. With what had happened last night on North Lake, the time had come and he'd be finding out soon if he was ready.

"Have another cup of that tea, Father, and how about another good helping of honey to go with it," said Sada, knowing that the honey might just do the trick to give him the strength he would need.

Father Paul reached for the cup and began to drink slowly, sitting up a little straighter in his chair with each sip of the brew.

"It will be a busy day, Father," Sada continued, reaching for a writing tablet and pencil from the cupboard. Dollard, now sitting fully erect, looked at this old woman, wondering how she always seemed to know what he needed, even before it was known to him.

Another all nighter, that's what Father Paul was in for. Every Catholic family that lost someone had to be seen and he would stay with them for as long as he was needed. Taking pencil in hand, he made his first entry: 'Funeral home.' Except for Pico Stevens and Rob Church, Father Paul had no idea who had been lost. He put '2 out of 7' as the next note on the list.

~

It was late morning and the streets of Mount Olden were unusually empty. The few people Paul saw on the streets passed him without saying a word.

The front door of Ozymandias' Funeral Home was locked when on any other day it would have been opened by now.

"Was nothing the same?" Father Paul muttered to himself.

"It's you, Dollard. I was wondering who would be the first and here it is, the priest. For sure I thought it would be the chief," said Ozymandias.

"He's probably still asleep. I left him at five at the meeting hall and they were still going strong. I wouldn't be surprised if he got to sleep no more than an hour ago. I need to know who we lost, Oscar. Nine, is that right?"

"Nine," answered Ozymandias, as he locked the front door behind the priest. "I'm working in the back and I don't want people wandering in and out. I see the *Standard* already has the story," he said, handing the paper to Dollard, "and it's only a matter of time before this M. S. Hoffmann comes knocking at the door."

"I've already seen it. Sada dropped it off at the rectory."

"I hate these damn reporters," Oscar said, leading Father Paul back to the embalming room. "Always exploiting the misery of others, Dollard. They make people's sorrow into one of those soap operas they have on the radio. Were you out there, Dollard, did you see this Hoffmann reporter?"

"I was there, but I didn't notice the reporter. Conditions were so poor, no moon and the snow falling, Hoffmann could have been standing next to me and I wouldn't know anyone was there." Remembering Tom Olsen's sudden appearance at his side on the lake, Father Paul realized what he had just said wasn't exactly true. Still, he had no idea who M. S. Hoffman was.

The embalming room was spotless and empty, except for the equipment. This was not what Father Paul was expecting, not with nine bodies having been brought here some time during the night.

"Where are they?" he asked.

Oscar knew exactly what was being asked, having seen Dollard's face when they came into the room. Still, there was opportunity here.

"Who?" he answered.

"Nine people were brought in here, Oscar," Father Paul answered, trying to make himself as clear as could be.

"The deceased, you're asking about the deceased, Dollard. They're in the cold house. I can't keep the remains here, especially if they haven't been embalmed. Putrification, Dollard. The enemy of the undertaker."

"Yes of course. The bodies would be in the cold house," said Father Paul, annoyed at himself for not knowing. "Do you know who they are, Oscar?"

"I have their papers right here," he answered, pulling out a shoebox from one of the cabinets and dumping the contents on the embalming table. "Come over here if you want to look," he said to the priest, who was clearly uncomfortable with where Oscar had emptied the box. Although the stainless steel table was spotless, Father Paul knew what was on it yesterday and what would be on it later today.

"I took a quick look at this last night," Oscar reported. "Three are from St Anselm's; Rob Church, John Deluca and Neil Garlic. Two more, this Pico, and someone named Jill, Martin Jill, had Mass cards in their wallets so they might be

Catholic. Three were Methodists, I let the pastor know, and the last one had no identification."

Oscar could see Dollard was visibly shaken and quickly sat him down before he fainted. "Churches, Delucas and Garlics. Oh my good Jesus. Three good men, three large families. There must be at least ten to fifteen children between them, Garlic's wife is sick with emphysema and Deluca takes care of his in-laws. And what about the others? What of their families?"

Father Paul had been a priest for many years and knew about death and tragedy. This was not the first time that a parishioner was gone and it certainly wasn't the first time someone drowned in the lake. There were always accidents. Father Paul was no stranger to death; it was the magnitude of this tragedy that was so overwhelming.

"Good family, the Delucas," said Oscar. "Ann Deluca was always here when she was needed. Funeral directors see a lot and can tell a lot. This is a good woman. She was here for many a wake and it wasn't always for kin. If the grieving wife or mother needed someone to be at her side, it was Ann. How many children do you think she has, Dollard?"

"The Delucas have four. The youngest is preparing for her First Communion. The oldest can't be no more than thirteen, maybe fourteen."

"Deluca was an ice man. Is that so, Dollard? An ice man."

"He worked for the ice company. A cutter."

"The season is just coming and that family is going to be in trouble."

Father Paul was thinking the same thing. The busy season was just about to start. That meant whatever savings they had from last winter were certainly gone and the extra money John Deluca would have made for every block of ice he cut in North Lake would not be coming in. This was a family in trouble.

"I've got to give them a good funeral, Dollard. I'm not going to wait to see what Mrs. Deluca wants to do. I know what she's going to want. When it comes to spending her few cents on food for the children or a coffin for her husband, she's going to take him back to the house and dig a hole in the back yard. That shouldn't be his ending. He was a regular at church?"

"They both were. They came every Sunday and filled a pew."

"Then I've got to do right by him. Follow me."

Oscar Ozymandias led Father Paul through a back door to a small building made of cinder block. A lot of sawdust was mixed into the snow. The door was secured by a heavy chain and padlock. Oscar didn't want any visitors coming in when he was out. The walls were lined with two rows of block ice from floor to ceiling and a series of rooms were fashioned out of walls made of more ice. Sawdust bound the block together.

"Sawdust and wood chips keep the ice from melting. Close the door behind you, will you, Dollard. Got to keep the cold in. Stay close by and follow me."

With the door closed, they were in absolute darkness.

"Ouch!" howled Father Paul, feeling a sharp pain on his side.

"What happened? Are you all right?" asked Oscar.

"I banged against something."

"Stay put. I'm lighting a lantern."

A bright, blinding light reflected off the walls from all directions. Father Paul wasn't sure what he was seeing. Next to him a piece of plywood held up by two saw horses. Sawdust everywhere. Very cold, he was feeling very cold. He reached into his pocket for his gloves. Need to keep his hands warm. A very low ceiling, no more than seven feet from the ground. It felt like being in a box. Shapes, forms on plywood tables. The torch that had initially burnt bright, began to dim and with it, what was once clearly illuminated faded into shadows.

Father Paul's eyes barely adjusted to the muted shades of grey. In front of him, on the table he had banged against, were the bodies of two men. He recognized both. John Deluca and Neil Garlic.

Oscar Ozymandias, always gracious, showed his Tuesday dinner companion his place of business. There were five rooms in the icehouse, each room shaped and defined by floor to ceiling ice blocks. Two rooms had plywood tables, each able to accommodate three average sized men. Neil Garlic was no average sized man. He took up nearly half of a table. The other three rooms were for bodies that were already in coffins. Some were wood, some the heavy hardboard.

It was hard for Father Paul to keep track. One room led to the other, one darker than the other, easy to become confused, hard to keep track of the count. Uncertain of exactly what he was seeing. Affirmed in what he was seeing: broken bodies, broken lives, and families left behind.

"Wooden ones are county. They're already sealed shut and the internment will be later today or tomorrow in the county plot. There's no embalming for the county. That's why we have to bury them quickly. I'll use one of the wooden ones for John Deluca. A good man needs a good Christian burial. Roll that gurney over here, Dollard. Since this one is on the house, there's no need to wait for family to come and tell me what they want."

Father Paul, unable to move, watched in disbelief and fascination. Ozymandias, his contempt for this weak priest now seeping through the corner of his mouth, rolled the gurney next to John Deluca's side of the table; grabbed hold of the sheet the body was wrapped in, and with one tug had him just where he wanted him. Oscar was moving his merchandise, just like Mr Miller moved the sacks of flour in his warehouse.

"Grab the lantern, Dollard," Oscar ordered, as he started wheeling John Deluca toward the embalming room.

"One minute, Oscar. The Last Rites, I want to anoint them. Take me to the ones who you think are Catholic. I did Rob and Pico yesterday. We don't need to stop by Rob and Pico."

Oscar wasn't about to say what he was thinking. He had too much sense for that. 'Stop by.' These men were dead. You don't stop by the dead. And giving last rites when you don't know who you're giving them to? What do the sacraments mean if they are being peddled to just about anyone? Are we selling indulgences again? He saw this coming when he was in the seminary and this was the very reason he had left. Was he surprised by Dollard's hollow gesture to the dead? Not at all. Was he angry? Absolutely.

But Oscar said nothing as he guided him through the warren of rooms, back into daylight and air untainted by death.

~

Father Paul never thought he'd welcome being in an embalming room, but here he was and it was a relief. Anything was better than that house of ice with all its bodies.

"Do you need help with John?" he asked.

"I can manage just fine." And indeed he could. Father Paul watched as Oscar nimbly maneuvered John Deluca into position for the embalming.

"I don't know how you can do it, Oscar. It's good that you can, it has to be done, but I can only imagine how hard it must be."

"God's work, Dollard. It's all part of God's work. Assisting our Lord in preparing the soul for the resurrection. Now, how about staying around for the embalming? You can be my assistant. A little help doing God's work is the work of the angels."

There was no way Father Paul was going to help with the embalming. He had two good reasons. The first was the calls he had to make. Three of his congregants were dead and he had to be with their families. While important, this was second to the fact that he had almost fainted in the icehouse and there the bodies were intact.

"I need to be on my way, Oscar. Families to see. Oh yes, before I leave for the Delucas, a question."

"Yes, Dollard?"

"Nine men lost their lives last night."

"Yes?"

"Between the bodies and coffins, I think I counted ten."

"Ten?"

"Ten."

Oscar Ozymandias, his head in the embalming that he was about to perform and too tired to think straight, was confused.

"Ten? You counted ten. You must have made a mistake. Nine, Dollard, nine."

"Not ten?"

Father Paul knew this was no time for arguing, and given how poorly lit the cold house was, it would be easy to be mistaken. Still, he thought, between caskets and wrapped bodies, the number might have been ten.

Chapter Fourteen

Mae and Jane Stevens were the first to arrive. A dank smell clung to the walls and the sun streaming through the stained glass windows was no match for the cold air that filled the empty sanctuary.

"Just sit there, Mother, and stop worrying."

"What if this pew belongs to someone else?"

"Pews don't *belong* to people, nobody *owns* them. Just sit down, will ya, Mom!"

Jane Stevens had forgotten how annoying her mother could be. Mae was always wondering what the next person was thinking and always sure that it was some judgment about what she was thinking or doing. The longer Jane was away from her parents and in her own home with her children and husband, the more it rankled her when she heard her mama being her mama. Mae Stevens seemed to be getting worse since Mike passed and Jane feared with her mother now a widow, she'd be seeing more of her.

Getting to St Anselm's had been a struggle. Mother and daughter had something on their minds, something that was both puzzling and worrisome, and it was clear to Jane that the first person they needed to speak to was Father Paul. But her mother was reluctant, and they kept repeating the same conversation, like a stuck record on a Victrola.

"I don't think we should bother the Father about it, Janie."

"He's the one we need to start with, Ma."

"But he's so busy Janie, with it being Sunday and all."

"He'll find the time, Ma."

"With what happened at the lake, he's got more important things to think about. We can wait. We can wait, don't ya think, Janie?"

That's as much as Jane Stevens remembered. It wasn't all that was said; she was leaving out the part where she got impatient and had sharp words for her mother. She always left out that part on any of the thousands of times her mother's voice got stuck in her head.

"Just sit down, Ma, and stop it. Ya wouldn't have this worry if we had got here for early Mass the way I wanted. Then you could have had the whole damn church to yourself."

Jane, shocked by the words that had tumbled out of her own mouth, words that came near to blasphemy, quickly looked away from Mae and toward the crucifix, and while crossing herself, asked Jesus for forgiveness for blaspheming his house of worship. Jane didn't usually do things like this, and she took it as a sign of how disturbed she was by what she and her mother were here to talk to the Father about.

~

Late Mass on the first Sunday following the North Lake tragedy and the church was filling up. Father Paul was in the sacristy readying himself. This was a humble room in a humble church and nothing like the one in the cathedral where he was ordained. Everything was just the right size for a priest who felt more comfortable with the pastoral ministry than the sacramental. The plain pine wardrobe did well in holding his vestments, albs and stoles, and three shelves on the wall were enough for all his other priestly paraphernalia. Nothing elegant, fancy or ornate. The basics, just like the good Catholics of Mount Olden.

Father Paul had chosen black vestments to wear over his alb. Ordinarily it would have been green and although this was not a funeral mass, he felt it fitting. He'd be wearing his black vestments during many of the days to come and might as well start now. His congregation would understand, he thought, as he looked in the mirror and adjusted the sash.

Paul went to the door leading to the sanctuary, opened it slightly, and looked out at the pews.

Not an empty seat.

There should be a performer in every priest. There wasn't one in Paul Dollard. He thought he'd get over the stage fright with practice; he'd now had plenty of practice. He had said Mass thousands of times and it hadn't gotten easier. It was worse on Holy Days, especially Christmas and Easter, when the church was as full as it was now. Some day he hoped there would be a pill that would get him through. Some day.

~

Oscar Ozymandias didn't have to worry about stage fright. He delivered Mass to an empty house. There weren't even pews. There was, however, a sacristy and a sanctuary, and neither would be considered humble by any measure. Tucked away in the back of his funeral parlor in a place that could never be found, secure behind a nondescript pine door that was always locked, was a holy shrine that Oscar had taken great care in building. A carpenter of considerable skill, he was able to turn the simple into the ornate. The altar, he called it his alolere, was made of wood, hewn and polished to a fine silken surface, with five carved Greek crosses with gold leaf detail. Applying the gold and getting it to bond to the wood was no easy matter.

It took months to master the technique but when it was done, he had achieved perfection.

The tabernacle, also a treasure, involved thought and planning that began after he had been in the seminary no more than two or three months.

~

Oscar was a teenager when he went to the seminary. Most parents would have doubts about turning over so young a son to the church. Not Oscar's. They had given up on him long before he made the decision. He was what they called an incorrigible. Misbehaving? He had left misbehaving behind when he was seven or eight. At ten he was a full-blown delinquent and when he entered his teens, no one could control him.

By twelve even the local sheriff had given up. He had tried hollering, jail time, even beating the child. He'd never had to go that far with a youngster in all his years of policing. One day he came to the Ozymandias home – he would have liked to have had Oscar in tow but the boy was nowhere to be found – and told the parents it was time to send him away to a home for wayward youth run by Catholic brothers. When Oscar showed up, they were to call the sheriff and he'd take him away. No one ever ran away from the brothers so there'd be no worry about that.

Two weeks later Oscar was spotted in town and the sheriff grabbed him and took him to the school for wayward youth. After two years there, Oscar had his epiphany.

The church provided order and discipline, two things he had not had in his first fourteen years of life. There was also a very clear understanding of what was right and wrong, and what to do if you wanted to get to heaven. His parents, nominal

Baptists who never went to church and spent most of their leisure time drinking in local bars, provided none of this.

After two years in the boys' school, the principal took him on an overnight to the big city where the bishop was saying Mass. What a sight. There must have been hundreds, even a thousand people in that church and it was bigger than anything Oscar had ever imagined. When the bishop came in, it was a procession, and not a single person said a single word. Absolute silence. He wore special vestments with a purple sash around his waist and a tall pointed hat on his head. The bishop had a gold staff in his hand that was taller than him. It was wonderful.

Oscar filled the ride home with endless questions. The bishop was a priest, not a brother; he studied very hard at the seminary and followed every last teaching of the church. He never wavered no matter what the pressure, and there was always pressure. He dedicated his life to Jesus and was a prince in the service to our Lord. He is chosen, he works hard and he is called.

Oscar Ozymandias, on the ride home, had an epiphany. A bishop. That's what he was going to be, that's what he was going to do with his life.

The principal thought Oscar was reaching too high but didn't want to discourage the lad. After all, you never know.

They talked again the next day and Oscar said the same thing. A bishop. That was enough for the principal. This was no passing fancy. A long trip is begun with a first step. That night was the first Oscar spent in the seminary.

It took Oscar a few months to realize it wasn't going to work. In the beginning he was taken by having a room just for himself and special clothes to wear. The trouble began when he started questioning why his teachers weren't doing what they were teaching. The priests were amused at first by their new student, but his persistence soon provoked their irritation. Faced with their irritation, Oscar became more resolute in his orthodoxy. These priests, the men who were supposed to start him on the path to becoming a bishop, were just not Catholic enough. Things started to turn real ugly and Oscar realized if he continued the way he was going, he would soon be back with the brothers. Being nobody's fool, he made a conscious decision to keep what he was thinking to himself, learn what there was to learn, and wait till he was old enough to be on his own.

Oscar Ozymandias spent the next four years learning it all. He was especially taken with Latin and the Eucharist. He had done some traveling as part of his training and committed to memory every last detail of every sanctuary, altar and tabernacle he had come across.

Some day, some day.

Oscar's twentieth birthday went unnoticed by everyone but him. He was old enough to be on his own, and wise enough to know that the church was not the place to find salvation. Its teaching had strayed too far from the teachings of Christ and the Disciples.

Remarkably, the priest in charge of the seminary came to a similar conclusion. This young man was just not fitting in. As orthodox and literal as they were in bringing the teaching of Our Lord, the Apostles and the Church to this third decade of the twentieth century, they were convinced that in Oscar, they had a fanatic on their hands.

Three months after Oscar turned twenty, the head of the seminary sat down with him and told him that the priesthood was not his vocation.

Control, Oscar, control. No time for weakness, thought Oscar. He couldn't stop weakness seeping through his pores, as his face became engulfed by the heat of rage. No matter. The old wrinkled man in front of him, close enough so that he was breathing in the faint foul smell of piss, couldn't see his face even with thick lenses perched on his nose.

"One big lie!" he said, as he moved one step closer to a frail Monsignor Mathew, Rector of St Benedict Seminary. "The rubbish you teach. This has nothing to do with Christ's teachings. You offer salvation and give nothing more than the shadow of the Cross."

Those were Oscar Ozymandias' last words in the seminary as he placed his cassock, wrapped in brown paper and bound with white string, into the trash basket next to the priest's oversized mahogany desk. He was done with this place of sacrilege with all the trappings of indulgences. No humility or fidelity to the Gospel in this office.

~

Oscar had come to the seminary an aimless scruffy kid, a nobody with no one. Now a man, he had heard Christ's call to devotion and service. A man whose devotion to both word and deed far exceeded the paltry renditions by the priests at St Benedict's was now being cast into the desert as Christ had been.

His scapular clad teachers accused him of the failure of obedience. Obedience to what? A teaching and devotional that more than strayed from a sensible understanding of scripture. The words are the words. They give meaning to us for a reason. They are there to be followed, not twisted to give 'forgiveness' to an unfaithful flock. And towards what end, this pandering? To increase the numbers of the led? The coffers of the church? The priests called Oscar's words the words of the heretic. Oscar knew them to be the words of truth. This time it wasn't the Romans who were casting the disciple into the desert. This time it was the anointed servants of the church.

Oscar, affirmed in his faith, closed the Rector's door, leaving behind the lies of a false monastic life. They had given him a worn black overcoat, threadbare at the elbow and frayed at the hem, and a twenty-dollar bill. A meager offering to ease their minds for what they had put him through and what they were doing. He had come to St Benedict's with nothing and he was leaving with little more than nothing. And they called this charity.

Clean shaven, hair neatly combed with a touch of pomade to keep the stray strand where it belonged, and black trousers that he carefully ironed to achieve the crisp pleats that he liked so much; the priests said this was vanity, Oscar knew it to be pride. And with that he began the mile-long walk down the rutted dirt road that spilled out into the blacktop and the Greyhound to get him to the city. His plan: use half the money in his pocket for the bus and the other ten bucks for food and a place to sleep until he could find some work. He didn't know how long it would take to save enough money, but when he had enough he'd head back into the mountains and Mount Olden. You couldn't get any further away from the seminary and those damn priests than back into the mountains.

Oscar saw the bus making its way down the road and none too soon. The clouds were thickening and the air was full of that first winter storm that would make this back country almost impossible to get through until the first melt in late spring.

Yet with each deep breath came the sweetness that he knew was in front of him. A new beginning in a search that would lead to salvation, redemption and resurrection. And if he could only find it in a congregation of one, he was prepared for that, too.

He drifted from town to town, rooming in boarding houses, finding what work he could doing odd jobs for a day's pay. The thirteenth disciple, unattached and unburdened, silent in preaching the message of Christ as only he could understand it. He had been crucified once by the old men who had cast him out of the seminary. That, Oscar resolved, would never happen again.

Mount Olden was just another stop on the way, helping the local undertaker clean up the room where the deceased were readied, just another way of making a few bucks. Business was good and a day's work became a regular job, the first he had ever had. Oscar moved from mopping the floor of the embalming room to washing and dressing the bodies after old man Olsen had completed the embalming and restoration.

The possibilities escaped Oscar at first, until he realized that many of the clientele were Catholic. A proper burial was as important as a proper christening and he could, in his unique and private way, be part of a sacramental ministry.

~

"What time is it?" asked Jane Stevens, to no one in particular. "Eleven o'clock Mass is supposed to start at eleven o'clock."

"Hold your voice down, Janie," said Mae, as she looked around uneasily.

"He's already late. See?" she said, putting her watch under her mother's nose. It was no time to start snapping at her mother, but the looking around and worrying was getting to her.

"When it's time Father Paul will come. Just stop it and sit still."

Stop it and sit still. The very words that Jane said to her own children. Doesn't her mother know she's talking to a mother? Father Paul and St Anselm's, not the way it's supposed to be. At Jane's church the priest greets the people at the front door. He is there, he is always there. That's the way it was when she was growing up when Father Reilly was the pastor here. Jane couldn't wait to get back to her own parish.

If it wasn't for family business she wouldn't be at St Anselm's today. But she needed to be here, to talk to Father Paul. They had visited Papa at the funeral home, and they had questions.

~

Father Paul took one last look. Not an empty seat and lots of people standing.

Easy, Paul, he said to himself. Pick out one face and talk to that person. One face, one face.

It had worked before and he could only hope it would work today. A priest with stage fright. What irony, he thought. It's not like this was opening night or he was playing to a new crowd. He knew most of these people and they knew him.

You know the routine, he reminded himself. *Five parts, five parts. Introduction, Liturgy, Eucharist, Communion, Conclusion. How many times have you done it? How many times have you said it? Offered it? Don't worry what you call it, you've done it over and over.*

Paul felt the knot in his stomach getting tighter. The words never helped and with so many people in the church, he couldn't imagine anything working, even a shot from the bottle he kept tucked away to help with some of the more difficult moments. This certainly was one of them and he knew the whiskey would be no match for his butterflies. *Damn Latin. Why Lord, why Latin?*

Paul kneeled in front of the cross in the sacristy, asking for the strength to see him through this test of faith. Jesus never failed him. As painful as this was, he'd get to the *Ite, missa est.*

One last look in the mirror, a final adjustment to the stole, and Father Paul entered the church for the eleven o'clock Mass.

"In nominen.

In nomine Patris, et Filii et Spiritus Sancti".

The Mass had begun. Fifteen minutes late and with one false start, but it had begun.

~

Oscar was playing to an empty house and that was just fine. There was no one he knew who could recognize his excellence so what difference did it make? In any event, he was not here doing what he was doing for the common man's adoration. He was deeply rooted in his religion, in the sacrament and the literal intent of the teachings of the disciples. What he was about to do needed to be done if God's voice was to be heard and Christ's path to be followed.

"Gratia Domini nostri Jesu Christi.

Et caritas Dei

et communicatio Sancti Spiritus.

Sit cum omnibus vobis."

Silence.

"Pax vobis."

The Mass had begun. Oscar liked the silence, imagining the congregation responding with the '*Et cum spiritu,*' and he thought the *Pax vobis* a wonderful touch. They were the words that the bishop offered when delivering the mass, and Oscar had every reason to believe that if he and the church had been a good match, becoming a bishop would have just been the beginning.

"A magnificent sanctuary," Ozymandias said aloud, straightening the purple skullcap, having dispensed with the miter some years back. The tabernacle, of course, was what he was most proud of.

And no wonder that he had devoted so much time and energy to creating this one piece that made up his sanctuary. After all, it and the Eucharist, that sacred part of the Mass where Christ becomes part of us through the symbolic transformation of wine to blood and bread to flesh, was what all this was about.

~

"Now just shush, Janie," said Mae to her daughter, who was mumbling under her breath. No one could hear Jane but her mother, but to Mae Stevens, it was as if her daughter were yelling at the top of her lungs.

"Dreadful, Mother, dreadful," she said, whispering in her mother's ear so that the others could not hear. "He hasn't gotten one sentence right."

A more sympathetic person would have noticed the torture this man was going through; his face flushed and perspiring from every piece of exposed skin. Jane Stevens noticed none of this, attending only to the Latin and the many mistakes the priest was making.

Mae wanted to listen to no more of her daughter's ministrations, turning in a way that left her ear far out of reach. If Janie wanted to continue her whispering, she'd be talking into Mae's shoulder.

"Verbum Domini."

"Laus tibi, Christe."

It was time for the homily and Paul, no matter what the Gospel for the day, had a way of bringing the Lord's word to the struggles of the people of Mount Olden. Today Paul had a good idea about what was on everyone's mind.

"You listen to today's reading and in it you hear the call. Listen to the Lord's word and hear His wisdom.

"We, the followers are on the road and last night it led us to a place where men went to help men who needed help. Not all who went to the water knew who was standing at their side, not all who went down to the water came back. Two men were once on the road to Emmaus and they didn't know the stranger amongst them.

"Could He have been amongst us last night? Can we ever know? Some will say if He were there, last night would not have happened. Others will say if He was there it was to let us know what happened had purpose.

"Look to me for the answer and I tell you I have no answer to offer. What I do offer is this Mass and the power it has in bringing us, this community, together. Our Church asks us to believe in moments like these and it offers us this Mass to help with our suffering.

"The first gatherings were to keep our Lord, Our Savior's word alive, keep Him alive in our communal memory. In the memory there is the healing and in the healing there is salvation.

"We gather today, like the Disciples did then, to keep in our memory our dear brothers who we lost last night.

"We gather today to be with those amongst us who lost their husbands, brothers and sons, last night. We gather today to begin the healing and offer our community to this most holy purpose.

"And now we receive the living Christ through the body and blood as we receive this bread and wine. And with it, forgiveness of our sins."

Jane, unimpressed, looked up and beyond the altar to Christ Our Lord on the cross, a crown of thorns on his head, the only bearer of comfort and salvation on this day of tragedy.

~

Oscar was ready for the Transubstantiation, the reason for everything he was doing today. He had to take advantage of opportunity and there was never any assurance when good fortune would come again. The unexpected death of Vern Wasby was such opportunity.

"Benedictus es, Domine,
Deus universi, quia de tua largitate
accepimus panem,
quem timi offerimuus,
fractum terrae
et operis manuum hominum:
ex qu nobis fiet
panis vitae.

Oscar opened the tabernacle, reached for the ciborium, and placed it on the altar. It was empty. It always was since he made it a point not to leave the host in such an unattended state. He then returned to the sacristy and two large chests, one a refrigerator and the other a freezer, that were covered with elegantly embroidered tapestries depicting the ascension of Our Lord. He carefully pulled back the cover, making sure to fold it in the right places. He opened the freezer, saw many of the shelves were empty and then the refrigerator, which he had filled with seven bundles, wrapped in brown paper and fastened with white cord. Handling each bundle with supreme care, he placed them on a cart and rolled them into the sanctuary.

"*Orate, fratres, ut meum ac vetrum*
sacrificium acceptabile fit apud Deum Patrem
omnipotentem."

Each package had been carefully labeled 'fresh' or 'embalmed', and in each the meat had been cut into two-inch strips; the perfect size. Oscar separated them and placed them carefully on his exquisitely carved altar.

"*Vere Sanctus es, Domine, fons omnis santitatis.*
Haec ergo dona, quaesumus,
Spiritus tui rore santifica,
ut nobis Corpus et Sanguis fiant
Domini nostri
Jesu Christi.

Done. Oscar returned the packages to the cart, making sure not to mix them up, and pushed it back to the sacristy.

Each, now with the Sign of the Cross and the day's date as a record that they were made ready to be transformed from mere meat to the flesh of Christ, went back into the freezer, the fresh on the upper shelves and the embalmed on the lower. The embalmed for the deceased and the fresh for Oscar once it was pickled. Many more packages of fresh since there was a lot of waste when it came to pickling.

The altar was again empty, except for the ciborium. Oscar returned to the tabernacle, removed a large jar marked *pickled*, plucked out a strip of meat, and placed it into the awaiting receptacle.

"*ACCIPITE ET MANDUCATE EX HOC OMNES:*
HOC ES ENIN CORPUS MEUM
QUOD PRO VOBIS TRADETUR."

Now came the part that Oscar liked the best. He placed the morsel of meat on his outstretched tongue and brought it into his mouth. It always happened at this moment, a sense of well-being, renewal, a first step towards walking in the path of Him. He leaned his head back, looked up at the crucifix and dropped to one knee, slowly chewing and swallowing.

"Ecce Angus Dei,
ecce qui tollitpeccata mundi.
Beati qui ad cenam Agni
vocati sunt.
Corpuis Christi.
Amen."

Not exactly as it is written or the way its supposed to be said, but good enough for Oscar. And as for the Latin, perfect, absolutely perfect.

The Pope could do no better, he thought.

~

"Dominus vobiscum."

"Et cum spiritu tuo," responded to the congregation to Father Paul, and with that the Mass came to an end.

"Come, Janie, let's get to the back so we can catch the Father."

"Stay put, Mother. Let the others go. There is plenty of time."

"We don't want to miss him. There are others who may need to see him also."

"Just sit, Mama. Sit!"

In a matter of minutes all the pews had emptied and Father Paul was heading back to the altar.

"Father, over here," beckoned Mae. "We need a minute of your time."

"Mae, Jane, God be with you."

"Wonderful sermon, Father. Wonderful."

Jane knew her mother was buttering up the priest before she raised her questions. This was another thing on Jane's list of things she hated about her mother. She always had to ingratiate before she asked anything of anyone, and her false kindness was often off the mark, just like now. The homily had nothing to do with the gospel and the Latin was the worse she had ever heard. How did this priest get away with it, Jane Stevens wondered.

"I'm glad you liked it, Mae. Now you wanted to speak to me?"

"We do, Father."

"Here or in the rectory?"

"Here is fine," said Jane, looking around to make sure they were alone in the church.

"So what is it? How can I be helpful? It has to do with Mike's passing?"

This man asks so many questions, thought Jane. She saw this as his weakness and she hated weakness. It reminded her too much of Mama.

"It has to do with Mike, Father. Ya see, after what happened at the lake, we went over to Mr. Ozymandias," began Mae, shifting nervously in the pew. "There were lots of bodies, they were everywhere. Nine, Mr. O. said. Good thing Mike was the only other one there. Running out of room, Mr. O. said."

So I was right, Father Paul thought. He had counted ten bodies. Mike Stevens was the tenth. It was late, it had been a long and stressful night for everyone. Oscar must have been confused.

"Mama, tell him why we're here. Get to the point," said Jane, with a clear bite in her voice that embarrassed Mae. It was one thing for her daughter to be insulting when it was just the two of them. Now there was someone else and it wasn't just anyone. It was Father Paul. What would he think of her, that her own child talked to her this way?

Mae got red in the face and started to stumble with her words. Janie used this as yet another reason to be insulting as she took over, the way a mother does when she gives a child one chance to speak her mind and then intervenes as if the child were no longer there. Paul, seeing what was happening but not knowing what to do, just listened. He couldn't think of how to rescue Mae Stevens from humiliation at the hand of her daughter.

"Father, Mama and I went to the funeral home to see how the undertaker had done with Papa. We were especially concerned with all that happened and all that Mr. Ozymandias had to do.

"Papa was perfect. It's been a few weeks now since his passing and he looks better than the day he left us. Mr. O. even filled out his face so he doesn't look so wasted," said Jane.

"The stain, Janie. Tell Father about the stain." Now it was Mae's turn to be the director, but unlike her daughter, there was no contempt in her voice. Rather, she was trying to be helpful to a child who may have forgotten something. Jane had forgotten nothing. She knew what she was doing as she turned to her mother and gave her one of those looks.

"I know what I'm doing, Mama, and I know why we're here."

Each word pushed Mae further back in her seat and further away from the conversation.

"Father, the man looked wonderful and that's why I noticed... It looked like red dribble had come from the corner of his mouth and there was an odd smell coming from him that was stronger than all the fluid Mr. Ozymandias had pumped in. Now I didn't know Mama had seen it and she didn't know that I had. We let Mr. O. know that my brother was expected in the week and he said with how he had prepared Papa and keeping him in cold storage, we'd still be okay.

On the walk home Mama and I talked, she about how good he looked, me about the dribble and smell. Mama noticed it also but didn't know there was something to make of it.

"'Blood, Janie and something rotting inside him, that's what that was,' Mama answered matter of factly. She thought this was what was supposed to be, Father."

"That's the truth, Father Paul. This was the first time I'd been around anyone who'd been embalmed. When we lost kin we'd bury them ourselves. I thought what I was seeing and what I was smelling was the way it was supposed to be."

"But tell Father what you told me, Mama. Tell him what we were seeing." Jane needed Father Paul to be as distressed as they if he were going to help and she knew she needed her mother to tell the rest if that was to happen.

"We was seeing blood and smelling rotten flesh, Father."

"Yes?" Paul said aloud. He wasn't asking a question as much as letting them know he was listening and encouraging Mae to go on.

Mae, sitting quietly, had finished.

"Is there something I'm not understanding?"

Nothing. Not a word from Mae or Jane. No test. Father Paul could tell that. Still, these women were here because what they had seen had bothered them, and he didn't know what that was, although they both seemed to think they had told him.

"There is something I'm not getting here," he said as gently as he could.

"Mama is sure she knows what we were seeing and if she's right, there's something very wrong," said Jane, taking over for her mother. "On the way from the funeral home she told me the story about her uncle who had mysteriously died many years ago when I was just a little one. It was in the dead of winter and they laid him out for two days. You could do that without him stinking since they brought him outside to the shed when the family wasn't viewing. A day after he died, a peculiar stain came out of his mouth and down his chin and he started emitting an odd odor. Not from deep down, like what happens with putrification, but right near where his mouth is. As little as I was, my nose remembers that smell even to this day and that's what I was smelling coming from Papa. Tell Father Paul the rest, Mama, about what happened next."

"Well, Father," Mae began, picking up where her daughter had left off, "everyone noticed what we was seeing and smelling. It was that obvious and that unnatural. It was Mike, he went over to his dead brother and took a good look. It was hard to get his jaws wide open with that rigor mortis and all, but Mike did it. He then started fishing around deep inside his dead brother's throat with something, I can't rightly remember what he used, and pulled out this hunk of meat. The closer that meat got to his lips, the more it was a-stinking and when we got it out, it was still oozing. Maybe a piece of liver, we thought, since there was still blood in it. Anyway, that was the odor, the red on his mouth was dried blood, and the mystery of my brother-in-law's death was no longer a mystery; he had choked on a piece of raw meat. Now what he was doing eating it, we never knew. But for sure, that's what killed him."

"Raw meat isn't what killed my Papa, Father Paul," said Jane, picking up the story. "It was that cancer. I saw what I saw and smelled what I smelled when I went to visit Papa at Ozymandias. I didn't know what it was but did know it shouldn't have been. And with what Mama told me, now that I know what I was seeing, something is wrong, very wrong!"

Stella Reese's brother Henry and a missing stomach, Joseph Peterson and the ear, the boy with the missing privates and now this. Father Paul said nothing to Mae and Jane Stevens. They didn't have to know what he was thinking, at least not yet. As for now? There were questions, and although very serious questions, they would have to wait until Tuesday when he and Oscar sat down for their weekly meal.

Chapter Fifteen

"A lifetime in a week, wouldn't you say, Oscar? If only we could take this particular lifetime away and start all over again. Here we were last week, never thinking that anything like this could happen, and now look what we have."

That's what we're here for, thought Oscar Ozymandias.

He knew enough not to speak up when Dollard started with his soppy sentimentality. He and the priest were the bottom feeders on people's misery. He knew it and the priest should know it. Sure, it had been a terrible week for those who had lost family. It had been a wonderful week in the funeral business. The town, in its generosity, had paid for all the funerals.

Generosity? Generous to him, certainly, but not to the townies who would foot the bill when the council raised taxes. Under ordinary circumstances, at least four of the deceased would have been buried by family in the woods. Just do the math and you'd know Mount Olden had spent one pretty penny, a penny that was going to land right into Oscar's pocket. *A bad week, Dollard? A very good week for me and I bet for you.* There were more nickels, dimes and quarters in the church basket this week than last. He'd put money on that.

"Father, Mr O." It was Jake, pad and pencil in hand, ready to take the order. Meatloaf, spaghetti, spaghetti, meatloaf. Why, wondered Oscar, did this man have to write anything down? Most times the only choice was between the

burgundy and the Chianti and for as long as he had been
coming it was always the burgundy.

"The usual, Jake."

"Okay Mr O. You, Father, the usual?"

"That's just fine. Did we thank you for the coffee and
donuts the other night? We really needed them."

Jake accepted the thanks by tipping his head and
saluting with his pencil.

"How many years has it been since you're in Mount
Olden, Oscar?"

"It feels like forever, Dollard."

"No, how many years?" Paul asked again, with
uncustomary impatience.

"Maybe ten, a little more, a little less."

"How did you wind up here?" asked Paul, his eyes
locked on Oscar's as he leaned over the table, so close that he
could see a bead of perspiration forming on Oscar's brow.

Questions, why the questions? Oscar had made it a
point to keep his business to himself. A private man in a public
business. He had carved that on a piece of wood and placed it
in his sanctuary as a reminder. What was Dollard up to? For
as many Tuesday nights that they had together, for all the tea
he had with Father Reilly, he steered clear of his life before he
came to Mount Olden. It was effortless, no one asked and he
didn't volunteer. Now, all of a sudden, questions.

"It was the next town on the road. I stopped, got work
and stayed."

"Olsen's?

"Olsen's. My first and last stop."

"What did you make of Tom? The old man's son."

Tom Olsen. Better to be talking about Tom than
himself. Still, until he knew where this was going, he wasn't
going to feel right.

"Jake."

"Yes, Mr O?"

"Another glass," he said, holding up an empty glass that only a few minutes ago had been filled with the house burgundy.

"Your third?"

"My second, Dollard. Only number two. The third is still to come. And from the looks of it you'll be on your second pitcher of water in no time."

A laugh, a break in the tension, a drop of perspiration under the collar that only Oscar knew about.

"So what's with all the questions?"

"I'm just curious about Tom. A strange fellow. On the lake the other night, he was right next to me without my knowing he was there. Made me nervous. Not too many people make me nervous. This man did."

"He's strange, all right, I'd say that about him," answered Oscar, not giving the priest any more than was needed, hoping Dollard would get back to the stuff they usually talked about; upcoming funerals, sick calls, life in the pulpit.

"He was at Olsen's when you got there?"

"He was always there. He was the old man's right hand. Did everything. Made calls, opened a vault, an expert on preservative treatments, even the makeup. Everything that had to do with the remains, an expert. Now for the business end of it, a disaster. But otherwise, very competent. He taught me everything and believe me, Dollard, there is a lot to the 'everything.'"

A lot more to this than becoming a priest, thought Oscar. He wouldn't dare say this aloud, no one in Mount Olden knew that he was once a student at the seminary. Some things are better kept to oneself. Still, he knew both, preparation for the priesthood and funeral directing, and there was no question about which was the more difficult to master.

"How'd he do with your getting the business?" asked Paul.

"Now that was and still is a problem. He felt betrayed. He had every expectation that his father would hand it down to him. I knew that wasn't going to happen, anyone who spent any time in Olsen's knew that wasn't going to happen. Tom Olsen had no idea. There was a lot of ill feeling between everyone for a long time. He did his part though, and that was always puzzling."

"His part?"

"Part of the deal was his mentoring me. I was convinced that wouldn't happen because of the circumstances. It did happen and he did it very well."

"Any idea why?" Father Paul asked.

"He liked – no, he *needed* to be in the building. Again, not the business end or even the people end. He liked working with – no, I mean *on* the remains. No matter what has to be done, he does it and never complains. Training me let him stay around the bodies a little longer."

"You didn't keep him on after you took over. How come?"

Paul asking questions, Oscar hearing an interrogation. The sweat on his brow was joined by a ring of moisture under his collar and a dampness across his back. Good that what he felt could not be seen.

"What's all this about? You're holding back on me. A priest not being forthright. Imagine that."

"Bear with me, Oscar," the priest said, laughing. "You're absolutely right. My curiosity about Tom Olsen is not as innocent as I would like. Just answer a few more questions and then I'll tell you what's on my mind. So why didn't he stay on?"

At least this doesn't have to do with me, thought Oscar. So long as the spotlight was on someone, anyone but himself, Oscar Ozymandias was on solid ground.

"I didn't offer him a job."

"Because?"

"The easy answer was money. This business came with a big note. How many years has it been and I'm still paying on it. At the beginning I certainly wasn't about to pay anyone's salary but mine and I was taking very little out of the business."

"That was the easy answer?"

"That's the easy one."

"So now let's get to hard."

"Odd, odd, odd. He was almost inseparable from the embalming room. Table, sink, exchanger, instruments, Tom Olsen. Another piece of equipment, that's how I came to think of him. When it was time for him to move on, he wouldn't. As obvious as I had to be, that's how dense he was. Rude, Dollard. I'd be downright rude and he'd still show up the next day. I went so far as to change every lock in the building, fearing that he would take it upon himself to come uninvited and just be there."

"How'd you get him to stop?"

"I'm not sure I did," answered Oscar, thinking of the many times over the years he'd had to shoo Olsen away, just like he was a stray cat smelling something tasty. He meant no harm and he never got close enough to anything Oscar wanted to keep just to himself.

If nothing else, Oscar was cautious, and clever. This grown-up juvenile was no challenge. Still, who likes cats knocking over teacups in the cupboard?

"He still comes around. I guess this business is a part of him. He has some ill feelings about my being here and not him. Strange bird. He keeps his father as the saint and me the opportunist. What happened couldn't have been more different. The old man sought me out, it was his idea."

"Why didn't he give it to Tom?"

"Don't really know. It wasn't the money," answered Oscar, aware that his dinner companion's attention was now moving away from him and on to Tom Olsen. Redirection, unnoticed deflection, masterful. "I barely had enough for the down payment, it was very little, and the monthly payments came right out of the business. Maybe it had to do with Tom not having a head for numbers, maybe the old man knew his son's strange ways and wanted to get him out of here. Lots of maybe's and I'm here and he's always looking to hang around."

Oscar could have filled three Tuesday nights with Tom Olsen stories. He didn't like this man, could have destroyed him, but had to restrain himself. Mount Olden, as big as it was, was a very small town and a businessman in the business that Oscar was in had to stay above the fray. There were others who talked about Tom and that was enough.

The stories ranged from Tom the eccentric to lock your doors when that peculiar youngling of Old Man Olsen comes around. Never married, never had a close friend, always living on the edge. Oscar knew him to be harmless, others felt differently. And for the priest, this was the first time there had been any curiosity and Oscar still didn't know where they were heading. This was not a 'news of the day' conversation that had been the cornerstone of their weekly ritual. Spirited, gossipy, even spicy, until Father Paul started moving to the point of it all.

"The Stevens came by St Anselm's last Sunday."

"The mother – and daughter?" Oscar knew about Jane Stevens and her aversion to Father Paul's bumbling Mass delivery.

"Came for the late Mass and hung around. They needed to talk to me. They had questions about Mike."

Not what Oscar expected and certainly not what he wanted to hear.

"Something wrong?" he asked.

"Strange is more like it. Had to do with the body."

"First rate," Oscar asserted, letting anyone who wanted to listen, there was no one in Tilly's who was in earshot, that when it came to his business, he was the best. "Not an easy restoration. You know what that man looked like when we brought him in? Not a single bit of fat left. Eyes sunken, cheeks collapsed, color grey. The man was wearing the heartache of his death on his face. I seen bad, Dollard. Mike Stevens was a challenge and they got a masterful piece of work in what I gave them. When that boy comes home from the service to say goodbye to his father, the man he sees will nearly look as good as the picture they gave me. I also gave them one good price. You hear me, Dollard. You get what I'm saying?" Oscar's voice was getting louder and there was no knowing where it would have stopped if it hadn't been for Father Paul interrupting him.

"They said there were stains."

"Stains?" exclaimed Oscar, catching Father Paul in mid sentence.

"A red stain starting at the corner of his mouth and going down to his collar. Could that have been the fluid you use?"

"Impossible. I work with care, extreme care. Nothing I use could cause this discoloration. They must be mistaken."

"There's more," continued Father Paul. "There was an odor. They said they smelled a foul odor as if something was rotting."

"Dollard, what are these women talking about? Rubbish. Rubbish. There is no one in this state who could have given them what I gave them. They have him back, at least for the time they need until the boy comes home. And now I have to hear this? A man can take but so much."

"Easy Oscar, easy. They could be mistaken," said Father Paul, as he reached across the table and placed a reassuring hand on Oscar's arm.

"They certainly are mistaken."

"When's the last time you saw Mike?"

"The night I did the restoration. He's been in the coffin since then and in cold storage. The only way to make sure the body holds up. It couldn't start going bad with all I did. They smelled something? Can't be. Maybe it was the embalming fluid? Maybe it was the fluid?"

"Would that make for the same odor of decay?" asked Paul.

"Absolutely not. No!"

"They were quite sure they were smelling something rotting. In fact they said it was coming from his mouth."

"Dollard, are you listening to me!"

"Oscar, you and I have no argument. Let's put this to rest. Jake, a check. Let's go over to your place and take a look."

"Yes, let's take a look."

~

No idle words passed between them as they walked from Tilly's to the funeral home. The snow on the ground and the bitter cold of the wind would have been enough to explain the silence. This had nothing to do with the silence. Each was lost in his own thoughts about what had just happened.

Not the usual weekly dinner companion, Paul was thinking. Arrogance wrapped in clever sarcasm, curt, abrupt, this was the Tuesday night Oscar. He would even go as far as making not too subtle judgments about Paul as a priest that would largely go unnoticed if Paul didn't have these same doubts about himself.

Tonight was different.

Anger, that was it. He was seeing, almost feeling, the undertaker's anger. The more Oscar tried to hold it in, the more Paul felt its explosiveness. A challenge by an old lady and her not-so-nice daughter and this man was on the prowl and ready to attack.

What's with you, Oscar? thought Paul. *What did I say, what did they say to get you into this state? A mistake, if they had noticed anything it could be nothing more than a mistake.*

Paul had been around grieving families enough to know they often gave others little room for the mistakes that we all make every day of our lives. A place where the rouge and powder didn't take, a piece of Mike that escaped the embalming fluids and now had an odor; so what?

Always the priest, always in the space of another man's pain, Paul's thought went to wondering what could have happened to make this man think he needed to be anything but human. The suffering that he must feel each and every day of his life because we all have feet of clay. Isn't that what the teachings of Christ tell us? A man with no charity, either for himself or others.

Paul knew this about Oscar and now he was seeing it with all its power and ferocity. *Poor man, poor soul. How can I help? How can I ease your tortured suffering so you can have peace from yourself?*

Focus, Oscar commanded himself, as he began the walk back to the funeral home. He hardly noticed Dollard, who was having a difficult time keeping up with his brisk pace. No matter. He had things to think about, maybe to worry about. This was the business of the moment, not thinking about a sickly out-of-shape priest who couldn't keep up with him.

A stain, a smell. That daughter. Trouble, I knew it. What trouble? What could she be seeing, smelling? They came to see him. Put him in the viewing room. Right. That's what you did. The lid. The lid. They opened it, they closed it. They didn't say a word, they didn't say anything. Concentrate, visualize, remember, Oscar commanded himself. He had a knack for doing just that, taking himself back in time and remembering everything that happened down to the smallest detail. If he were there, the memories of what went on were somewhere inside him. It was just a matter of eliminating all distraction and reaching down for the prize. Tonight was the detail of the embalming of one Michael R. Stevens.

"Concentrate. It's the details, man. The details! From the top."

"Oscar, what was that?" asked Father Paul, whose wandering mind was suddenly jolted by the first words spoken since they had left the restaurant.

"Nothing, nothing, just thinking aloud. It's getting cold and the snow's starting. Let's just keep walking."

It had, the snow that is, and it was coming down hard. It had started falling and neither man had noticed until now. If Father Paul had been able to see Oscar, it would have been his pale sweaty face. If he had been able to hear his thoughts, it would have been of a man who was getting very worried.

Focus, concentrate, remember the details, Oscar thought, trying to walk through each and every moment with

Mike Stevens while making sure not a single word crossed his lips. He didn't need Dollard asking again what he had said. *After the embalming you send Willy on his way. He leaves, you go to the door and make sure it is locked. You go back to the sacristy. You are looking for the package. It is still cold, you placed it on the table and it is still cold. Of course, it was in the freezer chest. The chest, go back to the chest. The latch, take the lock off, open the chest. Which tray, which tray! Damn it, which tray did you reach for? To the left, that's the one. It had to be that one! It needed to be treated, the host needed to be treated. The tray to the right is raw, fresh, frozen and untreated. You wouldn't take a packet from there, Oscar? You would know better. You knew who was receiving communion, you knew. The left, not the center.*

What's that? What's that! It's coming from outside, the noise is coming from outside. The other side of the wall, the back of the house, there's someone back there. Damn, a can, knocked over. A cat? No cat. Too heavy for a cat to knock over. Olsen, maybe damn Olsen. He came back again. He wants to see the bodies. That would be just like the bastard. Did I lock the cold house? Yes, of course. The key is where it should be and I only put it there when I'm finished, when I've locked up. He won't be able to get in, if it's him. Who else could it be? It has to be him.

The packet is getting soft. Good. Rub it. Good. Put it in the calabria until you are ready. Good.'

"Oscar. Oscar, we're here."

Yes they were there, in front of Ozymandias' Funeral Home and Oscar had no certainty about whether he had taken the packet of meat from the left or center of the ice chest.

~

"I'll need your help in getting him. Grab that gurney and follow me." Oscar didn't need anyone's help, not when it came to moving the merchandise, but he wasn't about to let Dollard know that. In fact, he had long decided that he wasn't going to let the priest know anything about who he was, how he got to this town and certainly not how he did business.

"Grab the one on the left, that should be Stevens. I'll be back in a minute. I need to make sure the embalming room is ready." Oscar couldn't stop talking to himself or worrying. By nature he was a thorough man and wouldn't have a second thought about being careless and leaving something behind. Now he had to make sure before he brought Dollard into the room.

"Damn, Oscar, this is some heavy casket. Who's in here?"

"You got the wrong one, for God's sake," Oscar said angrily. "The next one, the next shelf over. Wait a minute, let me get over there and you'll give me a hand."

Rolling the gurney alongside the casket, he directed Father Paul to lift one end while he lifted the other.

"Easy, Dollard, easy, or you'll send poor Stevens flying." A word of caution just in time. Father Paul, expecting this casket to weigh as much as the first, had nearly upset the coffin.

"What's in that coffin?" asked Paul, pointing to the first he laid his hands on.

"Not what, Dollard, who."

"Of course. Who."

"Come, Dollard, let's get on with it."

Good that the question of who was left in the cold house, thought Ozymandias, as the two men wheeled Mike Stevens through the back door. The answer to who was Pico, a man with no one but the county to worry about how he'd be buried, and what was left of Vern Wasby. Except for the good meat of the harvest, there was a lot left, and put that together with Pico, and you have one heavy coffin.

"What do we do now?" asked Father Paul as they wheeled Mike to the embalming table.

"First thing we got to do is open the box and see what the Stevens ladies were talking about," Oscar said, beginning to regain his composure. Whatever it was, he'd deal with it. But they didn't say anything to him. They saw something, they smelled something and they didn't say a word. The answer was obvious; whatever they think they noticed shouldn't have been there and it was there because Oscar Ozymandias had been party to something that shouldn't be. In their silence, there was an accusation. What could they have seen? If nothing else, he was always careful, especially when it came to his fulfilling his spiritual obligation.

Relax, Oscar, you can handle it, was his last thought before gently opening the coffin, exposing a very dead Michael Stevens. Father Paul, staring at Oscar's handiwork, crossed himself and the body in front of him as the lid swung open.

The mouth, the red going down to the collar; which side. It would have to be the right unless Mae or Jane moved Mike's head on the pillow. The head was as Oscar had left it and yes, there was the stain.

"There it is, Dollard, there," Oscar said, pointing to the discoloration. For a moment Father Paul forgot that this was a man he had known and brought himself as close as Oscar now was. Two professionals examining an offending piece of skin.

"Probably some embalming fluid," commented Oscar. "That can happen every now and then. See the makeup, the grease and powder. Over here, Dollard," he said pointing to a specific spot on Mike's cheek. "It was properly applied but sometimes it sinks in and if there is an underlying stain, and that can happen when you use as much as I put in, this can happen. Had to use quite a bit because the burial might be as long as a month away."

There was no noticeable odor until Father Paul started sniffing in and around Mike's face. When he got to the mouth, which appeared shut, he pulled back quickly.

"There, Oscar, take a whiff of that. Do you smell it? What do you make of it?"

Oscar leaned over and took a deep breath. Father Paul was right, the smell was there. Not what the Stevens women probably smelt when they opened a coffin that had been closed for more than a week, but it was there.

"Yes, I smell it. Decay. We're smelling decay."

"Should that be happening?"

"It can. Always a possibility that the chemicals missed something."

Father Paul leaned over one more time, his nose brushing against the dead man's lips. "I don't know Oscar. It smells like there's something rotten in there. We're not going to know unless we take a look."

Take a look. What to do? Oscar had never been in a position like this before. He didn't want to arouse suspicion and if he thought something was amiss, he'd be asking what the priest was asking.

"I'll have to open him up."

Unexpected news. Open him up? What was Ozymandias saying? Father Paul didn't have to say a word. His face said it all.

"The mouth doesn't stay closed by itself. I threw a few sutures in there. Hand me the scalpel."

Paul handed it to him and turned his head away, not sure he wanted to see what Oscar was about to do.

"This way, Dollard. You're asking for it. The least you can do is watch what's happening. You'll survive and be assured, it's a bloodless procedure."

Oscar Ozymandias was playing with him and Father Paul knew it. Bloodless. If Oscar was as good as he said he was, there shouldn't be a drop of blood left in the body. As for watching, it didn't take a keen observer to know that Father Paul was squeamish about what the undertaker was doing. Still, he had to face the Stevens family and to do that, he had to know if something was not right.

Oscar knew what was going on, what would be found and the questions that would be asked. Take the initiative, be curious, be shocked, outraged. Got that, Oscar?

"Turn the light on and give me the tweezers."

Mike Stevens looked dreadful under the harsh light of the hanging bulb. The makeup was starting to dry and crack, and the grey lifeless skin was coming through.

"We'll have to fix him up again," he said to Father Paul. "I'm surprised the Mrs or the daughter didn't say anything about this. Okay, Mr. Stevens, here we go. This is not going to be easy, Dollard, the jaw is locked. Okay, there it is," Oscar said, leaning over and peering into Mike's mouth. "Got it. The sutures are cut. Let's see if there's any play at all with the jaw. A little. Dollard, put these tweezers over there and get me the next size. Yes, that's it. Good. Let me have them."

Ozymandias slid the instrument into the partially open mouth and started feeling, probing, and pulling. "There's something in there, I can feel it. See if you can find a tweezer with longer prongs. No, not those. Yes, that will do. Now I need a little hands on help." He really didn't, but this wasn't going to be easy for him, so he certainly wasn't going to make it easy for the priest. "Come here and hold his jaw down. Come on, don't be squeamish. If I'm to find out if there's anything in there, I need some help."

What choice did Paul have? He'd been around the dead, that was part of his job. But what Oscar was asking him to do now, never. Touching the skin that by now had lost anything that made it human took every bit of courage. He had to believe what Oscar was asking was necessary. It was only that assurance that kept him standing on his feet.

"Good, I have a good grip on it. Whew, the odor is getting strong."

Father Paul also smelt it and wasn't sure how long he could last.

"Get me that jar of camphor. Yes, that's the jar. Hand it over."

Oscar took it from the priest, dabbed a little of its contents on his index finger and rubbed it right under his nose. "Do like I did," he commanded. "It helps with the odor."

One last tug and Oscar had it. Clamped in the tweezers was a piece of rotting meat approximately two inches long and a half-inch thick.

"Oh crap." Oscar exclaimed. "What the hell is this doing here? Tampering, someone has been tampering with the body. I don't know what this means or why it was put down his throat, but someone very sick has been up to no good. I think I got it all. Let me have that bottle, Dollard. Need to lavage the oral cavity to disinfect anything that's still down there. I think I got it all but you never know."

"We need to talk," said Father Paul.

"We need to talk, but first I have to take care of Mr. Stevens. Ten minutes, that's all it will take. You look terrible, Dollard. You're not going to faint on me, are you?"

"It's getting close."

"Go into the office. I'll finish up and wheel the body back to storage. I can handle that by myself. Go inside and I'll meet you there."

A few minutes to sew Mike up again, a few minutes to think about what comes next. Be as flabbergasted as the priest and let him do the talking. Decided? Yes, decided and done.

~

"Defiling a body, very serious, Oscar, very serious. What do you think?"

"I don't know what to think. In all my years, in all my years." Of course Oscar knew what to think. Careless, just careless. The host had come from the center and not the left. Right cooked, center raw, left treated. "That was deliberately put down the deceased's throat by someone."

"No possibility that this was part of Mike's last supper?" asked Father Paul, looking, searching, and reaching for an explanation that would make this an accident rather than the sacrilege he knew it to be.

An interesting possibility, thought Oscar. Mistakes happen. The wrong host in Mike was an example of that and if this were an accident, it might put this to rest. A small sacrifice, admitting fallibility to a priest. Of course, if he had made the mistake, it would have been an insult to his very core. Purging the digestive tract is elemental in the funeral business. Not doing it right would be the same as a priest not getting the Latin right and Oscar knew what he thought of Dollard because of that.

Still, there was an appeal to admitting that he had made a mistake that would explain it all. Hell, Catchum was at his side when he purged the body of any food that was left behind and even if he weren't, someone some day would be asking

Mae Stevens why she gave her dying husband a piece of beef when he was shriveled on his death bed.

Nice try, Oscar said to himself. *Now stop reaching and stick to the truth, or at least most of the truth. The more lies, the greater the chance of getting caught.*

"Part of the procedure, Dollard, is purging the body of everything. Everything. That includes bowel and anything in the stomach." Then, without a moment of thought or change of expression, he added, "As basic to the funeral business as preparing the host is in yours." He loved himself for his wit and sense of irony. Even in a moment like this, when most average men would be squirming and sweating, he hadn't lost his essential Oscar brilliance. A brilliant piece of irony without a touch of sarcasm. That was the hard part and he knew it.

"So someone did this?" Father Paul asked to no one in particular even though Ozymandias was no more than three feet from him. "But why? Something is very wrong. Sick. Sick. What do you think?"

"I don't know," answered Oscar, and as if for emphasis, he said it again. So far, this was the hardest thing being asked of him. Oscar had something to say about everything and in matters of opinion, he was quite convinced that his was right.

Of course, in the matter at hand he knew exactly what had happened and the why of it.

Could he say his reason for doing what he did was because of priests like Paul Dollard? Could he say that he faulted the Church for pandering to the whim of the times? Could he say that he did what he did to poor Mike Stevens so that he would be welcome through the gates of heaven when he made the same journey as our Lord and Savior?

"I haven't got the slightest, Dollard. Who did it? Why they did it? I have no idea. And the fact that it had to have happened right here in my place, is the most distressing part of it all." Good, he said what neither man had said. Obvious but not said. Now let the priest talk. If there was ever a place for silence, Oscar thought, it was now.

"Other things have happened here, Oscar."

Keep your mouth shut, Ozymandias thought. *Be disciplined. Be quiet and listen. How much could he know? How much is out there? Don't even try to explain. Don't dignify this misfit with any explanation. There is no offence here, no crime.*

Was harm done to the good Catholics who received a sacrament after they were gone that would assure that they got to where they were going? Who would have done that? No one whose feet walk this earth now.

There was a man once who would understand. There was a man who would have done just what I am doing now.

He's not here, I am.

Look who has been left to spread His word. Dullards with stiff collars. Admit to nothing Oscar, you've done nothing wrong. Will you be discovered, found out, exposed? Maybe some day, and like Him, you might have to make the sacrifice. A little price to pay. If not for a death there wouldn't have been a resurrection and without resurrection, no salvation.

"There's more than just Mike Stevens, Oscar. Joseph, Oscar. We spoke about him. Do you remember?"

Ozymandias nodded, yes he remembered very clearly. So that was one and he had handled it very well. He remembered that also. This, thought Oscar, was the beginning of the list. Stevens, Joseph, and... how many did Dollard have?

Just stay calm, Oscar, he cautioned himself. *Whatever he has, no matter how many on that list, you can handle it.*

You're smarter than this man. Remember that, no matter what.
You're smarter.

In his mind, he absolutely believed that. His palms had a different answer; his hands were starting to sweat. He clenched his hands and started to methodically, nervously move his thumbs up and down his bent index fingers. He didn't know he was doing it and Father Paul didn't see it.

"There was Stella Reese's brother, Henry. She told me a story about him when he was laid out in Olsen's. Closed coffin, there had been a terrible accident and they kept the coffin closed. She was alone with him, she opened the coffin, his mid section was gone. She knew what he should look like and when she saw him, she said there was nothing where his stomach should have been. She didn't dare actually look. She put her hands on him. That's how she said she knew. How could she know? That's what I thought, Oscar. How could she know? The story stuck with me enough to put it into my journal, but it was so fantastic that I figured she had to be mistaken. Strange things happen to people who are in mourning. Now with Mike and what we have just seen, and with Henry, this is not the fabrication of a grieving sister."

Father Paul let out one deep breath, leaned back in his chair, and looked at Ozymandias. He was done. Oscar too, let out a deep breath; the priest had finished with his list.

"I don't know what to say," Oscar responded, waiting to hear what was going to be asked of him. "Henry Reese, I remember him. There was something about him and the Rough Riders."

"That's right, he was the one," said Father Paul, trying to coax Oscar's memory.

"I was working for Jonas Olsen at the time. A closed coffin, an accident. I remember."

"These are the three we know about, there may be more. I have to do something, Oscar."

"What's to do, Dollard? I can help you with Stevens, we both saw what happened with him. But the others? I'm not doubting you with Joseph, but even you aren't sure about that, and as for Henry, that happened a long time ago."

"It's Tom Olsen that I'm thinking about. He's been around for all three. What you've told me about him and what I've seen myself has me thinking about him. Always around, even now that the place is yours, I'm thinking that he may be the one who's doing this."

"What do you want to do?"

"I'm not sure. There are certainly questions that need asking."

"Questions?"

"I need to be absolutely sure Tom was here when all this happened."

"Careful, Dollard. You don't want to let too many people know what's happening and what you're thinking. This is all a very nasty business and I'd be absolutely sure before letting anyone know what you're up to before making the accusation."

Accusation, this was an accusation. Once the town of Mount Olden got wind of what was happening, things would never be the same. Once Tom Olsen's name was mentioned, there could be hell to pay.

"What are you thinking? Tell me my next step, Oscar. I can't do nothing."

"Who else knows of your suspicions, Dollard?"

"Well, just you. I have to let the sheriff know. That would make three of us."

"I'd hold off on the sheriff, at least for a while. Once he knows what you're thinking, this all becomes very public."

"What are you suggesting, Oscar?"

"Old man Olsen had his records. They're here somewhere. At least let me find out if Tom was in town when he did Henry Reese's funeral. That would be a start."

"We would have to know that, wouldn't we? Agreed. How long would that take?"

"A few days, maybe a week. There's a lot of boxes in the basement and I haven't been down there in years. With all these burials in the next few days, it may be a while before I can get down there and go through everything. We've got to find out what's going on so I'll start as soon as I can. A few days."

"We do have to know if Tom was there. Without him being there all we know is something has happened, and if that's the case, I wouldn't know where to begin."

"As soon as possible, Dollard. We'll find out if he was there and if he wasn't we'll figure out what to do next."

~

Oscar Ozymandias remembered Henry Reese very well. He was his first harvesting. He had thought about doing it, planned everything to the last detail, and waited for an opportunity. It came when Tom Olsen was thrown in jail by the sheriff for five days for public intoxication and general rowdiness, leaving him in charge of the embalming at Olsen's. When Henry Reese was brought in and it was clear that there would be a closed casket, it was time. Now, years later, a priest tells him it wasn't as perfect as he thought. What to do next? Ozymandias wasn't sure. He did know he'd have to figure something out very soon because Paul Dollard would only have to ask a few people a few questions to know Tom Olsen could not have been involved with Henry Reese.

And when Dollard started asking his questions, the sheriff would certainly be first on his list.

Chapter Sixteen

Anger, resentment, despair. What else was there to feel when Jonas Olsen made his decision?

"Grandfather, father and son, that's the way it's supposed to be. It's mine, not his, mine, and now you're going to give it away. Not fair, do you hear me? Not fair!'

Words that were never heard by the person who needed to hear them. Words that were never said by the person who needed to say them. As many hours as Tom Olsen rehearsed this speech standing in front of the mirror, he never could muster the courage to confront his father.

Jonas Olsen's decision shouldn't have come as a surprise. Maybe it was the strength of the wish or his being slow in figuring things out. Probably a little of each. If only desire and the aptitude to be a good mechanic in the embalming room were enough.

Olsen's was a family operation located in a building that was also the family's home. In fact, a stairway from the kitchen of the two-bedroom apartment on the second floor led right into the showroom where the bereaved could choose from one of the eight coffins on display.

Tom liked the ones with the brass side rails because they made it easier for him to climb in and play. An imaginative child, he invented any number of games for his own amusement. While most other children his age were playing hide and seek in the woods, he was crawling into the boxes. The top lids were always open so prospective customers could see the comfort they were buying for their deceased relative. Tom was small enough to squeeze into the bottom part where he would stay motionless, waiting for someone to miss him and come looking. There was many a time when it took hours before he was missed. His ability to stay quiet and out of the way for so long? Mr and Mrs Olsen saw this as sign that their only child was blessed with great fortitude and discipline.

When Tom became too big for the bottom half, playing the deceased became his favorite game. He still had to wait to be discovered but now he'd dress in his Sunday best, lying perfectly still with a crucifix on his chest and hands folded. His parents viewed this as a sign of their son's sense of humor. Once a child no older than Tom was laid out in one of the coffins. He had drowned in the lake and was to be waked that evening. When Ma came looking for him it took her a moment to figure out which child was her son. This story was told and retold over and over at the dinner table and after each time, the family had a good laugh.

Now for school, it was Tom's dread and who could blame him? He was downright awful with anything that had to do with words or numbers. The kids made fun of him because he could do nothing right, and his father was the man who dealt with dead bodies. Everyone knew where Tom lived and what was stored in the cold house behind the funeral home.

Tom didn't make it easy for himself either, since he didn't know how to keep his mouth shut. He was forever talking about the comings and goings in the embalming room and went so far as to bring in a couple of fingers that had been separated from a customer who had a nasty accident that resulted in his demise. The fingers were to be buried with him, but since the funeral was a couple of days away Tom saw no harm in bringing them for show and tell in the school yard.

Rather than sparking curiosity, he was greeted with the other children's disgust. Fortunately, the teachers didn't believe the wild story the children told about dismembered digits. It was so beyond reason that Miss Clark was convinced this was just another instance of the children telling stories to get Tom in trouble.

Tom, no fool, spent as little time as possible with his school mates and as much time in the funeral home as he could. This was a little worrisome to his mother, his not having friends and all, but Jonas Olsen told his wife to just let the boy be.

When Tom was twelve he assisted with his first embalming. He was no stranger to the room, the eight caskets in the show room couldn't hold a child's attention very long.

Mosel Green, all 340 pounds of her, had come to a sudden and unexpected end. It was as if her body had decided it couldn't go on carrying all that flesh around anymore. He had never seen such a large body before and when he was sure his father wasn't looking he did some inspecting. There are a lot of folds and hanging parts when you weigh that much and you're no more than five and a half feet tall. He had seen privates before, but Miss Green had the biggest breasts he ever encountered.

"Sorry this happened to you, ma'am," he said to Mosel. He was always talking to the deceased and out of respect, was always polite. "You are one large woman." He couldn't see her very privates, there was a towel covering them, but everything else was exposed. "How did you manage to carry them around?" he asked, pointing to the breasts. He knew they were breasts because of the nipples. If not for those two distinguishing features, they could have been just another hunk of flesh hanging on the frame.

"Lot of heft here," Tom said as he put his two hands around each and lifted. He looked under the left one and discovered a rash and a white crusty substance that emitted an odor. "Yuck. We'll have to do something about that when we wash you up."

"What are you doing, son?"

"Look at the size of her, Pa."

"That's why I need the help, boy. Go get me the trocars."

Tom couldn't have asked for more, he loved those trocars. He had touched them, felt them, even practiced by sneaking one out and going to the pumpkin patch on the other side of town. It took only one pumpkin season for him to get pretty good with it. He even went as far as to approach some of the bodies when he was sure his Pa wasn't looking. Now it looked like he was going to have a chance to use one for real. The stories he'd be able to tell when he went to school. He never learned.

"Here, son," his father said, handing him one of the instruments. "Just aim at where I'm pointing and give it a firm but gentle push."

Tom, having watched his father many times, knew exactly where to place the sharpened edge. "Just move your hand, Pa. Don't want to nick you." It was a little hard to get in, this was no pumpkin.

"A little harder, son. That's a big belly that Miss Green has there. There you go. Soon you'll have that baby just where you want it and she'll start to drain."

And that's exactly what happened. Absolute manual precision and only twelve years old. This also became dinnertime fare, but instead of laughter, there was admiration and pride. No wonder Tom thought he'd be the third Olsen in the business.

~

Running a funeral home is a business and that's where Jonas had doubts about his only son. He'd certainly have to know how to read, write and do numbers; there's a lot of bookkeeping and inventorying. If you're not careful you could wind up with more coffins than you need, or even worse, not enough. When a six-footer needs the deluxe mahogany and all you have is birch for a five footer, credit has got to be good with the coffin company. Can't wait two weeks to straighten things out. That's one of the things that people didn't understand about Jonas' line of work. Everyone gets caught on the bodies and what gets done to them. This was certainly the case with his son.

But what about the pressure? When the deceased arrives, everything has to be in place. No putting it off, no waiting for a part to arrive. You die, you get buried. If the second part can't happen exactly when you need it, like getting the right coffin or floral arrangement, you might as well put the body in the ground yourself. It's a lot cheaper and the deceased is exactly where they're going to wind up anyway. In order for everything to happen like clockwork, to have on hand what's needed or be able to get it immediately, you have to run a tight business and that means good books and good books means good writing and arithmetic. Tom had neither.

Then there were the people skills. A funeral director has to deal with the public. The Olsens knew this was beyond their son. They found this out the first day he went to school. He just didn't fit in. No friends, the butt of the joke, no ability to sweet talk. No writing, no adding. The best the senior Olsen could hope for was to sell the business and have enough money for their old age and a few extra dollars for their not-quite-right son.

When Oscar Ozymandias walked through the front door looking for a job, Jonas knew he had his answer. Oscar was a serious-minded man who was smart and smooth. He said he was looking for a place to call home, and he was thinking about the funeral business because it helped families with 'transitions', and the deceased with going on to meet his maker.

Jonas hadn't thought about things quite like that before. Yes, that's exactly what he was doing and what was needed. It was what a funeral home had to be to its community and that's exactly why Tom wasn't up to the task. Jonas decided to keep an eye on his new employee, maybe he'd be the right person.

Tom had no reservation about teaching Oscar everything he knew and no awareness that he was preparing his competition for a battle that he was sure to lose. The teaching made him feel real important for the first time in his life.

Oscar excelled. He learned the technique, both embalming and restoration. When Tom went on one of his drinking binges, his only companion in life his muscatel, Oscar was there.

~

Oscar and the seminary, a round peg in so many holes. The obvious was his devotion and his teachers' cavalier application of ritual to practice. At first tolerant, they attributed this upstart's argumentative pronouncements to his adjustment to monastic life. But they soon became weary of the constant assault on their adherence to church doctrine and ritual, and the bold challenges to their authority.

Not so obvious, at least to Oscar, was his radiating contempt for his teacher's intellectual rigidity when it came to

Socratic exploration of foundational elements in the theology. They wanted him to be punctual, maintain silence during devotions and clean every wall, floor and bathroom. They called it developing discipline. Oscar called it rubbish.

It was the Eucharist that was the explosion that led to expulsion. As Oscar read it, the Gospels were clear: Jesus could not have been clearer. A sign of devotion, recognition of union and salvation. 'Take of my *flesh*.'

But where did the bread come in? Whose idea was that anyway? Matthew, Mark and Luke and the time of year of the Last Supper. A Seder connection. The day of unleavened bread, or a day after the first day of unleavened bread. What difference does it make? These were Jews, all of them, including Jesus. Passover and bread: no bread! But there was meat. Why not meat? Made more sense then bread. Except if we consider the times, the masses, the logistics. How easy a piece of bread and now a wafer. Cheap and easy to store. But even there Oscar wondered, in what he would describe as his epiphany. Cure the meat, whether it came from a steer, sheep or goat. The perfect substitute for human flesh.

Oscar wanted to discuss theology. The monks who were charged to turn this unruly adolescent into a Prince of the Church declared him hopeless. Oscar, like Moses, cast to wander in the desert for eternity, knew in his heart he was right and they were wrong. With this resolve he would stick to strict adherence to ritual and wait to be summoned to his Mount Sinai for the answer to the mystery of the Communion.

Oscar's Mount Sinai was Mount Olden. The Burning Bush, the message of opportunity that apprenticing at Olsen's Funeral Home offered. He heard Jesus' call, take of my body, and he willingly signed on.

A couple of years after Oscar arrived, Jonas got sick. Doc Radler said it was his heart and he needed to take it easy for at least six months. An undertaker can't take it easy for six months. Unable to handle the pressure that comes with an unwell Papa, Tom went on a drinking spree that lasted a full two weeks. This made a difficult decision easier.

Feeling he had no choice in the matter, Jonas Olsen announced that Oscar would take over until his health was restored and the Doc gave him the okay to go back to work.

Oscar, without Jonas or Tom, seemed to be working night and day. Luckily there were no disasters at the lake, just the usual business; old people dying and one or two accidents that didn't require major restoration. These months completed the education of Oscar Ozymandias. He wanted this business. He could do it himself and he could increase volume. People were dying in Mt Olden who weren't coming to Olsen. The market was there.

There was no mistaking that Oscar Ozymandias was the one and with illness taking Jonas so suddenly, the old man decided to do what needed to be done sooner rather than later. He called his son in first, explained what he was doing and that he expected Tom to help Oscar ease into the business.

His conversation with Oscar was about the business, the terms and the payments. Oscar would pay for the business out of the business. Oscar was pleased and Tom got drunk and violent, going up and down the main street breaking windows. In a matter of minutes everyone in town knew of Tom's tantrum, that's what they called it, and there wasn't a single person who was surprised by it. They expected this and worse from that crazy son of Jonas Olsen.

The sheriff had his fill of Tom and threw him in jail for almost a week. He knew he was taking a chance giving such a stiff sentence to the son of a local business owner, but this time young Olsen had just gone too far.

Jail is a good place to think about things. Five days after being locked up, the door swung open and Tom Olsen left with a new resolve. First, he would help Oscar out because that was the only way he could be near his one and only love, the funeral home. The second was he would look to God for the strength to live with helping that no-good bastard Oscar Ozymandias who had stolen what was rightfully his from under his nose.

It was hard enough for Father Paul to stand at the altar for Sunday Mass and now he had all this stuff about the defiling of the dead to deal with. Oscar's advice had been prudent, so he discussed his suspicions with no one. Oscar said he'd be able to check some records to see if Tom Olsen was working in the funeral home when Henry was butchered. Harsh? What other word can fit with what was described. If it was true, the man's stomach had been cut from him. In a few days he'd hear from Oscar and then know what to do. In the meantime it was another Sunday and there were masses to be said.

Father Paul did okay until he came to the eleven o'clock. He had both hands firmly fixed on the altar, leaned forward and there in the sixth pew was Tom Olsen. He so seldom came, why now?

Was this another trial, another test? Hadn't he proven himself by now? Probably not because if he had, the Lord wouldn't have visited Olsen on him, or if he had, He would have given him the fortitude not to worry about stuttering in front of all these people. *Please don't stutter.* If only he had a little of Father Reilly in him, a master of the liturgy who knew every last word and phrase, and didn't need to have the missal open in case he forgot.

Reilly was a good man with little passion, a workhorse for his church and for his God. Come Sunday when he was in his priestly robes standing before his flock, he never made a mistake as he moved effortlessly through the Mass. He must have had bad days but you'd never know it from sitting in the church when he was saying Mass.

Not so with Father Paul. Any upset and he had problems somewhere with the Mass. Tom Olsen being in church was a big time problem. Still, he knew he'd get through it, he always did. He took one deep breath, took a large drink of water from the pitcher he always kept beneath the lectern, began with the Introductory Rites, and before he knew it he was up to the *Dominus vobiscum* and a moment later, *Ite, missa est.*

~

He recognized the voice immediately, having heard it last on the lake only a few days before.

"I need to confess, Father," said Tom, unshaven, clothes disheveled and with more than a whiff of alcohol lingering on each of his words so early on this Sunday morning. "It can't wait. I need to confess. I need to do it now, Father."

Discomfort moved to curiosity. It had been years since he had heard his last confession and now this sudden sense of urgency.

"Come, Tom, let's go over to the confessional. When is the last time you confessed, my son?"

"Father, I have sinned."

"Your last confession?" the priest asked again.

Nothing could stop Tom Olsen, certainly not a question from Father Paul. "I done wrong, Father. I'm doing wrong. It's hate that's eating me up now. I had my rights and they were taken from me. Just snatched from right under my nose. Took me away from the only thing that had any meaning. I hang around where I need to be, but I can't get close enough to do what I should be doing. That is except for sometimes. Sometimes I get close enough and then I do. Do you follow me, Father? Do you understand?"

Paul understood more than he wanted to. Tom hadn't exactly said it, but wasn't he confirming the suspicions he had shared with Oscar?

"You fear you have done something very wrong, my son?"

"It's what I'm thinking to do that worries me, Father, not what I've done. What was mine was taken from me and I know who did it. He knows that I know and he acts like what he did is okay. Every day it gets rubbed into my nose. Every day everyone who I see knows what he did and what happened. Sometimes I get so angry, Father, that I want to do something terrible. I get so angry that I want to eat him alive. Do you know what I mean, Father? Can you understand how I've been wronged? I've been driven to this thinking and I fear that someday the thinking might become doing."

Tom Olsen stood, swung open the confessional door, almost tripping as he bolted from the church. No penance, no Hail Marys, no nothing but an enraged man. And a shaken Father Paul. It took very little to imagine this sick man defiling the dead.

Chapter Seventeen

Oscar had never been so busy. Not only were there the accident victims, but three old Methodists had died. That was for the best. If they had been Catholic it would have meant even more of Dollard. For now, he had to get more coffins, and some help. It was more than moving the deceased; he couldn't keep up with the embalming. Willy Catchum could assist, but the only one who knew how to do it all, the embalming and restoration, was Tom Olsen. In the next few days there'd be at least eight funerals and funerals can't wait. He'd need both men and the work had to start after lunch.

It would be another week before Oscar would again sit down for a Sunday afternoon meal. Nothing came between him and Sunday dinner. *Take the time and do it right,* he said to himself. The stew, a bourguignon, was already prepared, and needed only to be heated. He liked it that way, giving the seasoning a chance to infuse the meat.

Presentation. Who better than an undertaker knows the importance of presentation? The floral arrangement, for example, was very important. Flowers were already in the room where Sylvan Taylor, one of the Methodists, was to be waked. Bleeding hearts in the shape of a heart spelled 'Dear Father'. He plucked two. In the next room, a large bouquet of mixed roses for one of the men who had been lost in the accident; he took one white and one yellow.

"Be tasteful, not excessive," he said aloud.

Oscar had an assortment of vases in all sizes for his summer customers who often brought freshly cut flower from their gardens. He didn't charge for their use. In the winter he had a special arrangement with the town florist and supplied all store-bought flowers as part of the funeral package. A good businessman takes advantage of every opportunity.

The flowers, adorned by a few sprigs of green, were just what the table needed. Now for the wine. A split of merlot. Perfect. A deep dish and salad plate for mixed greens, a setting from his silver chest and a checkered cloth napkin. Oscar moved a few steps back and took it all in. He moved the high stem goblet a little to the left. Now all that remained was ladling some of the stew into the tureen and he was done. Music, yes music. He cranked up the Victrola, reached for Verdi, and he was set.

Oscar Ozymandias had hoped for a peaceful half hour, but the moment he sat, the thinking began and with it, worry. In five days all the deceased would be comfortably in the ground and he would again have to deal with the priest. There were too many people who remembered the Reese funeral and it wasn't Henry Reese they remembered, it was Tom. He had already started his drinking when he went for the call, and once he had brought the body back to the funeral home he went on the rampage that landed him in jail for five days.

Whatever happened to the body couldn't have happened when Tom was there. Once Dollard asked the question to the first person he saw, Tom Olsen would be crossed off the priest's list and the finger would point to Oscar.

"So far Dollard is the only one who suspects anything. Dollard, have to do something about Dollard. A priest, a prince, the shoes of the fisherman. He could be the last. The host from the host. Yes of course. It will all be over if only it could be him."

"Veerbum tuum, per quod cuncta fecisti: quem misisti nobis Salvatorem et Redemptorem, incarnatum et Spiritu Sancto et exVirgine natum,'" Oscar said aloud, holding the goblet up to the crucifix on the kitchen wall. *"'By the power of the Holy Spirit, he took the flesh that was born of the Virgin Mary.'"* He reached for a piece of meat; *"'TAKE THIS, ALL OF YOU, AND EAT IT: THIS IS MY BODY WHICH WILL BE GIVEN UP FOR YOU.'*

"I will call you to the highest calling, Father Paul Dollard. In the very sanctuary that lives inside these walls, you too will have your resurrection and when I take in the consecrated flesh that will be your salvation, I will receive salvation. In you, my host, I will be able to find the path to righteousness and will have to take no more. You will be my last communion, my work will be done and I will live the life of the ordinary man once again."

An unexpected delight was the stew, and with redemption, partaking in this delicacy would come to an end. But with redemption comes sacrifice, he reminded himself, wiping his mouth with his napkin.

With the decision made, all that was left were the details. Oscar's genius was in the details. How to do it, how to get what he needed, how not to get caught. The details.

~

Working out a plan came to a crashing halt. Someone was downstairs. He must have left the front door open. Not like Oscar to forget to lock a door behind him. Carelessness was a concern, he couldn't afford to be making mistakes like this when so much was happening. Must be that damn Olsen.

Oscar took the napkin from his lap, had one final sip from the goblet, and wiped the corners of his mouth. He hated interruptions when he was eating but there was no choice; he didn't want anyone wandering around in places where they didn't belong.

"Who's down there?" Oscar called out as he came down the stairs.

"Ah, you're here, Ozymandias. It's me, Father Paul."

"What are you doing here? Shouldn't you be at St Anselm's saying Mass?"

"Mass is over, Oscar. We need to talk. A matter of some urgency."

What now? thought Ozymandias. This wasn't stopping. Ordinarily a man with strong nerves, Oscar was starting to feel the pressure of so many things that couldn't wait.

"Dollard, you saw what was doing in the cold house. Now there are three more. Please, can't this wait?"

"It really can't. It's about you and Tom Olsen and it's important."

"Then come upstairs. I was having a bite before I went back to work. Come upstairs and join me. You can talk while we eat."

~

Father Paul had never been in Oscar's living quarters and was taken by his taste and the wealth that had obviously gone into everything he was seeing. He had done enough traveling to recognize an oriental rug. Oscar had three. There was a crucifix in each room that could all be icons and many silver pieces in the breakfront. A silver bowl casually adorned a wooden coffee table that was surrounded by several chairs and a couch.

"Stickly?" asked Father Paul.

"Impressive. You know about Stickly, do you, Dollard?"

"I once took a trip to Santa Fe. You have so many beautiful things here, Oscar. All this in Mount Olden. A well-kept secret."

"It's my home, not the funeral parlor," Oscar responded crisply. "Have one," he said to the priest, who seemed to be staring at the chocolates on the coffee table.

"Chocolate? Oh, actually I was looking at the bowl. It looks so much like a paten."

Couldn't be, Father Paul thought. *Not something people usually use as a candy bowl.* He couldn't take his eyes off it.

"Come now," said Oscar, reaching for the bowl and being a little more insistent that the priest have a sweet. "It's time to receive communion," he said with smile on his face.

Laughing, Father Paul said he really couldn't.

"Sacrilege?"

"Sacrilege? Don't be silly, Oscar. The sugar. Diabetes."

"You?"

"Me."

"With all our Tuesdays, how is it that I don't know that?"

"It never came up, I guess. Not part of the Mount Olden weekly news," answered Father Paul, slipping down into one of the two rocking chairs.

"Comfortable?"

"Comfortable."

"I'll be right back," said Oscar as he walked to the kitchen, returning a few minutes later with a spread, wafers and two glasses that he filled from a decanter already on the table.

"I'm keeping you."

"You're keeping me from nothing. Remember, first I eat and then I work. This is Sunday and I make it a point to treat myself very well on Sundays. This is supposed to be a day of rest. If nothing else, at least my midday meal can be that. Please, help yourself," said Oscar, as he reached for a cracker and put some of the spread on it. "Pate, liver pate. It goes so well with the port. Have some," he said as he filled his and the priest's wine glass. "Take the host from your host," he chuckled.

"I'm not supposed to, I should be careful. Well, maybe one."

Oscar, an excellent judge of people, knew Paul's reluctance was for his benefit. Knowing the priest and his appetite, if this were sitting on his kitchen table and that housekeeper of his wasn't around; he'd probably be eating the pate with a soup spoon.

"How long have you been a diabetic?"

"For as long as I can remember."

"I still can't understand why I don't know that after all these years of eating at Tilly's?"

Father Paul knew the answer to that question; he wasn't a very good patient although he did try to avoid desserts and could only remember a few lapses at Tilly's. When alone, and fortunately there were only a few times a week when Stella wasn't hovering, he'd occasionally cheat.

"How did you find out?"

"When I was a kid I just wasn't right. My folks took me to the company doctor the mine owner had for us. Doc Steele was mainly there to give the miners something for the cough and get them back to work. That made him an expert in coughing and no expert in diabetes. Still, when my mother brought me to him because I just wasn't right and had no sign of a cold, he listened carefully, asked what I had been eating, had me urinate in a bottle, and after taking a strong whiff of my pee, told my folks to keep me away from sugar. I was pretty good for a while and started feeling better until the summer came and then I sneaked ice cream and candy. As soon as I did, the bad feelings would come again. They took me to Father Coviello, he was our parish priest, and he had a good talking to me. It worked for a week until the heat came back."

"Do you do anything about it now?" Oscar asked, as he watched Dollard mindlessly reach for his third chocolate.

"I did when I was in the seminary. Their doctor took it very seriously, put me on insulin, had me come in every few weeks for a test, and was strict about diet. Not a problem in the seminary where we live with less. Part of being in the Order."

"And in Mount Olden?"

"Look at me," Father Paul answered, holding up his hand with another piece of chocolate in his fingers. "In Mount Olden it's an impossibility. Look at this. It could be my eighth piece and I wouldn't know it."

"Your fourth," said Oscar.

"You see what I mean?"

"So you do nothing?"

"Almost nothing. I go to Doc Radler and he gives me insulin."

"So he knows about it?"

"I had no choice."

"No choice?"

"A couple of years ago I cut my toe and it had the hardest time healing. Radler knew what he was looking at right away. Asked if I was diabetic and then told me about what happens with healing. Said it would only get worse and how long that takes depends on how I take care of myself. He gave me some insulin and syringes and told me how to take a little more or less depending on how I felt. It didn't seem very scientific but you know the doctor. Anyway, it seems to be working all these years. So far I've only had one of what he called a crisis. A few years ago I got really sick and Sada had to get him to see me in the rectory. He knew from looking at me that I hadn't been taking care of myself. He was almost as good as Father Coviello. I took care for at least three months and then started slipping again."

"You've managed to keep this secret."

"The doc, the pharmacist, Sada and now you. Sada's had to inject me when I didn't have the strength to do it myself. Sometimes the whole thing seems to get out of whack so quickly.

"Being a country priest is hard enough and you've been to Mass enough to know that being up there in front of everyone, especially when the pews are filled, is not easy for me. The town knowing about the diabetes would only make that harder."

"I understand," answered Oscar to the question that wasn't asked but clearly understood. He also understood that this man was speaking to him in a way that he hadn't during all the years they had known each other. How did he feel about this new intimacy? Certainly no closer to the priest who couldn't get the Mass right and bent the ministering of the sacraments at will. Contempt, not concern; that's what he felt before these revelations and that's what he felt now. The information, however, might be very useful.

"Give me a moment to put down another setting. You'll have some dinner and we'll talk about what's so important."

Oscar left and Father Paul thought about his candor. It was good to have Oscar know his secret; he felt a little less burdened by it. Father Paul stayed in the sitting room and Oscar quickly took his goblet and returned it to the cupboard, wine and all, and took out another setting for his guest. The candy bowl, he said something about that. He said nothing about the wafers. Maybe he was too involved with the chocolate to notice that they were remarkably similar to the stock and trade of a priest and the Eucharist. He could take no chances with the goblet. Too much coincidence could lead to too many questions.

"We're ready. Just grab the wine glasses and come in."

"The decanter?"

"Leave it. We'll be drinking a merlot."

Port and now merlot. Paul couldn't remember ever having a merlot. Oscar took the glasses from him, rinsed them out and filled them from the decanter on the kitchen table.

"Lovely dishes, Oscar."

"Help yourself," he said, handing the priest the ladle. "It's still warm."

"What is it?"

"A bourguignon."

"Very good and a little gamey," Paul said, having plucked a small piece of the meat from his plate.

"I do some hunting. Do my own butchering and freeze the game. Do you think it's a little peppery?"

"Not at all," Paul answered.

"I do love the sprinkling of fresh parsley. Lends some color."

"Color?" answered Paul, as he leaned over the plate and began pawing at the stew with his fork.

The subtle smirk on Oscar's face went unnoticed as Dollard continued his methodical search that Oscar knew would come up empty. There was no parsley in the stew.

"I usually use leeks but this is with shallots. Have another taste and let me know what you think."

Paul picked up his spoon, tilted his plate, brought some of the broth into his mouth and began to pucker his lips.

"Not that way, Dollard. Didn't your vows include acquiring a sensibility in judging a dish well-prepared? With a piece of meat, the flavor is in the meat."

Paul, embarrassed by Oscar's playful rebuke, did as he was told. A small piece of meat in sauce, slowly chewed, slowly savored and a smile of satisfaction, although in fact he couldn't tell the difference between a leek, shallot, or the plain old onions that Sada used.

"The verdict, Dollard?"

"Delicious."

"Splendid," Oscar answered, as he filled his goblet one more time, and the priest's plate with one more ample helping of meat before returning to the matters at hand.

"So now tell me why the visit, what is this 'urgency?'"

Paul had nearly forgotten the reason for his visit. He needed to be careful. Priests are not supposed to violate the sanctity of the confessional booth. Still, what he heard did cause alarm and given his suspicions, he feared Oscar was in danger.

"Tom Olsen is not balanced. He's saying things that have me worried."

"Worried?"

"About you."

Dollard obviously had information and Oscar knew where it had to come from. The damn priest just didn't get it straight. The confessional is a sacrament. Sacred for god's sake. His obligation is to keep it. Still, the church had said that this is a man to carry the words of Our Lord and Savior and that would have to be good enough for Oscar Ozymandias, given what he knew had to be done.

"He's out to get you, Oscar."

"That boy has always had hard feelings toward me because of the business. His father made the right decision and Tom to this day benefits from it. Now that his parents are gone the monthly payment goes to him. It's enough to keep him fed and housed."

"He came an inch from saying he was going to do something drastic, hurt you, harm you. Look, Oscar, it's a fact that someone has been tampering with the bodies and now more than ever I am certain it Olsen, sabotaging you. It's time to go to the chief."

"Easy, Dollard," Oscar said, trying to think quickly. "Until we know that he was here to do what we think he did, we can't make the accusation. He's smart enough to talk himself out of anything he said. We don't want to scare him away."

"What about your safety?"

"He needs me too much right now to do any harm. He knows this business is never going to be his, and with the little work I throw his way he has access to the departed, and he needs that to do what he's doing. In fact, he'll be working for me for the next few days, both Willy Catchum and him, because of all the funerals. I'll keep an eye on him."

"And if he tries something?"

"With Willy and I here, he won't."

"Then how should we proceed?"

"It's too much for me to think about for one day. Come back tomorrow evening. Nine should do me, and we can have a light supper. We'll talk then."

With that Oscar stood up, cleared the dishes and took a bowl of chocolate mousse from the refrigerator. He set down two bowls and two spoons.

"I shouldn't."

"Yes, of course. How thoughtless of me, Dollard."

"Well, maybe a taste."

"Are you sure?"

Before Oscar had finished the sentence, the priest had filled his bowl.

~

With the priest gone, Oscar began to clean up. He abhorred clutter and crumbs. First, everything back in the cupboards that belonged in the cupboards. He picked up the dessert bowl, moved it to the table's edge and brushed into it any hint of the meal just eaten. How clean the bowl was, except for the crumbs. So clean that the slightest hint of the mousse that once lived in it was completely gone, having found its new home in a diabetic's stomach.

"He's gone and thank goodness. How weak of intellect, character and above all, discipline. An illness that put an end to more of my customers than I can count and this man, with the least of encouragement, consuming the poison that will someday kill him."

And with that, a smile emerged across a face that usually was implacable.

Chapter Eighteen

Oscar slept well Sunday night, and was out of bed long before his usual six am wake up. After a very close shave and more than usual 'mirror time', he reached for a lab coat and carefully buttoned it, top to bottom. There would be no time today to change his starched white shirt or crisply ironed trousers if either became soiled or stained.

Today's schedule called for four funerals, two wakes and three embalmings. He took out a large piece of brown paper, taped it to the wall in front of the embalming table, and wrote three names across the top; O. Catchum, Olsen. Along the side he noted the names of the nine deceased.

"It only works if you keep the lines straight and parallel," he said aloud as he drew a grid.

He took a step back, looked at his handy work, and smiled. "Perfect."

Now all that was left was filling in the boxes. Who would do what to whom, and when? If everything went as planned, he'd be able to send Willy and Tom home by seven and sit down for dinner with Dollard by eight.

Now for a cup of coffee, a muffin, and work.

~

"How you gonna manage this, Father Paul?"

"I don't know, Sada."

"Who's first?"

"Don't know that either."

"Four funerals in one day has to be a record. You sure got to put that down in the journal."

Paul looked at the writing tablet in front of him. Four names, four men. Three he knew and one a stranger. Not the usual, saying a funeral Mass for someone he didn't know, but this was not a usual time. So many people dead from one single accident; it was unheard of. He knew the church would be filled all day, some to say goodbye to someone they knew, others because they had to have a place to go with how they felt about what happened. In either case, Father Paul would be playing to a standing room only crowd. The thought of it, and his left hand began to shake.

"Take your medicine, Father?"

"Sure, Sada, sure," he said without looking up from the pad.

He didn't remember if he had taken his insulin shot. Maybe he had, probably he hadn't. He was not very good at remembering. Three, four times a day. Too much to keep in mind.

'Did you take it, didn't you take it; how much did you take?' The questions he asked every day when he remembered there was a question to ask. Most of the time he forgot.

"Sada," he called. She was busy in the kitchen doing something. She was always doing something: cleaning, straightening, preparing. The older she got the more she couldn't sit still.

"Rob Church," he said. "How many kids? And what about Pico Stevens, doesn't he have a wife?"

The questions were getting Father Paul even more nervous. His worst fear in times like this was getting confused and mixing things up. It happened once and it only took once to make the memory stick to his insides. It was his first year at

St Anselm's and like this time, it was a day for more than one burial. The masses were at ten and eleven; two men had passed leaving two wives, two families. He got it all mixed up; the men who had passed, the names of their wives, their children. The congregants at both services were shocked, he was mortified, and the nights that followed, sleepless. And that was with only two funerals.

"Say it again, Sada, and slowly." He had divided his paper in quarters, put a name in each box and underlined it. Family? Work? Church? He needed some information about each man and he had to make sure it got into the right box.

"Speak up, Sada. I can't hear you."

Sada knew everything. If there was something to be known about any of Mount Olden's Catholics, she knew it. Thank God for her, thought the priest, as he wrote everything down with his right hand, and reached into the top drawer of his desk with his left hand. In the back was a box of Oreos. He kept them there, well hidden, for times when he needed a little soothing. He knew he had to get some control back, but that would have to wait. Taking care of himself was the last thing on his mind.

~

Tom Olsen did not need a list, all he needed was some self-control. He wasn't surprised when the call came to help in the embalming room. He knew Ozymandias couldn't do it all alone. Being so close to Oscar Ozymandias was his test. All those bodies from the accident; the funeral parlor itself – everything should have been his. He wanted to kill the bastard. He thought the priest hearing his confession might help. It didn't.

It was a long time since Tom was in the embalming room, a scalpel in his hands, inserting the lines, pumping the fluids and oh, how he loved the trocars. Usually Oscar called him only for the crap – the picking up, the lifting, the hauling.

Now, though, he needed help with the stuff Tom loved. *Control, Tom,* he said over and over. *Start trouble and he'll throw you out. This may be your last chance to be so close. Don't screw it up.*

On most days, Tom Olsen would have already had three beers, while the rest of Mount Olden hadn't even had their morning juice and coffee. He stopped drinking the night he got the call from Ozymandias. A man who has three beers for breakfast feels like dirt when he hasn't had even one. He took a handful of aspirin, put on his hat and coat and headed for his day of work, hoping the aspirin would do the trick.

~

"Take a good look," said Oscar to Willy and Tom, pointing to the large sheet of brown paper on the wall. "We've got to stay as close to the schedule as possible. If you're falling behind, have a good reason. If you haven't got one, work harder and catch up."

Too much was happening in the cold house and Oscar didn't want any visitors. All the work for the day was already where it had to be.

The funerals were scheduled two and a half hours apart, giving Willy, who had changed into the black suit and would be driving the hearse, enough time to go back and forth. The four caskets with the deceased securely inside were in the showroom. Each was labeled so there would be no mistakes.

The embalming was left to Tom and the three bodies were already waiting for him. He also had to tend to the wakes. There wasn't much do. The two Methodists, in their open caskets, were already in the parlor on either side of this very large room. One was scheduled for twelve, the other for three and if there was some overlap, that's the way it would have to be. Tom's job was to stand at the front door fifteen minutes before each wake and to get the folks to move on after the first.

"You're going to be dealing with the public, Olsen, and each person coming is a potential customer. Change into this when you go into the parlor," said Oscar, as he handed him a pair of black slacks and a white shirt. "We don't need you going in there with your apron and rubber gloves. And for God's sake, look in the mirror before you go through the door. All I need is for any one of them to see you splattered with blood. Do you understand?"

"Relax, Oscar, I understand," he answered resentfully, reacting to how Oscar spoke to him, not to what he had said. Changing his clothes had never occurred to him.

Oscar's job? The overseer. He'd spend the day going from the funeral home, to church, to the cemetery, keeping things going, keeping everything on schedule. It was the only way he'd be sure everything got done.

He removed the lab coat, strung his pocket watch across the vest of his three-piece black suit, slid into his jacket and carefully placed a folded hanky into the breast pocket. One final look in a mirror; Oscar Ozymandias was ready.

~

The impossible day was more than half over and everything was almost on track. The first wake had started, Tom was beginning the second embalming and the funerals were running a little late. Probably Dollard rambling on with his homilies.

"Olsen, I have to run a few errands," Oscar said, leaving through the back to make sure the cold house was locked. Tom, thoroughly involved with Number Two – he gave each of his charges a number – was positioning a trocar and hardly noticed what Oscar had said.

"Sure, sure, later," he answered, his mind concentrating on what he was doing, not on what he was saying.

~

As busy as he was, Oscar had not forgotten about his dinner guest. His first stop was the market, his second the bakery.

"Mr. Ozymandias, you're the last person I expected to see today. How many funerals, how many wakes?"

Kurt Croppins had come to Mount Olden from some European city, bringing with him a thick Germanic accent and a cultivated skill in preparing the richest baked goods imaginable. Today, Oscar settled for a pound of petit fours and a seven-layer chocolate cake.

"It will be a long day, Kurt, and I know when it is finally over, I will need one of your treats to ready myself for tomorrow."

The next stop, the pharmacy. "Here you go, Henry," he said to the pharmacist, handing him the box of cookies.

"Well, thank you, Mr O. What can I do for you?"

"The usual and a lot of it."

The usual was alcohol, rubber gloves and syringes for injecting the embalming fluid under the skin.

"You know where it is. Should I put this on account?"

"Of course," answered Oscar, always the businessman.

Henry's back room had every medicine imaginable. A worktable in the center had a balance scale capable of precise measurements, a mortar and pestle, and empty bottles of varying sizes. Oscar loaded a cart with bottles of antiseptic solution, alcohol, rubber tubing and an assortment of syringes.

Shelf after shelf of different colored crocks filled with powders, some labeled, others not, bottles filled with liquids, jars of pills, and vials of medicines in cigar boxes.

How does this idiot find anything in this mess? thought Oscar. Lord knows he had his assortment of chemicals in the embalming room and each was clearly marked and lived in its rightful place, easy to find and retrieve. Not here.

Now to the upper shelves. Oscar reached up and beyond a mortar and pestle to a shoe box he knew from watching Henry was filled with morphine bottles. He reached for morphine and the vials of insulin on a nearby shelf. These items he placed deep in his pocket. They would not be listed on his invoice or found on his account.

"Damn, damn, damn," he said, as a pestle tumbled off the shelf, knocked down in his haste to return the morphine.

"You okay back there, Mr. O? I'll be right with you."

"Just fine, Henry. Just a pestle. Nothing broke. Stay put. Almost done. Out in a minute."

As he left the store room, Oscar could feel the emerging moisture accumulating in the palms of his hands and hoped it didn't betray him in the tone of his voice.

Another one of Henry's steady customers was coming into the back room as Oscar was pushing his loaded cart to the door.

"You, Radler, you're shopping?"

"Oscar. Did you leave anything on the shelf?" Doc Radler asked, pointing to the cart.

"Not much," smiled Oscar. "Unbelievably busy. But of course you know that. I have all those certificates that you signed in my office."

"The certificates, did you keep a copy for me?"

"I have a big box with your name on it," Oscar answered smugly.

"Don't be impertinent with me, Ozymandias. What works for me, works for you and vice versa. Remember who's the doctor between the two of us and who's the undertaker," he said to himself, as much as he said it to Oscar Ozymandias. It was the drinking. The more he needed to keep himself going, the more he had to remind himself that it was he, and not the bottle that was in charge of his life.

"Easy now, let's not take offense. I'm simply saying I have the box, I have what you need, and you're covered. I want you to know I have everything," Oscar said emphatically as a small grin appeared at the corner of his mouth.

Authorizing a funeral director to forge a physician's signature on a death certificate was enough for a doctor to lose his medical license, or even go to jail. Radler knew it and now he knew that Ozymandias did, too.

"By the way, I had dinner with Father Paul, Radler. The man doesn't look good. Sweaty, tired, dragging himself and he had an odor about him. Told me he's a diabetic and under your care."

"He sees me from time to time," the doctor answered.

"You should keep an eye on him. He's not taking care of himself."

~

With all his shopping loaded in his trunk, Oscar took his time getting back to the funeral home, pleased at his good fortune in running into Doc Radler.

Willy was waiting for him when he pulled up with the car.

"Done with the funerals, Willy?"

"Everyone is tucked in safe and sound."

"Excellent, Willy. It's starting to snow and it smells like a big one. Unpack the truck and then you can go."

The last few people were leaving the wake, another good sign. Still on schedule. Not so when he got to the embalming room. Tom was in the middle of Number Three. He was only up to the infusion and hadn't done any of the cosmetics.

"What's going on here?"

No answer.

"Do you hear me, man!"

"I'm doing the best I can," Tom finally responded.

"Just finish up with the infusion. I'll do the rest later."

Tom, feeling the shakes coming on, needed a drink more than ever. It took everything he had not to explode, and thank God for that. He knew if he broke up property that didn't belong to him or even better, took a swing at someone, the sheriff would send him to the state prison. He had warned him as much.

Oscar unlocked the cold house and tucked all but Number Three in for the night. He would deal with him after Olsen left.

"Olsen, it's already six o'clock. Get this finished in a half hour and then you're done. Here's your pay. Just let yourself out and close the front door behind you. I'm going upstairs."

Oscar made one last swing to ensure that everything that needed to be was locked. His final stop was the front door, where he tripped a switch that relayed a signal in his apartment every time the front door opened. That's how he'd know when Tom Olsen finally left. He got to work in the kitchen.

The day was much too short for Tom. It would be a long time before he'd be doing another embalming. Maybe that's why he took his time over it. He wanted it to be absolutely perfect. He'd have to hurry up with this last one and hope that the infusion wasn't too fast.

Thirty minutes came and went and no buzzer in the upstairs apartment. Another ten minutes and Oscar started to get nervous. A lingering Olsen could abort everything he had planned.

"Stay put," he said to himself softly, hoping that he could have the resolve to listen to his words rather than acting on the unease rising in his body. How long is a minute? Unendurable when so much is riding on its quick passage.

At exactly ten minutes to seven the buzzer sounded and a heavily bundled Tom Olsen headed into a stormy night, looking for his first beer of the day.

Chapter Nineteen

Oscar looked out of the kitchen window. White. No trees, no street, no sky. White. The second storm of a season that had not just begun and from the looks of things, would be worse than anything he had seen in all his winters in Mount Olden. The windows were rattled by the winds blowing out of the northeast, a branch banged against a window pane. This was going to be a big one. The only comfort, the warmth in the kitchen, the smells from the oven. The roast was well on its way.

He went downstairs, needing to get a good look at what was happening outside. The snow was already drifting and the path to his front door was hidden under a blanket of white. The businessman in him was relieved that it had started after his day had finished. The survivor, and if nothing else Oscar prided himself on being a survivor, was worried. Would Father Paul Dollard come out on a night like this? Still the optimist, he opened the garage door for the guest that he hoped would come soon.

Ozymandias checked each window and turned off every light on the first floor. The only illumination that remained came from a few lit candles and whatever street light managed to make its way in from the raging storm outside. Anyone who was a stranger to this home would not have made it from the front door to the stairs leading to the apartment. Oscar, who had made this trip thousands of times, could do it blindfolded.

~

The muffled sound of a car on the street. One of the few cars he'd heard passing by since the snow became heavy. He turned towards the front door. The headlights shone through the windows and created shadows that moved restlessly on the walls. The sign of the cross appeared, then disappeared.

A sign, clearly a sign.

Important and holy work is to be done tonight, Oscar told himself. This will be a night of sacrifice, harvest and resurrection. And if all goes as it should, two men will be forever free; a man of the cloth will return to his Lord, no longer tortured by the daily obligation of saying the mass, and the other, having found the ultimate host, will no longer be driven to take in dead men's flesh.

The table was set; the good china, silverware and lace tablecloth. The meat was well on its way, the candied yams and sugar-glazed carrots simmering, the salad and desserts made, including Kurt's wonderfully rich chocolate cake, now on an elegant serving plate.

A few more details: Oscar placed a brown apothecary bottle next to the liquors and filled a syringe with one hundred units of insulin, then taped it to the underside of the dinner table where he and his guest would soon be eating. Everything done, everything ready. All that was left was the waiting and praying that the storm wouldn't keep the priest at home.

Oscar was lost in Mozart's *Requiem* and his glass of sherry when he realized the noise intruding on his solitude was the buzzer. Someone had come through the front door. A loud noise, something had fallen to the floor. More noise; furniture moving.

"Who's down there?"

"It's me, Oscar. Father Paul."

"Stay put until I turn on a light. You're liable to trip and break your neck." Not a bad outcome but very unlikely, Oscar thought as he smiled to no one but himself.

"Ah, you made it," he said with relief, as he laid eyes on this man whose Eucharistic sacrifice would lead to absolution and redemption.

"The snow has lightened up although from the looks of it, it will start up in an hour or two."

"I left the garage door opened."

"Yes, very considerate. I pulled in and closed it behind me. Is that okay?"

"Very good. I've cooked us a wonderful supper, but first let's sit down and have a drink."

"The bathroom first, Oscar. These last few days it seems like I'm there more than any other place."

This time the priest's visit was no surprise. Chocolates were still on the coffee table but this time in a bowl, not a paten, and the pate was surrounded with crackers from the grocery store.

"What will you be drinking?" Oscar asked when the priest returned after relieving himself.

"Water, a large glass of water."

"Water, Dollard? When did this become the beverage of choice?"

"Very thirsty these last few days."

"You're looking a bit under the weather."

"I've been very tired."

"Something to do with the diabetes?"

"That and what we've all been put through the days since the accident."

"Taking the medicine?" Oscar asked, already knowing the answer to this, and his compliance with the diet. Father Paul had already eaten his second chocolate.

"Not the way I'm supposed to."

"Supposed to?"

"Today I injected twice, yesterday once."

"And how many times a day should you be injecting?"

"Four times. I won't carry the kit with me. It's hard enough doing what I have to do, especially now, without having to stop and remember to give myself the injections. This has happened to me many times before, Oscar, so you needn't worry. Next week I'll get back on track with the diet and medicine."

Father Paul's answers didn't cause Oscar a drop of concern. He was delighted at the opportunity just dropped in his lap. Still, appropriate behavior was demanded so he ended the subject of his guest's health with a statement of general concern, even if it was an understatement of his observations. "For whatever reason, Dollard, you don't quite look yourself."

"Frankly, Oscar, with this storm and with how I feel, I had every intention of staying home and being in bed by now. I would have done just that if it weren't for a visitor today at St Anselm's."

This smelled of trouble. Just like the fruity odor coming from the priest, Oscar could tell that what he was about to hear was something that could cause complications.

"A man came by the rectory looking for his nephew. The family comes from somewhere in Ohio and this boy must be in his early to mid twenties, moves from place to place looking for work, calls home once a week. It's been two weeks since they heard from him and the last several calls have come from Mount Olden. The family name is Wasby."

It's the details that kill you, thought Oscar.

"I got this horrible feeling, Oscar, another one of Olsen's victims."

The man had an obituary in his wallet, both parents dead, an only child, and now a damned uncle shows up. It's always something. No matter how thorough the planning, it's always something.

"That's one huge step, Dollard," said Oscar, trying to inject prudent caution into the priest's considerations.

"Where's the 'huge step'? I don't see a huge step," Paul answered testily.

"Follow me closely, Dollard. The uncle says the boy's a drifter, so it's not unreasonable to think that he's left town already."

"He didn't say drifter, Oscar. The boy travels from town to town looking for work and they're hiring now, getting ready for harvesting."

"Well, if he'd been working for them we'd know about it from last night," replied Oscar, now with a taste of annoyance in his voice. "It was all hands and they have everyone's name, the ones that made it off the ice and the ones we brought back here."

"Oscar," interrupted Father Paul. "What are we arguing about? What is happening here?"

Now it was Ozymandias' turn to interrupt as he began in a low, measured voice of thoughtful authority. "If in fact this Wasby fellow was still in Mount Olden, and that would mean he did get the job, that puts him on the ice that night. And if there is no accounting for him either alive or dead, we need to consider the possibility that he's still under the ice and we won't know that until the spring thaw."

"Olsen, Tom Olsen. I think he might have something to do with this. With the body," answered Father Paul, as clearly as he could.

"The final possibility," conceded Oscar, "is that Olsen has done something with the body. For that he'd need an embalming room. He hasn't been here and the nearest one is some distance away. Olsen hasn't left town since the accident. And let's not forget about the remains, even if he had a place to do the mutilating. It's one thing to do some butchering, close the coffin and put it into the ground where the evidence will eventually disappear as the body decomposes. You see, Dollard, to do that there has to be a death certificate, and without it there is no burial. We have no death certificate for this Wasby, so there's no way of disposing of the remains. Tom Olsen may be crazy but he's not stupid. Too many reasons why your worst case scenario just couldn't play out."

"Or maybe it could, Oscar. Listen to me and see if this works."

Ozymandias understood that nothing was going to stop this damn priest. He took a deep breath to clear Dollard's toxic thoughts that now surrounded him.

Too late and too close to the end to let this idiot unnerve you. Settle down, he told himself. Just listen, just settle down.

"The night of the accident there was nothing but confusion," said Paul. "The sheriff couldn't even make sense of it when we had everyone who was there at the meeting hall. Lots of bodies and lots of Tom in and out of this place. Where were you that night? Can you say for sure he couldn't have brought a body in here and done the butchering? What would he have to do and how long would it take?"

"Just like slaughtering a steer. Purge the body and butcher the meat. Maybe an hour if you know what you are doing."

"Does Tom know what he's doing?"

"He's a master of it."

"Could he have had an hour alone here that night?"

"Easily."

"So there you have it," the priest said conclusively.

"Not exactly," said Oscar, thinking that logic would allow them both to leave this dark world of speculation and return to why Oscar had invited Father Paul to his apartment for dinner. "Remember, even with a steer, there are still remains. What does he do with the remains?"

"Yes. The remains, that's the easiest part. He buries them."

"How? There's no death certificate."

"This part I was sure you'd have the answer to, Oscar. All these coffins, Oscar, all the funerals in these past few days. A hip here, a shoulder there. Who would know?"

"No one, Dollard, no one."

He'd figured it out, the priest had figured it out. Almost.

"What are you proposing?" he asked the priest.

"That we go to your cold house and take a look."

"What if we find nothing? More than half of the departed have already been interred."

"In either case it's time to go to the sheriff. Even if we don't find something here, there's good reason to think Vern Wasby's parts are in caskets that have already been buried."

"You're talking about exhuming bodies. There are still too many possibilities for so drastic a move. I say we wait on telling the sheriff."

"Oscar, I'm going tomorrow. You're welcome to come along but if you don't, I'll understand."

"So be it. That certainly makes clear what needs to be done tonight. First we eat. I don't want to overcook the roast or eat it cold. After dinner we'll take a look in the cold house."

~

Father Paul was much slower in getting up than he had been in sitting down. The bowl of chocolates was half empty and Oscar had not had one. This, no doubt, explained his sickly look and unsteadiness on his feet.

"I don't know how I'm going to manage dinner, Oscar, with the way I'm feeling."

"Looks like you've got too much sugar in you. I have something that should make you feel better and as long as you stay away from the vegetables, there's sugar in them, and stick with the meat and salad, you'll be all right."

"Let's see what happens," he said, reaching for Oscar's arm to steady himself.

Oscar sat the priest down in a kitchen chair and reached under the table to feel for the syringe. It was there, securely taped just where he left it. He poured wine for himself and iced tea for Dollard. Iced tea in winter and it snowing? The priest didn't even ask, he was feeling that poorly.

"Ah, Dollard, it needs a bit more ice," said Oscar, as he turned his back to his guest, glass in hand, and reached for the brown bottle. He poured a precise measure of its contents into the tea and stirred vigorously. Just enough for what he needed it to do.

"Drink it all. In ten minutes you'll feel better."

The roast, nestled in a ring of vegetables, was on a silver serving tray, settling on the counter. Oscar placed it on the table, a fitting centerpiece. "A crown roast of lamb," he said with a flourish.

Whatever Oscar had given Father Paul was starting to do its job. He looked at that roast and his appetite sprang to life. He had never seen such a magnificent thing. Clearly these were lamb chops, but instead of lying flat on a plate, which is how they were served to him on the few occasions when he had lamb, they were standing in a tight circle, with the bone facing up. Each chop had a little white paper cap and in the center of the roast was a stuffing of some sort.

"Maybe one, Oscar, and just a little of the vegetables."

"You're feeling better?"

"Much better. What did you give me?"

"You are asking the alchemist for his secrets? Be satisfied with 'better'. Now, are you sure about the vegetables? Lots of sugar."

"Tomorrow I'll worry about the sugar."

One chop became two, two became four and with that the priest was feeling better and better. He began talking and couldn't stop and after he became bored with his own words, he became silly, giggled, and told Oscar jokes he hadn't remembered for years. Some were clever, and witty, others bawdy and downright filthy. By the time Oscar presented the desserts, the priest was making no sense at all. He wasted no attention on words as he devoted himself totally to Kurt Croppin's chocolate cake.

When he could eat no more he felt a sudden rush of fatigue and in the one lucid moment before he passed out, he asked Oscar what the hell had he done, what had he given him.

He knew, and Oscar was pleased that he did.

Father Paul's limbs grew limp and his body started to slump forward, prompting Oscar to lay a strong hand on the back of his collar.

"Easy does it, Father Paul Dollard," said Oscar, as he gently let the priest's head come to rest beside the silver setting. He let his hand linger beneath Dollard's nose. A faint but barely noticeable respiration. "Nicely done, Oscar. Just enough, not too much. Well dosed. A master. Morphine now and insulin for dessert."

A content Oscar Ozymandias turned back to his setting and continued eating the chop on his plate. He swallowed carefully, washed it down with some wine, wiped his hands and mouth with his cloth napkin, and walked around the table to a slumped Father Paul Dollard. He was out. The breathing was shallow and to the casual observer, he looked dead and on his way to heaven.

Chapter Twenty

"Radler, it's Oscar Ozymandias."

"Doctor, Ozymandias, doctor," came a slightly slurred voice on the other end of the phone. "What is it now?"

"Father Paul."

"What about him?" Radler asked impatiently, in between sips from whatever he was drinking.

"The man is dead, Radler, dead."

That was enough to almost sober the doctor up. "What the hell are you talking about?

"He passed out at my kitchen table and now I can't find a pulse."

"Holy shit. No pulse. Are you sure?"

"Who the hell do you think you're asking? I know when I'm not getting a pulse."

"Tell me what happened?"

"You know better than I."

"What the hell does that mean?" the doctor responded with concern creeping into his voice.

"He was under your care. When did you see him last?"

"Months ago."

"Months ago? The man was a diabetic, he didn't take care of himself and you can't remember when you saw him last?"

"Look, Ozymandias, I'm the doctor and not accountable to you in any way. You have no right speaking to me this way."

"That's right, you're the doctor and that's the problem. The man had fruity breath. You don't have to be a doctor to know he was in trouble. What happened here? I'll tell you what happened here. The man came to visit and was sick in a way that I haven't seen before. He said he didn't need to call you because he had his insulin with him. He went into the bathroom, did what he had to do, and while we were having a few nibbles about an hour later he became visibly sick. At the dinner table he crashed, he slumped over and seemed to faint. This was all beyond me. I tried to arouse him. He was unarousable. His body started to jerk, I didn't know what was happening and when I searched for the pulse at the femoral, nothing."

"My God, my God," was all the doctor could say.

"I went into the bathroom. The syringe was on the sink and next to it empty vials of insulin. Empty, Radler. If they were all full he had to have taken more than a hundred units. Could this have happened if he took it all?"

Oscar already knew the answer and was not surprised when the doctor said yes.

"If you hadn't seen him in months, how could he have so much medicine?"

Oscar knew the answer to this also; the doctor must have been leaving scripts for the priest in the pharmacy. Prescribing without taking urine, unheard of. How would the patient know how much to take and how often? This would be the question that everyone in Mt Olden would be asking unless the doctor handled this carefully and the undertaker kept his mouth shut.

"What do you want me to do, Doc?"

The fact that he all of a sudden became Doc didn't go unnoticed by Radler. This, he knew, was Ozymandias' way of saying they could work out a deal.

"You're absolutely sure there's no pulse?"

"No pulse, I'm sure."

"It's snowing and it looks like it's going to be coming down heavy again. There's nothing I could do if I were there. Do what you have to do to keep him for me tomorrow. We don't know for sure what killed him so it would be premature to think of a diabetic coma or anything having to do with the diabetes. Do you understand, Ozymandias?"

"Continue." Oscar wasn't going to give this man an inch.

"People are going to demand knowing why a community leader, a parish priest, is dead," said the doctor. "I'll be over early in the morning. Have everything ready for an autopsy. And Oscar, I'll need a blank death certificate."

The only thing left for Oscar Ozymandias to do was inject the insulin to finish Dollard off. He'd have to wait until the autopsy for the harvest and only the smallest of pieces was needed for Oscar to have this final communion and at last be free of his curse.

There was time and there was dinner to finish.

~

Oscar heard it. He heard nothing else, no door, no bumping into furniture. He heard it; the buzzer. Someone had just come in, closed the door without making a sound, and unlike Father Paul, knew where every piece of furniture was downstairs. There was not much Oscar could do now other than be done with eating and look concerned and distraught.

Footsteps on the stairs.

Who would know about the internal stairway and who would be so bold as to come up to the private living quarters without being invited?

"Ozymandias, it's me." More footsteps.

Although slightly slurred, Oscar didn't need a name to know who the voice belonged to. "You, Olsen. What are you doing here?"

Tom, having had a few, continued talking before he got to the kitchen and laid his eyes on Father Paul. "I was walking by and saw fresh tire tracks going towards the garage. Thought you had to make another pick up and might need some help."

A few more steps and he was face to face with what had just happened. Shaking his head vigorously, he tried to shed whatever was left of the drink that clouded what he was seeing. Now more sober, he looked again. What he saw was just as it was a moment ago. Shocked, he said in a voice that was too soft and humble to be his own, "Oscar, my God, what has happened?"

"He's dead, Olsen, dead."

"How could that be?" he asked, badly shaken by what was obvious.

"He came for dinner. He was not feeling well. Bad turned to worse and worse turned to this. I spoke to Doc Radler. Might have been the diabetes, you know Father Paul was diabetic, but the doc thinks it was probably something else. A heart attack, an aneurysm. Something like that. Anyway, he's going to perform an autopsy tomorrow so I've got to get everything ready and get Father out to the cold house. I need a hand."

"What do you need me to do?"

"Go downstairs and put the lights on. When you come back you'll help me carry him."

Tom left and Oscar thought, very close, but even if he had come a few minutes before, what would he have seen? Nothing, the same thing. Perfect planning that now needed a minor adjustment. In fact, the more witnesses to this calamity, the better off he was. No suspicions, that's what he liked.

Oscar reached for his lab coat, removed the syringe from under the table, sheathed the needle and placed it in his pocket. He didn't want any idle hands finding something where it didn't belong. Now all he had to do was wait for Tom.

"Did you have any difficulty finding the switches?"

The shock of a dead Father Paul had gone enough for Tom to feel the insult in Oscar's question. Of course he knew where the switches were. Hadn't this been home, the place he had been raised? Everything downstairs; the show room, the embalming room, all of it, hadn't it all been his playground when he was growing up? Of course he knew where the lights were and he was convinced Ozymandias knew that too. Lucky for that bastard that he was sobering up and it would be a sacrilege to do what he wanted with a dead Father Paul in the building.

"Everything's ready."

"Good. You take the feet and I'll take him under the arms." Oscar, always thinking, had to keep Olsen away from anything that had a pulse, anything that would let him know he was carrying a live rather than dead Father Paul.

"Be careful going down, he's dead weight."

This was a difficult one-man carry, a detail that Oscar considered but had not planned for. He knew he couldn't keep Dollard in the kitchen overnight. He had to be in the cold house to avoid putrification. The sudden appearance of Olsen was his answer and as long as he had him holding the priest by the feet, he was wearing heavy snow boots that came up mid calf, everything would be all right.

Two strong men and one comatose priest. With a little pushing, pulling and bending just the right place, all three were soon in the embalming room.

"Not on the embalming table," said Oscar sternly. "Just the feet, stay away from the rest of him. We're going to put him on the gurney and then you back off. Do you understand, Olsen? This is a coroner's case. The less we touch the body, the better it is."

He's doing it again, talking down as if I were stupid, thought Tom. Too many people in the past treated him that way and he didn't have to take it from this man. Even if the bastard hadn't stolen what was his, he'd still hate his guts.

"You got a mouth on you, Ozymandias. Coroner's case. You're going to tell me about coroner's cases? You're one miserable fuck, do you hear me?" Tom, feeling control slip through his fingers, was a second away from picking something up and breaking a window. He never aimed for people, that much could be said for him. But there had been a lot of shattered glass and a lot of nights in a cell.

Oscar now had the last details set. Tom was another witness to Dollard's unexpected demise and the body was now out of the apartment and on a gurney downstairs. He too, like the agitated Olsen, was not about to spare any words.

"Keep this up and this will the last time you set foot in this room!" Oscar knew exactly what he was doing and how high he had just raised the stakes for Olsen.

Knowing that he could never return to the embalming room was a terrible thing to happen to Tom Olsen. The beer made the decision for him. If he were to back down he would forever be under the power of this evil man. Tom reached down for the nearest objects, two trocars, and aimed one at the glass-fronted cabinet next to where Ozymandias was standing. It found its mark, missing Oscar's head by no more than a few inches. Readying himself for a quick retreat, he moved to the priest's head and reached down for a final goodbye before racing to the door.

Tom Olsen froze. Everything in him came to an absolute stop. He moved his hand from the priest's temple, letting his fingers trace a path to the bulging artery on Father Paul's neck. A pulse. He knew for sure he was feeling a pulse.

"This man is alive," he said softly, so he could hear the words that went with what his fingers had just told him. He looked at Oscar. "He's alive, you bastard. If I know it then you know it. What the hell are you doing? What have you done to him?"

Oscar knew this only son of Jonas Olsen was no match for him as long as he stayed calm and kept his wits about him.

"Take it easy, Olsen. This man is dying. He's been sick for many years and he's dying."

"You did something to him. If he's dying, it's because you did something."

"Don't be reckless. It's no good for me and certainly no good for you."

"Call the doctor."

"I called the doctor. He knows everything.'

"Give me the phone. I don't believe you. I don't believe a word you're saying. Give me the phone, Oscar."

Tom reached for the phone, Oscar reached for him. Everything was now happening too fast for words. Both men fell backwards, Tom on the embalming table, Oscar on Tom.

"Olsen, think for a moment, where can this end? If the man is not dead, he certainly is dying. He injected himself and now he's in a coma. If we just let him be he'll pass. If we call the doctor and tell him to come running, and if there is anything he can do to reverse this, Dollard will be an invalid with no brain for the rest of his life. Is that what he would want? And if you do something to me, they'll blame you. There are many people over the years that have heard you threaten my life. If something happens to me, it's going to happen to you."

"The priest knows. Father Paul knows what happened here."

Oscar grasped Olsen's jaw, forcing him to look at Dollard's lifeless body. "Look at him, man, he's not going to speak to anyone and whatever he knows will be buried with him in a pine box."

"You're a liar, you fuck, a liar," screamed Olsen as he began to struggle under Oscar's firm grip.

Oscar Ozymandias realized that this man was not to be reasoned with. Even if he understood the hopelessness of his situation, he'd get drunk one day and run up and down Main Street yelling about the undertaker who buried the priest when he was still alive. From that moment on no one in Mount Olden would ever trust Oscar.

Oscar saw clearly what had to be done. With one hand firmly keeping Tom Olsen on the embalming table, he reached into his pocket for the filled syringe.

Tom, out of the corner of his eye, saw a hand coming up to him and in it something shiny that he couldn't make out. Sensing danger, he quickly moved his body away and with it, Ozymandias almost lost his balance. Oscar firmly grasped his neck and standing with one leg barely touching the floor, put his other leg squarely on Tom's rib cage and applied every bit of pressure he could. All this while bringing the syringe with its one hundred plus units of insulin closer to the fleshy part of Olsen's arm.

Barely able to catch his breath and all too aware that he was about to get stuck with a needle, Tom positioned the sharp end of the trocar that he still had in his hand directly under Oscar's solar plexus. Oscar sensed it but paid it no mind.

For the moment his only concern was the needle in his hand and the thrashing body under his leg.

Tom made one last attempt to get free and when he did, Oscar pounced with all his weight and every bit of flesh of his body. Feeling the weight come down, Tom Olsen rested the blunt end of the trocar against his sternum and with his free hand, made sure it found its mark.

Oscar Ozymandias felt a sharp pain somewhere on his chest. He couldn't think about where it was coming from or how it got there. A sudden pain and then the sensation of something slipping smoothly inside him. Absolutely confused, he looked down to see six inches of a metal tube coming through his shirt, and a moment later, a pulsating stream of a warm thick red liquid spewing out of him. Did he know what had happened? Maybe. The moment before he tumbled off of Tom Olsen and onto the ground, his face spoke of absolute horror.

It took Tom Olsen a while to make the call. Covered in Oscar Ozymandias' blood, and holding a syringe with a lethal dose of insulin that was first meant for the priest and then for him, he called Doc Radler and then the sheriff. Was it too late for Father Paul? Would anyone believe the story that he would tell to explain what they were about to see?

Tom Olsen looked around the room, so familiar; the cabinets, the smell of the chemicals, the instruments. A small comfort while he waited for someone to come.

About The Author

Frederick Nenner is a medical ethicist and psychotherapist practicing in New York City for the past forty years. The themes and characters who inhabit this novel are informed by his professional life as an observer to the narrative of illness, suffering and death. His work in narrative medicine appeared in a number of publications including the *British Medical Journal*, *The Journal of Medical Ethics*, *The Journal of Palliative Medicine*, *Canadian Journal of Emergency Medicine* and the *Journal of the American Medical Association*.

frednenner.com

Made in the USA
Middletown, DE
03 December 2020

26169661R00163